The Black Fire Chronicles

The Hag

The Author acknowledges the Traditional Owners of the Country on which we live and work, paying respect to all Aboriginal and Torres Strait Islander Elders, past, present and emerging. The Author also acknowledges the Palawa people of Lutruwita, Tasmania, honouring their connection to Country.

Dedication

To my dear friend Penny-Maree. Thank you for your constant encouragement and enthusiasm, your wisdom and advice. You are an angel on earth!

And to my lovely and talented friend, Helen. Without your support, I would have retired to the garden, The Black Fire Chronicles locked inside my imagination. Thank you isn't enough.

You create your own universe as you go along.
~ *Winston Churchill*
Dogs do speak, but only to those who know how to listen.
~Orhan Pamuk

Contents

Introduction

Four years ago, Andrew Adler receives the surprise of his life when his beloved labrador Ralph begins to speak. Andrew's father is in grave danger, and with Ralph as his companion, the two become embroiled in a life and death adventure in the underground world of Vellistrian. Arch villains Owen, Secunda, and Torr unleash the devastating herb Black Fire on the world, part of a plot to create bedlam and gain control of the earth for their own evil purposes.

Fortunately, Andrew thwarts their plans. He rescues a young Pisal girl called Snow, and restores Jarl, the rightful king of Vellistrian, to the throne. Black Fire quickly disappears from the earth, and along with it, Ralph's ability to speak.

A year later, Andrew is watching the evening news on TV when he recognises the faces of Owen and Secunda in the guise of humans, both in powerful political positions. With no one to turn to, Andrew begs Ralph for help. The duo, along with Andrew's friends Leo and Teresa, become involved in a deadly adventure, as Black Fire consumes the earth.

Down below in Vellistrian, King Jarl is poisoned, and his new bride Snow must step into the breach as ruler of Vellistrian.

Andrew and his friends defeat the evil siblings Owen and Secunda, but at a significant cost: Owen disappears, stealing Ralph away with him.

Later, Andrew awakens to a dramatically altered world, where history has changed along with the victors. He discovers arch-enemy Owen is alive and well in World War Two Germany, meddling with events in a bid to make Andrew's life a misery. In a trip to Vellistrian, Andrew learns Queen Snow and the Pisal are experiencing similar woes. Snow advises Andrew that there is only one creature who can help: the mysterious hare known as the Seer.

Andrew meets the Seer and is tutored in the fine art of time stepping. He embarks on a dangerous journey into the past in an attempt to stop Owen. His time stepping into a faulty timeline is exciting but risky. Andrew learns his neighbours Mrs Jordan, Mr Lovell, and friend Angus are his guardians, in place to ensure he succeeds. But in a world that is ripping apart at the seams, Andrew feels he is running out of time. He passes on vital intelligence to Clementine Churchill, the wife of British Prime Minister Winston Churchill, after some daring encounters with Adolf Hitler and Albert Einstein.

With the combined help of Mrs Jordan, Angus, and new friend Daisy, Andrew thwarts his adversaries and finds Ralph. However, Ralph's time on earth is up, and he is relocated to a new life in Nostalgia with Queen Snow's parents. Heartbroken, Andrew visits Mrs Bargwana, in the hope she has another extraordinary dog. Instead, he receives a large British Shorthair cat, whose name is Winston.

Now read on...

CHAPTER ONE

"Is it cheating to get Winston Churchill's help with your history homework?" Sixteen-year-old Andrew Adler closed his textbook and turned to the British shorthair cat lounging on his bed.

The large grey cat lifted his head. "Would they believe you if you told them, Andrew? I think not. Besides, it may be history for you, but it is a large collection of memories for me."

Andrew grinned. "And pretty vivid memories, I guess, since you featured heavily in most of the twentieth century!"

A rumbling purr of pleasure erupted from Winston, and Andrew's mind strayed to the cat versus dog debate. His labrador Ralph had always thumped his tail as a sign of pleasure, but Winston could wake the dead with his purr. "Your purr is amazing," he said aloud. "It's like you're laughing." He scratched Winston behind the ears, and the cat lifted his head for a chin rub.

"That's the spot, Andrew, thank you. And you're right, I can't laugh anymore, so purring is the next best thing."

Andrew leaned back in his office chair and studied the cat. "Is this your first animal body, Winston?"

"It is. For whatever reason, the forces behind this deemed it necessary for me to return and help out - and in a rather clever disguise, if I may say so!"

Andrew flicked his long fringe off his face. He had dispensed with his longer hair, thinking he was too old for that kind of thing now he was sixteen. He'd kept the long blond fringe because he knew his mum still liked to ruffle his hair. He liked it too, but he wasn't about to admit it to his mother. "But why now?" he said aloud. "What's so special about now?"

Winston's bright orange eyes gleamed. "I think you can answer that one yourself, Andy. The time is drawing near."

"For what, though?" Six months had passed since Andrew's time stepping adventure, and whilst everything had returned to normal, he felt a nagging doubt: was it the end of things, or just the beginning? Andrew looked across at Winston again. The cat had stood up and was licking his paw before using it to wash his face. "Winston, the Seer told me he may never see me again. And the triplets from Vellistrian are gone. Surely it's all over?"

Winston paused in his grooming. "If that was true, Andrew, why am I here? In the past, I felt that I was walking with destiny - that I had a role to fulfil. And now, I feel it again." He scratched at his ear with a hind leg, and turned back to Andrew, his eyes unwavering. "Change is coming. We need to be on our guard."

He was echoing Andrew's own feelings, a sense of restlessness that he'd put down to resuming normal life, a natural reaction after jumping through time and negotiating with world leaders, Winston Churchill included. "I'm always on my guard after what happened last year."

"Good." Winston looked outside at the fading light. "However, we can't be on guard on an empty stomach. What's on the menu tonight? Champagne? Duck?" There was a hopeful light in his eyes.

Andrew laughed. "Afraid, not, Winston. Mum and Dad's budget doesn't stretch that far. How about a nice bowl of roo meat instead?"

"Roo meat?" The cat was horrified. "Is that what you've been feeding me all this time? Kangaroo meat?"

"Of course," Andrew said. "We have an abundance of kangaroos in Australia. It's a healthy, lean meat."

"But... but..." he spluttered, "I was gifted an albino kangaroo once. I'm not sure how I feel about eating one."

"Did you meet cows in the past, Winston? Or pigs, or ducks? You were happy enough to eat them!" Andrew teased him.

"It's not the same," the cat growled. He arched his back in a stretch, and leapt onto the floor. "I have a sudden desire to sit by the front door - your parents must be on their way home. My dog Rufus used to do the same thing, and I wondered how he knew. Evidently pets are quite attuned to their family. Where have they been all day?"

"Oh, I forgot to mention, Mum had her annual tests at the hospital for arthritis, and a follow-up doctor's appointment. You know how long these things take." Andrew cocked his head as a car crunched across the gravel in the driveway. "That'll be them now. I'll be back in a minute; I'll find out how she got on."

Winston nodded and lifted a paw to groom his whiskers. Andrew ambled down the passageway, calling out a greeting: "Oh good, you're back! Who's up for Chinese takeaway? I can pick it up if someone comes with me." He'd gotten his L-plates two weeks ago after his birthday, and he was eager for some driving practice. He reached the kitchen as his father entered the house alone. "Hey, Dad! How did Mum get on? Does she need a hand getting out of the car?"

"Andrew, sit down."

There was a flicker in his father's jaw that Andrew at first mistook for anger. He dropped meekly onto a chair and waited. Mr Adler swallowed, collecting himself, and Andrew gave his father an anxious glance. "Is everything okay?"

Mr Adler held up a finger, *wait*. He opened the cupboard above the fridge and pulled out a bottle of scotch. Sloshing an oversized nip into a glass, he threw the drink back, and poured another. Mr Adler rarely drank. This behaviour set off alarm bells in Andrew's mind.

His father joined him at the table. "They've kept your mother in over the weekend, Andy." He tossed back the second nip and stared through his son. "They're starting chemotherapy on Monday."

"Chemo?" Andrew swallowed. "For arthritis?" Beneath the table, Winston brushed against his legs. He touched the cat's fur, desperate to anchor himself in the room while he processed the foreign words of his father.

A tear appeared in the corner of Mr Adler's eye, and Andrew's heart rate accelerated. He couldn't remember the last time he had seen his father cry. *Have I ever seen him cry?*

"They decided to do a full bone scan after the X-ray showed some irregularities," Mr Adler said. "Much to everyone's surprise, they discovered something else."

He stopped, and a cold fear ran down Andrew's spine. "Dad, you're scaring me. What did they find?"

His father looked into his empty glass. "They found cancer."

CHAPTER TWO

"Hold on, I'm coming!" Mrs Jordan called out to the person hammering on her front door. *Goodness gracious,* she muttered as she padded down the hallway. *Don't they know it's the weekend? It's too early for this hullabaloo. I'm not even out of my pyjamas!*

She opened the door wide, and her neighbour Andrew tumbled inside. "I need to speak to you," he announced. He pushed past her and made his way into the kitchen. "I'll make tea."

She followed him down the hallway and watched silently as Andrew filled the kettle, turned it on, and placed teabags into two large mugs. Her neighbour had grown into a likeable young man, and his time stepping adventures had taught him to remain calm under pressure. But this morning, something was bubbling away beneath the surface - something important - and she would have to bide her time until he was ready to tell her.

Andrew remained silent as he made the tea, placing a dash of milk in Mrs Jordan's mug, and heaping two teaspoons of sugar into his own. He brought the cups over to the kitchen table and sank into a chair.

Mrs Jordan slid onto a chair of her own, and raised the steaming mug to her lips. She took a tentative first sip. "Ahh, lovely." She glanced at Andrew, noticing his flushed cheeks and downcast eyes. His tea was untouched, and there was a slight tremor about his mouth which he bit down on to control. She put a reassuring hand on his arm, but he jerked away.

He looked at her now, and in his eyes, she saw a frightened young child. "Mum's got bone cancer," he blurted.

"What?" Mrs Jordan jerked forwards in her chair. She placed her mug on the table, not trusting her shaking hands.

"The doctors told Dad it's aggressive. They're starting chemo on Monday." His tone was deceptively casual, but the wobble around his lips had returned.

"Oh, Andrew! This is dreadful news. How did this happen? Wasn't Helen getting regular checks?"

He took a gulp of tea. "She was. Every six months, but her last bone scan was two years ago."

"Good Heavens." Mrs Jordan removed her glasses and pressed a hand to her forehead. "I was afraid this would happen."

Andrew's eyes drilled into her. "Mrs Jordan? I'm in no mood for fluffiness. What were you afraid of?"

She gave him a guarded smile. "I don't suppose you remember the day you brought Ralph home? You were quite young."

"I was six," he growled. "What has that got to do with Mum?"

"Do you remember the accident?"

His aggression evaporated, replaced by curiosity. "What accident?"

"You had a car accident on the way home from Canberra. It was raining, your father hit a slippery patch and ran into the back of another car. More cosmetic than anything," she added, taking a much-needed slurp of tea. "While Peter and the other driver were exchanging details, your mother had an encounter with a strange young woman. Soon after, your mother fell ill, and Peter drove you all to the hospital." She gave Andrew a hard stare. "You don't remember any of this? I collected you and Ralph from the hospital and brought you home."

Andrew shook his head. "Not a bit of it. I remember being super excited about choosing Ralph. I must've worn myself out and fallen asleep."

Mrs Jordan sighed. "It's time we guardians sat down and explained a few things to you. There's no avoiding it. But in my defence, I was convinced the Seer sorted things out back then."

"Mrs J, you're making no sense!" Andrew cried. "What happened? Why was Mum in hospital?"

She bit her lip. "You'll have to ask your father. Once you've heard his side of the story, come back and see me."

"Why can't you tell me now?"

The little boy was back, and her heart ached for him. She had loved Andrew for all of his short life, and she longed to wrap him in her arms and make everything all right. But she couldn't, and she knew things were going to get worse before they got better. "You need to see both sides of the story, Andy," she explained gently. "You need to understand that the woman we're dealing with is incredibly dangerous."

"I thought we were just dealing with Mum's sickness!"

"I wish that's all it was," Mrs Jordan said. "Go," she prodded him. "Go back to your dad, and see what he has to say. His answers may surprise you."

She watched him dash along the hallway, slamming the front door behind him. A draught of cold air drifted into the kitchen, startling her from her thoughts. She nodded as she reached a decision. She left the kitchen and headed to her study, where she called up an instant messaging service on her laptop computer. She hesitated, the mouse hovering above the 'call' button, before she offered up a silent prayer and clicked on it.

Within moments, the head of a large hare appeared on the screen. "Hello, Dorothy," the Seer was polite but guarded. "To what do I owe this unexpected pleasure?"

Dorothy's mouth twisted into an unhappy smile. "It's good to see you too, Seer, but there's nothing pleasant about my call. It's about the Hag. She's back, and she's come to finish the job on Andrew's mother."

CHAPTER THREE

"Ah, there you are!" Mr Adler said as Andrew entered the kitchen through the back door. "I was looking all over for you. If we leave now, we can visit your mother before your soccer game this afternoon."

"I went next door to see Mrs Jordan... and give her the news," he answered.

"Oh. Of course." His father's eyes clouded over. "Thanks for letting Dorothy know, son."

"She was shocked," Andrew continued. "But she said this is not the first time Mum's been in hospital. Dad, is that true?" He gave his father a keen glance.

Mr Adler sighed, and looked at his watch. "Why don't we have this discussion in the car, Andy?"

"Sure."

They went outside, Mr Adler locking the house behind them. When he turned back to the car, Andrew was in the driver's seat, his L-plates already attached. "Before you say anything, I need the practice!" he said.

Mr Adler rolled his eyes, and got into the passenger seat. "Do you know where you're going?"

Andrew gave him a sly smile. "No, but I'm sure you'll tell me."

They made their way through the back streets of Parramatta, Mr Adler providing a bewildering set of instructions. "Turn left here, then right at that roundabout up the hill."

"I don't think I've ever been in this part of Parramatta before, Dad. How do you know where you're going?"

"I grew up here, remember?" Mr Adler grinned. "Many moons ago, I was the one with the learner's permit, and Mr Lovell was the one in the passenger seat. And he was a lot less easy-going than me! Left at the bottom of the hill. Watch for that pothole. Drive in there and you'll be lost forever."

Andrew glanced at his dad. "Mr Lovell taught you to drive?" This was news to him.

"Mr Lovell taught me many things, Andy. Things my own father was incapable of teaching me. Left at the T-junction. Remember to give way."

All of a sudden, they popped out near the rugby fields, and Andrew recognised where they were. "We're on the other side of the park! So, once I get onto Park Avenue, we're almost at the hospital."

"Correct. Well done, Andy! It's unusual to have that level of awareness when you're first driving."

Andrew basked in his father's praise, and he decided to let slip the comment about his dad's father. He knew very little about his grandfather, except that he fought in World War Two, and that he was named in his honour. Beyond that, all Andrew knew was that he had passed away when his dad was 16 years old. *My age,* he thought with a shiver.

"Dad, when was Mum in hospital the first time? Why don't I remember?" They were stopped at a set of lights, and Andrew turned to look at his father.

"You were six, Andy. It was the day we drove to Canberra to collect Ralph."

"What happened?" The lights turned green, and Andrew accelerated away, pushed the clutch in and changed gears.

"Nice change," Mr Adler said. "Start looking for a space in the right-hand lane. We have to turn right at the lights up ahead. Don't forget to indicate."

"Yes, Dad." He found a gap, switched his indicator on and moved into the right lane. He changed gears twice, and the car coasted along. "Mrs Jordan said she met us at the hospital, and took me and Ralph home."

"Did she?" Mr Adler frowned. "I called her on the way. Your mum took ill after we had a little fender bender on the highway."

"Do you remember seeing a strange woman?"

"Slow down, Andy! The lights have changed to orange. You have to keep your eye on what's happening down the road, not just what's in front of you!"

Andrew obediently braked, dropped back to second gear, and came to a stuttering halt in the right-hand turn lane. "Dad. The woman?"

"Yes, yes, I heard you!" Mr Adler said. "Look, it was such a long time ago. I'm worried sick about your mother, and you want me to recall some trivial information from ten years ago?"

"But Mrs Jordan thought the woman had something to do with mum getting sick!"

"I don't give a hoot what Dorothy thought!" Mr Adler snapped. "Your mother is lying in hospital with cancer, Andrew, and the best you can do is rattle on about a witch?"

Andrew stared at his father. "I never mentioned a witch." Behind them, a car horn beeped, and he realised the lights had changed. Cheeks burning, he threw the car into first gear, came off the clutch too fast and rabbit-hopped his way through the intersection.

"Clutch in," his father commanded, and Andrew eventually regained control of the car. "Up here, on the left, see that sign for parking?"

Andrew gave a brief nod, and turned his indicator on. There was an uneasy silence between the pair as Andrew drove into the car park.

CHAPTER FOUR

It was now Saturday evening, and Andrew had retreated to the safety of his bedroom and the company of Winston. He was part-way through recounting the visit to his mother in hospital. Sitting perched on the edge of his mother's bed, he had felt tongue-tied and awkward. When his father stepped into the corridor to chase down another blanket, Mrs Adler had seized the opportunity to speak alone with Andrew.

She had always reminded Andrew of a willy wagtail bird: the pocket dynamo of the backyard, hopping from place to place with a cheeky look on its face and a sashay of its tail feathers. His mum was the same; boundless energy and full of positivity, always thinking of others, and offering a kind word when he was down. Now the boot was on the other foot, and Andrew was at a loss to know what to say. He looked down at her with a forced smile, desperate to hide the monstrous fear growing inside him.

True to form, his mother took the initiative. "No matter what happens, Andy, everything's going to be okay." She clasped his hand and looked at him with those blue eyes he adored, their spark dulled by pain medication. "I'll get through this course of chemo, and then I'll be on the road to recovery. So, keep your chin up, promise me?"

He swallowed, tears forming behind his eyes. "I promise."

"Good." She smiled up at him. "You know, it's funny, dear. This reminds me of when I was in hospital after we collected Ralph."

"It does?" Andrew hid his surprise. His dad had resisted discussing the matter, but now his mother was volunteering the information to him.

"Yes. They thought I had encephalitis, an inflammation of the brain. I saw a couple of weird things, but I swear I saw a witch outside the window, it wasn't the inflammation."

Andrew felt a chill sweep through his body. "You saw a witch?"

She leaned back in the pillows and closed her eyes. "It was all a jumble after we had the car accident coming home. It was the day we collected Ralph, and he was beside himself, barking his head off when this nice young woman came to check on you. Your father and I were busy exchanging details with the other driver, and she thought she heard you crying."

"Do you remember what she looked like?" Andrew held his breath.

Mrs Adler pulled herself upright in the bed, grimacing in pain. "It's such a long time ago, dear. She had amazing blue eyes; I remember that much. She said something about you and Ralph being a magical pair, once I told her I couldn't have any further children."

"Mum, why on earth did you tell her that?"

"I don't know, dear." Her eyes were cloudy with confusion. "She was very caring. I remember she touched me on the arm, and then she was gone. We got back in the car, and I began to feel quite ill. Your father drove us straight to hospital. I think Dorothy took you and Ralph home."

"And you're telling me you saw a witch outside the window."

Mrs Adler nodded. "And a big rabbit as well. I was that muddled, I thought it was Easter, and that someone had dressed up as the Easter Bunny."

Before Andrew could answer, his father bustled into the room, bearing a warm blanket. "Here, Helen. I'll tuck this around you. Pop your arms inside the sheets."

Andrew released his mother's hand, kissed her on the cheek, and left his father to fuss around. The two Adler men, attempting to nurture the nurturer, and doing a clumsy job of it. His head whirling, he waited in the hallway, keeping an eye on the time. After fifteen minutes, he poked his head around the door. "Dad. I've got to get to the game."

"And did you win, Andrew?" Winston asked. He had listened without interruption to Andrew's summary, stretched out at the foot of the bed.

"It was a draw," Andrew sighed. "They're the top team, so it's better than a loss. They used to belt us last year."

"Progress," Winston said. "Do you think you've made similar progress with your mother's predicament?"

Andrew curled around on the bed to face Winston. "I have no idea! One minute Mrs Jordan is talking about a strange woman, the next my mum and dad are talking about a witch. And it sounds like she had a visit from the Seer at one point as well! It makes no sense." He shrugged. "But this all happened ages ago, it's not like this weird woman is around now."

"Can you be absolutely certain of that, Andrew?"

"What do you mean?"

Winston's eyes narrowed. "I saw something, and if you recall, you saw something too."

Andrew sat up. "When? What are you talking about?"

"Two weeks ago, you were visiting Leo for homework, and I was on the windowsill here, looking out the window." He raised a paw and pointed. "It must have been around 5pm, the street lights were just coming on, and I heard your mother in the kitchen, preparing the evening meal. I saw a woman hurrying out of your driveway, and you saw her too. Do you remember? You called out to her."

"I did," Andrew said, his eyes widening. "I was walking past Mr Lovell's house. I thought it was Mrs Jordan, but she didn't answer."

"Because it wasn't Mrs Jordan."

"And if it wasn't Mrs Jordan, who was the woman leaving our house?"

"My thoughts exactly, Andrew. Why don't you proceed next door and put that question to Mrs Jordan?"

Andrew glanced out the window to the dark street. "But it's late. I don't want to bother her, and I don't want to disturb Dad after the day we've had."

"Go through the window," Winston said. "I once made a daring prison escape through a window."

Andrew stared at his cat. "You were imprisoned? I must've missed that history lesson."

"I'll tell you later. For now, get to Mrs Jordan and start asking questions."

"Okay." Andrew pushed up the window, and an icy blast of air filled the room. "You know, it's not the first time I've gone out the window myself," he said to Winston.

"I'm not surprised. Remember to leave it open a finger-width so you can get back in. I'll be waiting for you." The cat retreated into the warmth of the bedding.

Andrew slung a leg over the windowsill. "Typical cat." He dropped to the ground, pulled the window down, and trotted next door.

He tapped lightly on the front door, and within a minute, Mrs Jordan was eyeballing him through the peephole in the front door. "Andrew! What is it?"

"I want to know who this woman is. My parents let slip that she's a witch. I want to know the whole story."

Chapter Five

"I need to see the Seer," Andrew announced once he was safely inside Mrs Jordan's kitchen. "I suppose I'll have to get permission again? Go through Vellistrian, and Snow?" He referred to the subterranean race of creatures he had discovered when he was 12 years old.

"What on earth for?" Mrs Jordan looked puzzled. "I'll call him up on messenger."

"You'll what?" Andrew swallowed his surprise.

Mrs Jordan gave him a cheeky wink. "This is the 21st century, Andy. Follow me." She took him down the hallway and into a small study. Sitting at a corner desk, she jiggled the mouse, awakening her laptop computer. She clicked on an icon at the bottom of the screen, and there was a resultant screech and purr akin to the dial-up noise of an old modem. Andrew grinned at this so-called 'modern' technology, but hastily stifled his mirth when the Seer's solemn face appeared on the screen.

"Dorothy, this is becoming a bit of a habit," the hare said, a note of disapproval in his voice.

"I know, but hear me out," Dorothy replied. "I've got Andrew here, and he needs some questions answered. I'll just swap seats with him." She gave Andrew her seat, and excused herself.

Andrew eased his long legs beneath the desk. For the first time in six months, he stared into the hare's face: his wise, dark eyes ringed by pristine white, the dappled fur, and the small portion of his large ears that fit into the frame. "I... I can't believe I can talk to you this way!" he said. "Why didn't I know about this?"

"You needed to develop your time stepping skills, Andrew. Calling me up via messenger would have resulted in laziness."

Andrew frowned. Was that a faint twitch of humour in the hare's whiskers? "You may laugh," he said, his voice stiff, "but I could've done with a hotline when the world was falling apart last year!"

"Of course," the Seer agreed. "But that avenue did not exist in the altered timeline, so it is a moot point. Now, what is it you wish to discuss with me?"

"You've heard about my mother?"

The hare bowed his head in acknowledgment. "I have, Andrew."

"Can you help her?" He made no attempt to hide the anguish in his voice.

"I cannot. You will recall I once mentioned that some events stand for all time? This is one of those times. I intervened once, many years ago, and with great reluctance. I will not intervene again."

"Oh, you *were* in the hospital with Mum! She told me she saw a big rabbit. Please. Isn't there something you can do?"

"There is something *you* can do." The Seer leaned forward, his whiskers filling the frame. "You can love and support your mother. Beyond that, we must wait and see."

"But what about this woman that Mrs Jordan mentioned? And the witch my mother saw?"

The Seer leaned back, brushing a paw through his whiskers. "She is one and the same, a creature known as the Hag, and her history is as long as mine. And it appears she has taken as great an interest in your family as she did with your guardians. An unhealthy interest, prompted by an old prophecy."

"A prophecy? Look, you're making no sense!" The walls closed in on Andrew, and he struggled to breathe. "Seer? What's happening?" The room pitched on its side, and his seat buckled. The laptop floated off the desk and careened towards his head. He uttered a feeble scream and clamped his eyes shut.

The impact never came, and when Andrew opened his eyes, he found himself relaxing in a worn armchair in Mrs Jordan's lounge room. A wood heater radiated warmth onto his legs, and across from him sat the Seer, a wily smile on his face.

"Hot chocolate?" Mrs Jordan enquired at his elbow. "Seer, I've made you some thyme tea."

Andrew's head swivelled between the pair. "What just happened?" he screamed. "We were talking on the laptop in the office..."

Mrs Jordan placed a steaming mug in his hands. "It's all right, dear. These slips happen from time to time." She placed the thyme tea on a side table by the hare, and sat down on the lounge. "The Seer obviously feels he needs to discuss the prophecy with you in person."

"Okay, enough wizardry." Andrew glared at them. "Tell me about this prophecy, and how it relates to me."

"The prophecy has been in existence for many years, awaiting the right moment in time when all the variables aligned," the Seer began. "We've had a number of false starts, but when you came along, we had high hopes. Listen well, Andrew, and tell me your thoughts on this prophecy:

> *When the long-haired Blond*
> *And the eloquent Hound unite*
> *The Heavens will weep*
> *At their love and light*
> *Disperse the four others*
> *In time*
> *In disguise*
> *Lest the Shrew discovers*
> *The ancient three rise up*
> *And defile the herb of darkness,*
> *The world will laugh*
> *And descend into madness*
> *Beyond and below*
> *The Blond conquers fear,*
> *The foes are defeated*
> *And the Hound disappears*
> *Guardians appear*
> *And recount their stories*
> *Wisdom is hard won*
> *Losses trump glories*
> *While Time distorts and the Veil recedes*
> *Make haste!*
> *As friends will fade*
> *And foes succeed*
> *Darkness will fall*
> *Families will crumble*
> *Distractions are many*
> *And the Blond will stumble*

When the star is complete
The Blond will ascend
Reunite the Divided
And bring the curse to an end

Andrew stared at the Seer, his heart rate accelerating. "That first bit, the long-haired blond, and the eloquent hound - that's me and Ralph, right?"

"Correct," the hare nodded.

"And Lucy told me it rained the day you collected Ralph," Mrs Jordan chimed in. "That's the heavens weeping."

"What was the next bit, Seer?" Andrew leaned forward. "Disperse the four others?"

"Ralph had four siblings. Once you made the connection with Ralph, we had to act quickly. They were separated and sent to different moments in time, some of them in disguise. All of Ralph's brothers and sisters were special, and we didn't want them falling into the wrong hands."

"Lest the Shrew discovers," Mrs Jordan added.

"Okay, I'm beginning to build a picture," Andrew said, his eyes narrowing. "The next bit, it was about a herb of darkness? That's got to be Black Fire, for sure. And let me guess, the ancient three are Owen, Secunda, and Torr. Ancient because they are Pisal, right?"

"Correct," the Seer answered. "*The world will laugh, and descend into madness.*"

"I can vouch for that," Mrs Jordan raised her hand. "They were crazy times. We thought Black Fire was a cure-all, but it was a back door for world domination."

"*Beyond and below, the Blond conquers fear, the foes are defeated, and the Hound disappears*" the Seer recited again. "Does that sound familiar, Andrew?"

"It's exactly what happened in Vellistrian!" Andrew pounded his fist in his hand. "And Ralph did disappear! I thought I was going to lose him."

"And now we have nearly caught up," the Seer said. "*Guardians appear, and recount their stories. Wisdom is hard won, Losses trump glories.*"

"That doesn't sound too promising!" Andrew said. "Am I going to fail?"

"No, Andrew," Mrs Jordan said. "The prophecy refers to the Guardians' losses. We have all experienced heartache to reach this point in time. And that makes us all the more determined to succeed," she added, her mouth set in a grim line.

"But there are hard times ahead, Dorothy. The prophecy has proven correct thus far, now we must be on our toes."

"For what, though?" Andrew asked. "It's all well and good having a prophecy, but what are we preparing for? What is this Hag creature intending to do?"

"Destroy us all," Mrs Jordan answered. "She touched your mother the day you collected Ralph. Helen would've died if the Seer hadn't stepped in and healed her. The Hag wanted you to suffer, Andrew, to blind you from the task at hand. Now she's come back to finish off the job."

"But why? Mum doesn't deserve this. Why isn't she coming after me?"

"Because of your guardians, Andrew," the Seer answered. "Your mother was a soft target - a 'cheap shot', as you humans like to call it. The Hag has never played fair, unfortunately. There is more to know, but now is not the time. Be aware that she can present as both a young and old woman. You must be on your guard, Andrew. She has searched for the blond - *you* - for many years, and now you are within her grasp. Keep your guardians close. Watch for her, and watch for her offsider. When together, they are powerful beyond reckoning."

"And who would her offsider be?" Andrew asked.

"Yes, that's a good question." Mrs Jordan caught the Seer's eye. "I thought Lucy and I took care of that particular problem when we were younger."

"You did," he responded. "But that was 30 years ago, Dorothy. She's had ample time to find another henchman, and I fear this time round she has recruited a formidable opponent."

"Who is it?" Andrew's heart thudded in his chest.

"I don't know," the Seer replied, deep concern etched on his face. "That knowledge is hidden from me."

Chapter Six

"You mean to tell me I'm the saviour of the universe, and I have to pit my skills against a crazy witch and her dangerous, unknown henchman?" Andrew fidgeted in his armchair. "I came to ask advice about my mum, not about saving the world!"

Mrs Jordan gave him a sympathetic look. "It's all tied together, Andy-Pandy. As guardians, we've been living with the knowledge - and the scars - of the Hag for a long time."

"And I sense there is some relief that Andrew is now aware of this, Dorothy," the Seer spoke up.

"Relief, yes." Mrs Jordan nodded. "But it's tinged with sadness, too. We hoped she wouldn't find a foothold, but she did... through Andrew's mum."

"What am I supposed to do now?" Andrew hated the forlorn tone in his voice. "I thought I'd be concentrating on Mum, and helping her through this."

"It's most important you do that, Andy," Mrs Jordan agreed.

"However, your mother is on her own path," the Seer added. "There are treatments your mother must undertake, and naturally, you will be there to comfort her. But I expect you to seek out your guardians and friends, who will in turn comfort and guide you."

"Too right," Mrs Jordan echoed. "Sickness is tough to deal with, for everyone involved. Come to us if you're feeling low, dear. Plus, we'll catch you up on everything we know about the Hag."

"And when the moment is right," the Seer said, "You and your guardians will pursue the Hag, and her wrongdoings will be redressed."

"Let me guess," Andrew said, his tone bitter, "I'll know when that moment is?"

"There will be no doubt," the Seer nodded gravely. "For now, spend time with your friends and guardians. They will ease your worries."

As he spoke, the Seer faded from sight, leaving Andrew and Mrs Jordan alone in the lounge. They sat in silence, the wood heater crackling in the background, until Mrs Jordan's cats crept into the room and flopped in front of the fire, flaming shadows flickering across their long white fur.

"I'd better go," Andrew said. "It's late."

"Go and see Teresa tomorrow, or Leo," Mrs Jordan said. "Tell them about your mum. And don't hide anything from them, Andy. You need their support."

Andrew stood up. "Goodnight. Thank you for calling the Seer."

She beamed at him. "We'll get through this, Andy. One way or another."

The following morning, Andrew dragged himself out of bed and made some breakfast. His father was nowhere to be found, and Andrew assumed he'd returned to the hospital to be with his mother.

He placed a bowl of food out for Winston, who had earlier demanded breakfast but had given up and hidden under the doona in protest. "I'm going out, Winston," he called to the cat. "I'll be back in a little while." He locked the back door but left the screen door ajar, so Winston could come and go through Ralph's old dog flap.

Out on the street, Andrew paused. He wanted to see Leo, but he knew his friend listened to an American science podcast on Sunday morning, and he wouldn't appreciate the interruption. Instead, he turned in the direction of Teresa's house. Like him, Teresa was an only child, and her Sundays were spent in the company of her parents. She'd be glad of the distraction.

A few minutes later, he knocked on Teresa's front door. Mr McKenzie answered, grunting when he saw Andrew. The relationship between the pair had been less than amicable for some time. Andrew had been willing to forgive Mr McKenzie's actions during the altered timeline of last year, but it seemed Teresa's father was unwilling to offer Andrew the same courtesy. Andrew's misadventure on the Navy aircraft carrier *The Australia* a couple of years ago had sealed his fate, and henceforward Andrew was known in the McKenzie household as 'that troublemaker'.

"Good morning, Mr McKenzie!" Andrew arranged his face into an exaggerated smile. "Would Teresa be home?"

"You know where to find her," Mr McKenzie replied. "Don't spend too long, she's got an assignment to finish. Unlike *others,*" he glared pointedly at Andrew, "Teresa has her future mapped out. Don't go and mess that up on her."

He stalked into the kitchen, leaving Andrew free to hasten away from his disapproval along the hallway to Teresa's bedroom. He found her sprawled across the floor, surrounded by English textbooks, and looking none too happy about it. She looked up and grinned as he came in. "Oh, you're a lifesaver! Reading Hamlet is driving me around the twist."

"Oliver Twist?"

She glared at him. "We're not doing Charles Dickens yet. Anyway, can I ask you a question?"

"To be, or not to be? *That* is the question," Andrew said in his best theatrical voice. He pushed aside a pile of books and joined her on the floor, a smirk on his face.

"Listen," she said, "I've had it up to here with 'to be or not to be', Hamlet does an excellent job of knocking people off, despite moaning about everything. It's so depressing! I give up." She snapped the book shut and sat up, stretching her arms above her head. "I suppose you've finished the assignment already? Anyway, how are you doing?"

"No, I haven't. And Mum has cancer." The words tumbled out of his mouth.

Teresa's mouth parted in surprise. "What?"

"I haven't finished the assignment."

"Not that bit." Her red curls bounced in irritation. "Did you just say your mum has..."

"Cancer. Yes. She was diagnosed on Friday." He thought he was doing okay, but all of a sudden, his throat closed over. "I... I'm scared, Teresa." He hung his head, his fringe hiding the hot tears on his cheeks.

"Oh, Andrew!" She scooted across the floor and gave him a hug. "That's awful news. Can they operate?"

"It's in her... her bones," he stuttered. "They start chemo t-tomorrow. But there's more! I saw Mrs Jordan last night, and I found out there's a prophecy being fulfilled, and I'm a big part of it."

Teresa tilted her head to one side, a concerned expression on her face. "A prophecy? What does that have to do with your mum?"

He stared at her, his face blotchy with tears. "I asked the same thing! It turns out there's some horrible creature - they call her the Hag - that's after me. And to get to me, she went through my mum. She's the one that made Mum sick." His mouth trembled, and the tears reappeared.

Teresa touched his arm. "I'm not going to pretend I understand what you mean, Andy, but if there's anything I can do, tell me. Your mum is like a second mum to me, I can't imagine what you're going through." She reached up and grabbed a box of tissues from her desk. "Here." She thrust some into his hands. "It's going to be okay. You mum will get through this, and you've got me, Leo, and Gus to support you. Mostly me, of course, because guys don't have the first idea about comforting anyone!"

He was laughing and crying as he blotted the tears on his face. "Thanks, Teresa, it means a lot." They were side by side on the floor, and he opened his arms to hug her. Their heads came together, and he glanced at her dark eyes beneath long eyelashes, and the bloom of colour on her cheeks. Besides Leo, Teresa was his oldest friend, but now something shifted in him, and he wanted something more than friendship. Her eyes widened as he tilted her chin upwards and his lips found hers. She pressed against him, her arms snaking around his neck. For a moment, Andrew forgot where he was, until he heard someone clearing their throat behind them. He broke away from Teresa's embrace and turned to find a red-faced Mr McKenzie in the doorway.

"I came to see if you wanted lunch," he scowled at them, "but apparently you've developed an appetite for something else."

Teresa's face turned a matching shade of red as her father stalked off. "You'd better go," she said to Andrew. "I've got some explaining to do!"

Andrew made his way to the front door, and Teresa darted after her father. As he shut the door behind him, he heard her pleading with Mr McKenzie: "Dad? Dad! It's not what you think... it was nothing!"

CHAPTER SEVEN

Andrew met up with best friend Leo at lunchtime the following day. He'd already filled Leo in on his mother's sickness, but now he shared the news of the prophecy... and the small matter of his failed first kiss with Teresa.

"You did WHAT?!" Leo yelled. The expression on his face was almost comical, and Andrew would have laughed if the whole episode hadn't been so painful.

"Shut up! She's coming," he admonished his friend, as Teresa made her way through the crowd of students towards them. She paused, clearly reluctant to join them. Her hesitancy was quickly replaced by relief as she spotted Gus approaching from the opposite direction. She waved to him and pointed to another table a short distance away from where Leo and Andrew were sitting. After giving them both an embarrassed look, she sat down with Gus, her back to the two boys.

"Hmph. Can't even face me." Andrew glared at Teresa.

"What actually happened?" Leo leaned forward, his voice lowering. "I was wondering when you'd have the guts to do something, you've liked her for ages."

"True, but my timing was awful." Andrew glanced into his lunchbox. He'd briefly crossed paths with his father at breakfast, before Mr Adler returned to the hospital for Mrs Adler's first chemotherapy session. Andrew had made his own lunch, a couple of ham and cheese sandwiches. He could still see the fingerprints in the bread where he'd squashed them together in haste. He closed his lunchbox, his appetite gone. The magpies in the backyard would snare some extra food when he got home from school. "The worst bit is that she seemed to like it," he said, blushing. "I know that sounds arrogant, but she didn't push me away - in fact *I* was the one that broke it off when I heard her father behind us."

"No way!" Leo's eyes popped behind his glasses. "What did he say? We all know how he feels about you."

"Let's just say he wasn't impressed with his daughter canoodling 'that troublemaker' as he likes to call me. She was horrified – daddy's little girl had slipped up, and she fell over herself to make things right with him. To hell with my feelings. She told him it didn't mean anything." He stared moodily into the distance.

"Cheer up, old man," Leo clapped him on the back. "You know she was just saying that to get back in daddy's good books."

"I'm not so sure." Andrew gazed at Teresa and Gus, their heads bent together as they sat side by side on the bench. "She's made no attempt to fix things up today. She was sympathetic about Mum, but she didn't want to hear a thing about the Hag and the prophecy."

"I've gotta admit, she's not Robinson Crusoe on that count. It sounds like the stuff of fairy tales." Scientific Leo had reappeared, complete with a sceptical look on his face.

"Leo!" Andrew lost patience. "You of all people should know better. You knew Ralph could talk, you know about Winston, and can I remind you again of the professor who tutored you last year?"

Leo shifted uncomfortably on the bench. "Andy, that's not fair."

"Life isn't fair!" Andrew shouted. There was a lull in the lunchtime conversation, and a number of students turned to look at him. Teresa twisted around in her seat, and the pair locked eyes. She offered him a melancholy smile, and in that moment, Andrew knew he couldn't compete with the love between father and daughter. He ripped his gaze away, turning back to Leo. "Life isn't fair," he repeated quietly. "Mum's in the hospital getting chemo, and now Mrs Jordan and the Seer are telling me I have to pursue a crazy old woman and her dangerous sidekick."

"What does Mr Lovell have to say about this? Isn't he one of your guardians as well?"

"He is," Andrew nodded. "And I'm going to see him when I get home from school."

A few benches over, Gus listened to Teresa's version of events. "Andrew was inconsolable," she explained, "And I was trying to comfort him, and he ended up kissing me. And then my dad saw. He was fuming, Gus! He hates Andrew, so now I'm in damage control, convincing Dad it was nothing, just a one-off because Andrew was in tears."

Gus remained silent. He noticed Teresa was quick to lay the blame at Andrew's feet, while admitting nothing about her own feelings.

"Anyway, he listened to me," Teresa continued. "I can be pretty convincing, and he obviously never expected Andrew to have the guts to kiss me. Neither did I, for that matter!"

She's lying to herself, Gus thought. *I've seen the way she looks at him, but she's scared of upsetting her father.* "Have you spoken to Andrew about this?" he asked. "Is he okay?"

She bit her lip. "No, I haven't, but I'm sure he'll understand. Besides, he was raving on about some other stuff - a prophecy, and a weird creature called the Hag. Do you have any idea what he was talking about?"

Oh no. A shiver ran through Gus. *It's HER fault that Mrs Adler is sick. Will we ever be free of that wretched woman?* His face was a mask, deliberately puzzled. "A prophecy?" he said aloud. "Sorry, I don't know what you're talking about. And I've never heard of a hag, unless we've moved onto the topic of fairy tales." Inwardly, his heart was hammering. *I must get to Dorothy and Patrick, and warn them.*

Teresa was relieved by his response. "Good, it's not just me that thinks he was rambling. It must be the stress."

"I think so too," Gus agreed. "Teresa, it's probably best you don't get too involved with Andrew at the moment." Her hands were clasped on the table in front of them, and he lightly touched her fingers. "He has too much going on with his mother, and a relationship will only complicate things. It's best you respect your father's wishes."

Teresa looked at him with trusting dark eyes and nodded. She packed up her lunch and bounded off to class, leaving Gus alone to brood. Had he done enough to convince her to stay away from Andrew? "I think so," he said under his breath. "I hope so. Her safety depends on it."

The school bell rang, and Gus decided to cut class. It was time for a crisis guardian meeting.

CHAPTER EIGHT

Half an hour later, Mrs Jordan heard a tap at the front door. Expecting another visit from Andrew, she was surprised to find Gus leaning on the door frame, a sour expression on his face. "Angus? Is everything all right?" Only she and Mr Lovell called him by his proper name, due to their long and colourful history.

"No. Everything is not all right." He shook his head in irritation. "Why didn't you tell me the Hag had returned?"

"We only figured it out on Saturday night. Why, what's the matter?"

"We need to talk with Patrick - *now*." He took Mrs Jordan's arm and pulled her through the doorway.

"All right, hold your horses!" She held up her hands. "Let me grab a jacket and we'll go."

Five minutes later, the pair huddled on Mr Lovell's doorstep. The door opened almost immediately, and Mr Lovell gave them a roguish grin. "Saw you coming. Figured we were having a council of war, or some such thing. Would one of you mind putting the kettle on?"

They were soon assembled in the old man's lounge room, Mr Lovell in his customary spot by the window, the other two sharing the floral-upholstered couch. They were an odd bunch to look at: an elderly man, a middle-aged woman, and a tall young man with blond hair who appeared to be about sixteen years of age. But looks are deceiving, and one had only to glance at the teenager's wise grey eyes to understand he had seen more than could be accounted for in a person of such tender years. The old man had survived war and heartbreak, and the woman had navigated her own losses. Their common bond? The guardianship of one Andrew Adler, and the deep scars they carried from a cruel and heartless adversary.

"The Hag," Gus spoke up. "I wish you'd told me immediately that she was back."

"Eh?" Mr Lovell jerked upright in his armchair. "No one told me, either!"

Mrs Jordan had the good sense to blush. "I'm sorry, really, I am, but there's been so much going on. Have you all heard about Helen Adler?" She updated the pair on Mrs Adler's health.

"That's awful," Mr Lovell muttered. "Do we know how it came about?"

"Think about it, Pat! You already know," Gus said. "It was HER, up to her old tricks again." There was a universal groan as they each pondered the repercussions of his statement. "And Andrew's gone and complicated things too," he continued. "He cried on Teresa's shoulder - which is completely understandable - but he ended up kissing her, and her father saw."

Mrs Jordan had a proud grin on her face. "Bless him. He finally had the courage to do something."

Gus turned on her. "No, Dorothy, it's not *bless him*, as you put it. At the moment, Teresa is chasing her tail, trying to placate her father. It's only a matter of time until she reaches stage two in this romantic fiasco."

"And what's stage two?" Mr Lovell grunted.

"Stage two is when Teresa decides to see Andrew behind her father's back."

"Look, my old brain cells are not functioning as well as they used to," Mr Lovell said. "Why does it matter?"

Gus shot the old man a furious look. "Pat, I'm older than you, and my brain's working just fine. And it matters because Teresa will become the Hag's next target."

There was a sharp intake of breath from Mrs Jordan. "My goodness, you're right. We can't let that happen! It will destroy Andrew."

"What do we do?" Mr Lovell said.

"We distract him," Gus said. "Keep him busy. Bring him up to date on how the Hag operates. Tell him your stories. Pat, yours alone will keep him busy for weeks! And it will take his mind off his mum."

"What are you going to do?" Mrs Jordan asked.

"You both know my story," Gus sighed. "I need to stay as far away from Andrew as I can, I don't want to jeopardise things. Plus, I'll run interference with Teresa, and try to keep her away from lover boy. The Hag must not find out that those two like each other." His eyes darted to the clock on the wall. "I'd better go. I skipped school to have this chat, and I don't want to be here when Andrew gets home from school. Are we clear on what to do?"

Mr Lovell and Mrs Jordan nodded. "And we won't mention your involvement with the Hag at all," Mrs Jordan said. "When he's ready, he'll come to you."

Gus's smile was half-hearted. "He may not believe my story. It would be better if he didn't." He excused himself, and left.

Mr Lovell glanced at Mrs Jordan. "So, we're taking a trip down memory lane. This won't be easy, Dorothy." His pale blue eyes shimmered with tears.

"You were there for me, Pat, and I'll be here for you," Dorothy squeezed his arm. "I'd be honoured to listen to your story." She planted a kiss on the old man's forehead, carried the empty cups to the kitchen and let herself out.

A short time later, Mr Lovell watched out his window as another tall, blond boy darted up the path to his front door.

Andrew had come to visit.

"Help yourself to a drink, Andrew. And I think there's some biscuits in the cupboard if you're hungry," Mr Lovell said as he ushered Andrew inside out of the cold. "Don't make me anything, I've just had one. Come into the lounge room when you're ready, the heater's on in there."

Andrew thanked his lucky stars. He was famished after skipping lunch, and he scoffed two Anzac biscuits while he waited for the kettle to boil. He made himself a tea and carefully carried his mug and another biscuit into the lounge.

"I've heard about your mother," Mr Lovell said as Andrew sat down. "Promise me you won't work yourself into a dither about this, son. People get sick all the time, and they also get better."

"Even after they've been touched by the Hag?" Andrew's eyes narrowed.

His question caught the old man off-guard. "Eh? Now don't go getting ahead of yourself. Nothing's set in stone."

"Except the prophecy," Andrew said. "You know, that thing where I suddenly become a superhero and save the day."

Mr Lovell gave him a stern glance. "As I said. Don't go getting ahead of yourself. As far as I'm concerned, you'll be doing nothing about the Hag and the prophecy until we know more about your mother's condition. Concentrate on your mother getting well, and then we'll deal with that other issue. Am I clear?"

"I guess," Andrew sighed.

"Good. Now what else have you got to tell me? I haven't seen you for a while. How's that new cat of yours going?"

"Winston's fine. He's a bit upset about eating kangaroo meat, but apart from that he's settling in well."

"I should think so! He was a tough old so-and-so when he was in human form, let me tell you."

"That's right," Andrew nodded, "you worked for him in the War Rooms in London. I'd forgotten."

"I knew him from another time as well, but I'll save that story for another day. How's soccer going this year?"

"We're not on top, but we're not on the bottom, either."

"Sounds like progress to me!" the old man grunted. "Is Angus still playing?"

"Of course. His experience is what gets us over the line."

"I daresay," Mr Lovell acknowledged. "Imagine how many games he's played! Several thousand, I'd wager. And Leo? Is he still playing?"

Andrew grinned. "Sport is not Leo's forte, as you well know. He dropped soccer to concentrate on his studies. Probably a good decision, the competition is pretty fierce this season. Some days I feel like an old man out on the field."

Mr Lovell threw his head back and guffawed. "Oh, Andrew, wait 'till you reach my age before you call yourself old. Do you have any idea what it's like to grow old?"

Andrew shook his head with a rueful grin. "Can't say I do just yet, Mr Lovell."

Mr Lovell sat back in his armchair. "It's like a thief stealing into your house one night and making away with your face. The next morning you look in the mirror, and there's an old bloke staring back at you. How did it happen? The young guy is still inside, thinking he can flirt with the cute girl who works in the newsagent on Lincoln Street - yeah, you know the one I mean!"

Andrew knew the girl. Rachel was seventeen, with glossy chestnut hair that fell halfway down her back, and dark eyes that were a treasure cavern of promises and secrets. The guys in Andrew's class drooled over her, and while he agreed she was pretty, she was not Teresa.

"But this old guy," Mr Lovell interrupted his thoughts, "He looks at you and shakes his head in pity. He knows those days are long gone."

"What about your first grey hair?" Andrew asked. "Or wrinkles?"

"You deny them all. Heck, I ripped out any grey hair I found for the first couple of years. In the end I gave up, there were far too many."

"Old age caught up with you, Mr Lovell," Andrew grinned. "How old are you, anyway?"

"Too old, son." He faced the window, staring at the faded blue winter sky that matched his eyes. "I stopped celebrating my birthday after something happened when I was ten years old." He passed an unsteady hand across his face.

"Can you tell me about it?"

Mr Lovell looked back at Andrew, wiping away a tear that had sprung unannounced from the corner of his eye. "It's time you heard it. We may need to do it in a few sittings though, Andy. It's a long story."

Andrew rose from his chair. "I'll put the kettle on."

Fifteen minutes later, the pair were back in the lounge drinking tea, while Andrew had refuelled with a couple more Anzac biscuits.

"It all began in 1900, Andrew. I was ten years old, and my older brother Andrew—" Mr Lovell held up his hand. "Yes, yes - you heard right, the year was 1900, and yes, my brother's name was Andrew too. I loved him more than anything else - anyone else - on the planet, but he was going away. Off to fight a 'glorious' war in Africa. He promised ten-year-old me he'd be back in time for tea. It was a joke, but I was desperate to believe him. And that's when I discovered that war rips the heart out of you, and I was determined to do something about it…"

CHAPTER NINE

Andrew sat out in the yard, his back against the peppercorn tree. Winston rested against his upper leg. It was Tuesday afternoon, and a cold wind blew down the side of the house and around the tree, ruffling his hair. He snuggled into the hood of his jacket and thrust his hands in his pockets. His mother was back home, and Mr Adler was insisting the house remain quiet to aid her recovery.

As quiet as a morgue, the thought surfaced in his mind. "Not a morgue," he mumbled. "She needs to rest after the treatment, that's all."

"Correct, Andrew," Winston lifted his head and licked a paw. "And you know she'd chew your ear for sitting out here instead of doing your homework."

"I can't concentrate!" He brushed an annoying piece of fringe off his face. "I'm wishing and hoping that mum recovers, then there's this business with the Hag and the prophecy, and then..." He hesitated, a blush rising on his cheeks.

"Yes?" Winston prompted him.

"I-I can't stop thinking about Teresa." He looked down. "There, I said it. I know I should be concentrating on Mum, but I can't get her out of my mind - even if she doesn't think about me the same way—"

"How do you know that?" The cat cut in on him. "I believe you said she responded enthusiastically to your kiss. Would that not suggest she reciprocates your interest?"

"I've got no idea!" Andrew moaned. "My head is full, and I don't want to think anymore." He gazed past Winston to the street, catching sight of Gus entering the driveway. He stood up and beckoned him over. "I'm outside," he explained. "I don't want to disturb Mum."

Gus joined the pair under the tree. "Mate, I'm so sorry. How's she doing?"

"She's had her first chemo treatment. She's tired. I heard things can get worse after a few sessions."

Gus frowned at him. "They can, but that doesn't mean it will happen to your mum. I've seen this before, and in times when they didn't have chemotherapy and radiation. Don't you give up on her, she needs your strength."

Andrew's shoulders slumped. "I'm not strong."

"You've no idea, have you?" Gus prodded him in the chest. "Think about everything you did last year, when the world was falling apart. I couldn't fix things, but you did!"

"I still needed your help."

"To some extent." Gus smiled. "We all need each other's help. That's the whole idea of us being guardians. Has Patrick started telling you his story?"

"He began yesterday. He told me about his brother going off to the Boer War, how he met the Seer for the first time, and how the Seer sent him to Africa to meet a young man who was being held captive. Apparently, this young man's name was Winston Churchill."

The grey cat shot to his feet. "As I live and breathe! You know this boy?"

Andrew and Gus looked at each other and burst out laughing. "He's not a boy anymore, Winston," Andrew said. "His name is Patrick Lovell, and he lives on the other side of that fence."

"Astounding!" Winston exclaimed. "Truly astounding. He was a good lad. We made our escape together and boarded a train outside Pretoria. We both fell asleep after the excitement of it all, and when I woke up, Patrick was gone. I'm pleased he made it home safe and sound."

"Do you see how all our lives are intertwined?" Gus turned to Andrew. "I'm never surprised when these things happen anymore. They call it serendipity, and that's why Winston is with us now."

Andrew shook his head in wonder. "I'm still pinching myself that Mr Lovell was born in 1890!"

"He skipped a few years, as you'll discover." Gus's grey eyes shone with the memory. "The point is, I helped Pat out on a few occasions, and he did the same for me. Nothing's changed, Andy. No matter what the obstacle, together we can get through this. Just concentrate on the positives."

"Hang on, what are these positives you speak of?" Andrew stared at him. "Not only am I dealing with Mum's sickness, but this Hag creature is back, and stronger than ever because of her new henchman. The prophecy made it sound like she's got a massive beef about something. How do you fight against such evil? What does she want from us?"

"She wants us to feel as bad as her."

"There's got to be more to it than that!" Andrew shook his head. "Have you come across her in the past, Gus? What do you know about her?"

The change in Gus was swift and surprising. "Nothing that will help you," he said, his voice cold. "Anyway, it's getting late, I'd better be off."

Andrew watched him hurry down the gravel driveway. He gave Winston a bewildered look. "Did I say something wrong?"

Winston stared at Gus's retreating figure. "No, you were merely curious. But as your friend pointed out, all our lives are intertwined. And it would seem Gus is not ready to share how his life and the Hag's were intertwined."

The days blurred together as the Adler household took on the burden of Mrs Adler's cancer treatment. Andrew stepped into the breach, assuming cleaning duties in the kitchen while his dad prepared simple, healthy meals for the family on the days they weren't at the hospital.

After he ran short of uniform shirts for school, Andrew taught himself to use the washing machine, and arranged wash days twice a week. His mother beamed with pride from her seat in the lounge room as he gathered in the washing after school. He waved and smiled back at her. He'd taken to placing the clothes immediately on hangers, thus bypassing most of the ironing. This was a real bonus since his school workload was also growing. *I'm so lucky to have Winston and Leo to help with my homework,* he thought as he carried the washing inside. *With Mum the way she is, it's hard to concentrate on anything.*

Nonetheless, Andrew knew when to take a break, and a cracking story was at hand a few short steps away at Mr Lovell's house.

The old man welcomed him inside. "Ready for the next part, son?"

"I can't wait, Mr Lovell."

"Good. Make us a cuppa. I'm feeling parched."

Andrew made the tea, and he discovered a packet of cream biscuits in the pantry. He threw four on a plate and headed to the lounge room. Mr Lovell was in his chair by the window, and he stretched out in his usual spot on the couch.

"We're up to World War One, or the Great War, as we called it. You've studied this at school, haven't you?"

"Yessir, you bet."

"Good. That saves me half an hour of explaining how it all came about. I'll skip to my mother waving me goodbye on the dock in Hobart, and her dismay at me taking along the toy soldier she made for me as a child."

"What?" Andrew gave him a confused look. "Why did you take a toy off to war?"

"He was my good luck charm - at that point, anyway. And it wasn't long before I met another chap with a good luck charm of his own. His name was Cecil Jordan."

"Jordan? Any relation to Mrs Jordan?"

Mr Lovell grimaced. "Don't get ahead of me, Andy. Cecil hailed from the Northern Rivers of New South Wales, and like me, he was pretty eager to join up and fight. I loved that man like the brother I lost, and until he was shot at Gallipoli, I believed he was just a normal bloke. That is, until the Seer showed up and insisted I look after Cecil."

"When you say *look after him*, did you nurse him back to health, or was there more to it than that?"

"A whole lot more!" The old man's eyes blazed.

Dorothy Jordan jerked awake in her seat. She had fallen asleep reading one of her favourite Agatha Christie books, *4:50 from Paddington,* and she felt groggy after her unplanned nap. Her mobile phone was buzzing on the small table beside her, and she snatched it up.

"I was beginning to think I'd have to leave you a message!" Lucy Bargwana's cheerful voice filled her ear.

"Apparently I've reached that age where I nap in the afternoons," Mrs Jordan replied.

There was a snort of mirth at the other end. "We're not *that* old, Dorothy. And there's really no time for napping now."

"Why on earth not?"

Mrs Bargwana's voice was breathy and excited. "There's been a fascinating influx of special cats down here in Canberra. I wanted you to be the first to know."

Mrs Jordan's mind darted away to her current pets, Napoleon and Josephine. The two Persians has been little trouble to care for, even when Andrew's special dog Ralph had still been in the picture. Despite his intelligence, Ralph had often switched into full-on dog mode, chasing the two cats around the back yard and over the fence. Little harm was done to the cats, although Ralph's life took a surprising turn after one particular chase, she recalled with a shiver. Now the two cats were well into their senior years, and content to spend the day curled up on a bed. Surely Lucy wasn't asking her to assume a greater responsibility with the special animals?

"Three of them are siblings, Dorothy." Mrs Bargwana cut in on her thoughts. "You'll recognise one of the names... it's Colleen."

"Colleen?" Mrs Jordan gasped. "As in Colleen O'Donnell?"

"That's right. She was your old neighbour in Hobart, wasn't she?"

"She was so much more than that, Lucy. She taught me to believe." Back in the 1970s, Colleen O'Donnell minded an eight-year-old Dorothy while her mother worked in the aftermath of the Tasman Bridge disaster. Dorothy remembered those few short weeks with immense fondness, as the old woman introduced her to a world of fairy tales just beyond her back door. "Didn't she have a brother she lost in World War One?"

"Yes, his name was Kevin. And there was an older sister called Deirdre, who was my mentor." She lowered her voice. "She was a snippy old thing. Blunt, with no time for fools. But she has a heart of gold beneath all that armour, and a huge knowledge that'll come in handy. I'll be looking after her. Colleen has come back for you."

"And Kevin?" Mrs Jordan asked.

"After I get off the phone with you, I'll prepare all the animals, load up the car and drive to Sydney. I have an idea Patrick would like to catch up with an old war comrade."

"Oh, he'll be delighted!" Mrs Jordan exclaimed. "He's been sharing his life story with Andrew, to help take his mind off his mother."

"That's really sweet of him. I can't imagine it would be an easy story to tell."

"It isn't, but Andrew needs to hear it. We've all made sacrifices, Lucy."

There was a pause at the other end. "I know," Mrs Bargwana said. "The time is drawing near, Dorothy. The return of the O'Donnells, Helen Adler's sickness, I can feel the shift. The Hag is making her move, and I'm worried."

The winter sun disappeared behind a bank of clouds, and Mrs Jordan shivered. "We kept her at bay in the past, we can do it again," she said. "We have to. We have no choice."

CHAPTER TEN

"Lambie, you're an absolute superstar for helping me with my homework!" Andrew shut his text book and gave Leo a friendly punch on the arm.

"Ouch." Leo winced. "And don't call me Lambie," he said, his tone defensive. "You know I've hated that nickname since, since..."

"Since you were tutored by Einstein. Yes, I know," Andrew winked at his friend. "But you'll always be Lambie to me." The boys had been friends for years, and early on, Andrew had discovered Leo's full name was Leo Alain Martin Bernard, which formed the perfect acronym LAMB. Leo blamed his French parents for the abundance of names, but he took the teasing in his stride.

It was almost lunchtime on Saturday, and the boys had ploughed through their maths and science assignments. Leo passed on a couple of tips he'd picked up from his scientist father, plus he explained a technique he learned from Einstein, which was attacking each problem from a different angle. "He was always going on about questioning," Leo explained as he stood up and stretched. "He said the world can't be changed unless we change our thinking. He believed *that* was the measure of intelligence - the ability to change."

A sudden stench hit Andrew's nostrils, and he waved a hand in front of his nose. "Smells like you've just had a change of your own! Man, that's evil. What did you eat last night?"

Leo's face reddened. "That wasn't me, it was Newton!" He pointed to the dog snoring beneath his desk.

"Wow. Maybe you'd better change his diet!"

"He's an old boy, Andy, and farts leak out of him. At least he's given up sleeping in the hallway, it wasn't good for his health. I lost count of the number of times we tripped over him, the poor old thing." He bent down and scratched Newton behind the ears. "When it's time for him to go, do you think you could put in a good word for me with Mrs Bargwana? It'd be brilliant to have the real Newton in dog form."

"Who, Bert Newton?" Andrew joked. "Olivia Newton-John?"

"You know who I mean!" Leo glared at him. "Sir Isaac Newton."

"You don't need him. Your marks are already astronomical. The universities will be falling over themselves to offer you a scholarship in a couple of years' time."

"Maybe." Leo gazed out his window, a distant look in his eyes. "What about you? Are you still keen to get into game design?"

"You bet. I love history, but I don't want to be some boring professor stuck in a university library. You'll laugh, but I had this idea about making an app. A game I want to call Time Stepping."

Leo grinned. "I wonder where that idea came from?"

Andrew held a finger to his lips. "Ssh. It's a secret. But I don't want to get ahead of myself. Right now, I'm listening to Mr Lovell's life story. It's been taking my mind off Mum."

Leo switched his gaze onto Andrew. "Is it working?" he said softly.

"Some days." Andrew dropped his eyes and straightened out the dog-eared pages of his exercise book. "I try not to think about the future, but it's not easy. They're telling me this Hag creature made Mum sick, and all I want to do is go after her, but they're saying it's not the right time!"

He threw his books on the bed and began to pace the room. "When *is* the right time? After Mum has died?"

"Aww, Andy, no!" Leo grabbed him by the arm. "Assumptions aren't allowed. That's not fair on your mum. Besides, you need to be around, supporting her, not running off to another place and time."

"You're right," Andrew sighed. "You're my voice of reason. I'll just have to bide my time and listen to Mr Lovell's war stories."

"Which war was he in?"

"All of them."

"Garbage," Leo snorted. "He'd be as old as Methuselah if that was true."

"He is. Maybe not up around the 900 mark, but he's over a hundred years old. Did I tell you he went to South Africa and met up with a young Winston Churchill?"

Leo whistled. "You guys seem to loop into and out of each other's lives! There has to be a scientific term for that." He bent towards his laptop and tapped a search into Google.

"There is," Andrew said from behind him. "It's called serendipity."

Leo turned around, his lips curled into a scornful smile. "And is this serendipity working on Teresa as well?"

"Oh, stick the knife in, why don't you?" Andrew's cheeks flamed. "You know as well as I do, she's avoiding me. In fact, she seems to be spending a lot of time with Gus instead."

"Sorry, Andy-Pandy." Leo flashed him a guilty look. "I didn't mean it! I have noticed her and Gus together. But he won't do anything, he knows you like her."

"Maybe, maybe not. I'm never quite sure what's going on in his mind, to be honest."

"He's one of your guardians, isn't he?" Leo reminded him. "He'll look after you."

Andrew didn't smile. "I hope so."

It was early Sunday morning, and Andrew braved the cold to retrieve his father's newspaper off the dewy front lawn. He spotted Mr Lovell bending down to collect his own, and he gave him a cheery wave. "When can we hear the next instalment?"

A flurry of emotions crossed the old man's face. "This next part is a tough one, Andy. Dorothy needs to hear it as well. Give me an hour, and we can start."

Andrew gave a quick nod. "I'll go and see her now."

Once the trio were settled in the lounge room, Mr Lovell continued his story of Gallipoli in 1915. An early morning swim with Cecil descended into a nightmare, when the old man's friend was shot by a sniper.

"Was he dead?" Andrew interrupted.

Mr Lovell's eyes were two hard stones. "He died in my arms. But as I dodged more bullets and dragged Cecil's lifeless body to shore, the beach and rocky hillside disappeared, replaced by a log cabin tucked within a pine tree forest."

And beckoning Mr Lovell inside was none other than an oversized hare. Cecil was laid to rest on a bed, and the Seer ushered the young Patrick into a room Andrew knew all too well: a cosy cavern lined with books, a well-worn chesterfield sofa, and the rich hues of a Persian carpet on the floor. The Seer calmed the shattered soldier with a thyme tea, and then removed an item resembling an old-fashioned school slate from his desk.

"It was a tablet computer, wasn't it?" Andrew said. "The Seer loves his modern gadgets."

"That may well be, but it was 1915, and a device like that was pure sorcery." The old man glared at him. "I'd just watched my friend die, then the Seer presents this portable movie screen and shows me Cecil's life continuing on as if he was still alive. I saw his wedding day, and the birth of two beautiful children. I saw grandchildren as well, one of whom took a liking to a sweet young girl called Dorothy Brown..." He gave Mrs Jordan a brief smile as she pulled a handkerchief from her sleeve and dabbed at her eyes. "I saw it all, and I asked the Seer why. It seemed pointless, with Cecil lying dead in the next room."

"Except he wasn't, was he?" Andrew tilted his head to one side. "Otherwise, Mrs Jordan wouldn't be Mrs Jordan."

"Clever lad." Mr Lovell nodded. "There was a noise behind the curtain, and the next minute Cecil appeared, took one look at the Seer, and passed out in shock. We laid him back on the bed, and that's when I discovered I was to be Cecil's guardian angel. Whatever happened, the Seer insisted that under no circumstance could Cecil die in war."

"Because his grandson had to marry Mrs Jordan?" Andrew asked.

"Yes, that, of course!" Mr Lovell's eyes grew fiery. "And one other thing: Cecil's daughter was my wife."

Serendipity. Leo had scoffed at the idea, but there was no denying it. The lives of Andrew's guardians had intertwined on many occasions over the years. But for what purpose? Back at home, Andrew stood at the kitchen sink washing the dishes from their evening meal. He knew there was more of the story to be told, but he couldn't help but hope some of this serendipity would rub off onto his mother. Surely some hero would emerge from the shadows and save the day?

He rinsed the plates and left them to dry on the dish rack. A sudden thought came to him: *he* was the person stepping from the shadows, according to the Seer's prophecy. No one was coming to save him - or his mother, for that matter. He would have to save himself.

The following day, Mrs Adler returned to hospital for another round of chemotherapy. Andrew's parents would not be home until later on, and he could not face sitting around in the empty house. He dropped his school bag in the hallway, gave Winston a friendly pat and some food, and proceeded next door for more of Mr Lovell's story.

Andrew let himself in the front door, and slipped into the old man's lounge room. His greeting died on his lips when he saw he was far from alone. "What's going on here? Mrs Jordan? And Mrs Bargwana - when did you arrive?" He gazed at the two women on the couch. "And where did all these cats come from?"

Lucy Bargwana removed a large ginger cat from her lap and stood to hug Andrew. "I had an influx of cats back home in Canberra, Andrew. It's the most I've received at once, so I thought I'd share the load. I drove up after lunch, and I've only recently arrived."

"Who are they?" Andrew asked, eyeing the ginger and near-identical pair of tortoiseshell cats.

"That can wait for the moment," Mrs Bargwana said with a mysterious smile. "Patrick is ready to continue, we can talk about the cats afterwards."

"It was soon after my early morning swim that an Irish contingent bolstered our numbers at Gallipoli," Mr Lovell said. "We were in desperate need of fortification after our huge losses back in April, and the Irish blokes were a bright and cheerful lot. One lad in particular caught my eye. He was a young one - as many of us were. Kevin was 18, with strawberry blond hair and a spray of freckles across his nose. His hazel eyes were as lively as his Irish accent, and he had a quick, almost pixie-like way of moving. One minute he was nowhere in sight, the next he was hovering by your elbow. He was a real pocket dynamo, keen as mustard and positive about everything..." The old man paused and cleared his throat. "And the best bit was that he knew about the Seer as well."

"Oh, come on, Mr Lovell—"

"It's true!" he insisted. "He and his two sisters used to play near some standing stones, growing up in Ireland. I gather they slipped through a portal and met up with the Seer. It's the only explanation I can come up with."

"You didn't ask him to explain?"

"We ran out of time." Mr Lovell's face fell. "I saved Cecil's life at the battle of Lone Pine, but I couldn't save Kevin. I found the mementos he held dear, and treasured them as my own in his memory: a lace handkerchief from his sisters, and a four-leaf clover tucked into a bible. I just wish I could've spoken more to him about his adventures in Ireland."

"And now you can," rumbled the large ginger cat from Mrs Bargwana's lap.

"What the hey?" The old man jerked upright in his chair. "That cat has an Irish accent!"

"Patrick," Mrs Bargwana spoke up, "I had very little choice about driving up here this afternoon, the cats were most insistent. Kevin's voice was one of the louder ones." She scratched the cat under his chin, and he purred in appreciation. "I'll be off now; the Seer has agreed to transport me home so I can attend to all the animals' needs." She placed Kevin on the old man's lap with a grin. "I imagine the two of you have a lot to catch up on! I'll be back in a few days to collect my car. I need to hear more of Patrick's story - I suspect the pieces of the puzzle will fall into place if we're all together."

CHAPTER ELEVEN

The next day, Andrew and Leo met up for lunch at school. Andrew was deep into his description of yesterday's cat invasion and Mr Lovell's story, when Teresa approached and perched at their table with a nervous smile.

"Hi guys, how are you? How's your mum, Andy?"

Leo's eyes flickered towards Andrew, who cleared his throat and said, "Hi Teresa, what's up?"

"I'm sorry to bother you. Have either of you seen Gus? I need to ask him something."

An ugly green monster twisted in Andrew's stomach. "You two seem to be spending a lot of time together."

"Oh, not really, we're just friends!" She had the grace to blush. "I wanted to ask him a history question. You guys aren't in my class, and he's incredible with history, you would swear he'd been there!"

The boys exchanged another look. "Yes, you would," Andrew said drily. "Have you checked the library? I know he spends a lot of time there."

Teresa smacked her forehead with her hand. "Why didn't I think of that? Okay, gotta run. Catch you later." She bolted off.

Leo gave Andrew an incredulous look. "She has no idea about Gus, does she?"

"Not a clue," he answered. "And let's keep it that way. She wouldn't leave him alone if she knew the truth. In her eyes he'd be some kind of rock star demigod - 'the boy that lived forever'." He gave a bitter laugh. "Can you imagine?"

Leo didn't smile. "Don't you think you should warn her?"

Andrew shrugged. "Gus doesn't have his talisman any more, he should age at the same rate as us. If she wants to follow him around like a lovesick puppy dog, she can. I can't stop her."

Teresa pushed open the door to the school library. She spotted Gus's familiar figure at a distant table; his head turned to gaze through the window at the playing fields beyond. She hurried across the room. "You're a hard man to find," she whispered as she sat down. "I've been looking everywhere for you! In the end I had to ask Andrew if he knew where you were."

"How's his mum?" Gus turned to face her, his grey eyes full of concern.

"He didn't say.... I did ask, though," she hastened to add. "I was after some help with history. That assignment on the Vietnam war has some curly bits to it!"

"I can come over to your house on the weekend, if that's okay."

Teresa detected a note of disinterest in his voice. "Are you all right, Gus?"

"I'm fine," he grunted. "The Vietnam war isn't my favourite topic though."

She frowned, her head tipped to one side. "Something's bothering you. Is there something going on between the two of you?"

He met her gaze. "What are you talking about?"

"You and Andrew. You both seem tense lately."

Gus continued to stare at her. Was she fishing for answers, wondering if a jealousy had arisen between the boys on her account?

"He has something to work through, Teresa. It's better if I'm not around."

"But his mother is sick. He needs all the support he can get."

Then why aren't you offering? he thought. "He doesn't need mine," he said aloud. "I've seen far too many people die; he doesn't need my dreary angle on it."

"But—"

"There are no buts." He cut her off. "It's just the way it is. I'll see you later on and help you with that assignment." He turned away, ending the conversation.

Speechless, Teresa rose and left the library.

"We were battle weary, and finally we were relieved by the 2nd Division." Mr Lovell dove into his story the moment Andrew returned home from school. "We had some down time in our billets, French towns designated safe and far beyond the reach of the booming guns at the front. We made our way into a town beyond Albert, and that was the first time I had the unlucky fortune of meeting the Hag."

"How did you know it was her?" Andrew asked.

"I didn't at first. She was just a suspicious-looking old woman with a couple of shifty companions and an enormous dog. An Irish Wolfhound, from memory. The point is, she killed a little blonde girl in the marketplace.

To this day, I still don't know how she did it. One minute the child was alive, the next this old woman touched her, and the little girl was stone-cold dead. And I was an excellent judge of stone-cold dead by that stage."

"What happened?" Andrew leaned forward on the couch.

"There was a stand-off between the Hag and her men, and the townsfolk and us soldiers. The townsfolk accused her of being a witch, while the poor mother of the child was in hysterics, weeping and wailing. We were all raising our weapons when the Hag singled me out. She saw the soldier doll on my pack, and somehow deduced it was mine. Quick as a flash, she ordered the dog to fetch it. I made a move to grab it, and the dog went for my throat. The next thing I knew, the huge brute was dead at my feet, killed by a sharp shot from Cecil."

"Wow, he saved your life as well."

"He did, but that was just the beginning of it. Within the space of a minute, she'd cursed me, ordered one of her men to kill another child, and I'd grabbed her and had a knife to her throat."

"What?" Andrew's eyes popped. "She cursed you?"

The old man's mouth tightened. "Yes... and there's more. The old crone in my arms transformed into a stunning woman with dark hair and the bluest of blue eyes. It scared me, Andrew. It was unnatural. She tried to wriggle from my grasp, and that's where the nasty scar on her cheek came from." He turned to glance out the window, his eyes staring into the distance. "I'll remember her shrieks to my dying days." He paused and turned back to Andrew, his pale eyes fiery. "But I'm not sorry. She's done far worse, and she must answer for that."

Andrew left Mr Lovell's house, hopping the fence into his front yard. He let himself into the house and heard a wretched cry from his parent's bedroom. "It's gone, Peter. Look at it! My hair!" He crept to the door and peeked into the room. His mouth parted as he saw his mother's blonde hair scattered across the sheets. Her fists tightened around the longest lengths, as if clutching a limp bunch of flowers. "What do I do now?" She cast the hair aside and buried her face in her hands.

Andrew snuck away. The sickness to date had been invisible to the naked eye, apart from his mother's tiredness and lack of appetite. Now there was no hiding it, and Andrew's heart ached for his mother. On his way to the kitchen, a shadow fell across the front door. After hearing Mr Lovell's tale of the Hag, he was on full alert. He tiptoed to the door and threw it open. "Who's there?" he growled.

Mrs Jordan yelped, her forefinger frozen on its way to the doorbell. Mortified, she threw a hand across her mouth to muffle the noise. "Andrew, what on earth? Don't ever do that again, I nearly dropped the casserole!"

Relief washed over him. "Sorry, Mrs J. I was worried you were some-one - something - else. Come on in." He ushered her into the kitchen, where he explained what he'd just witnessed.

"Oh, the poor dear." Her face crumpled in sympathy. "Sounds like I've arrived just in time. I made this casserole, and I've got something your mother might find useful." She handed the container of food to Andrew, then pulled some colourful material from her pocket. "Head scarves. A lady I knew in Hobart wore them years ago, and I thought it'd be perfect for your mum if she began to lose her hair."

For a brief moment, Andrew had a flashback to Mrs Jordan's hat obsession two years ago and he suppressed a smile. "That's really thoughtful, Mrs J. You're not just a guardian, you're a fairy godmother!"

Mrs Jordan beamed. "It's the least I can do. A fairy godmother from my past helped me remember it. Mrs Lee taught me all about plants, and how they offer protection."

Her words sparked a sudden thought. "Could you bring some for Mum?" he asked. "Do you think it would help?"

"I don't see why not. First of all, I have to teach Helen how to tie this around her head. Is she up for visitors?"

"I'll find out." Andrew put the food on the kitchen bench and went in search of his father.

Mr Adler's pale face relaxed into a smile. "Dorothy must be a mind reader. Go and get her, I'll let Helen know help is at hand."

CHAPTER TWELVE

E arly in the morning on the weekend, Andrew awoke to a message arriving on his phone. Rolling over in bed, he dislodged Winston from between his legs and grabbed his phone from the floor, charging cable still attached.

Andy-Pandy, I need you to do a favour for me. Napoleon and Josephine are to be returned to the animal hospital in Nostalgia. Can you take them for me? I thought you could catch up with Ralph at the same time.

He sat up in bed and rattled off a reply to Mrs Jordan:

Sure. I'll be over after breakfast.

Andrew silently prepared his food, fearful of waking his mother. He hovered over the kettle and switched it off before it fully boiled. It had a beep that could wake the dead, let alone his exhausted parents. He made tea, adding some cold water after removing the teabag. He added sugar and took a tentative sip. Perfect. Less than a year ago, he hated tea, but now it was his go-to drink. He had a slice of toast with vegemite, and last of all, he left a bowl of food out for Winston. He clicked the back door shut, trudged down the driveway, and vaulted the low picket fence in the front yard.

Moments later he was inside Mrs Jordan's kitchen, where he found his neighbour in the midst of a large pile of cat hair. The cats were doing all they could to avoid imprisonment in the two cat carriers on the floor. Mrs Jordan turned to him in despair. "They're none too happy about this, Andy, but it's for the best. They'll have their freedom shortly, and we can't have them escaping while you travel to Nostalgia."

"Here. I'll give you a hand."

Together, they wrestled the cats into the carriers and snapped the doors shut. "Phew," Mrs Jordan sighed. "It breaks my heart to see them go, but it's time. Now," she turned to him, hands on hips, "How are you going to do this?"

"I was about to ask you the same question." It was all well and good to time step by himself, but he was taking two important creatures with him.

Mrs Jordan paused, a hand on her chin. "Have you got the talisman I gave you for Christmas? You have a photo of Ralph inside it, don't you?"

He fished out the black, star-shaped necklace. "I wear it all the time, Mrs J."

"Good boy," she nodded. "Pop your arm on the cat carriers, and hold the necklace in your other hand. Now, picture Ralph in your mind, and Vellistrian, and see where you end up. I know you can do it, Andy-Pandy!"

I'm glad you think so, he thought as he crouched down, one hand grasping the handle of a carrier. He bent forward, clasped the dark necklace in his palm and, feeling like a contortionist, he hooked two fingers through the other handle. It had been a while since his last time step, and the last thing he wanted to do was lose one of the cats. He cleared his mind, focussing on Vellistrian, Ralph, and the animal hospital in Nostalgia.

His fears were unfounded, as he and the cats were immediately whisked away. Andrew held the two carriers in a white-knuckle grip, while his arms spun like manic clock hands. The cats emitted loud, frightened mewls from within their portable prisons.

After a few stomach-churning loop-the-loops and rolls, the trio landed, coming to rest on a smooth brown earthen floor. The cages had mysteriously disappeared in transit, prompting Andrew to wonder how he'd kept hold of the cats. Judging by their dirty looks, he presumed he had latched onto their tails. Thankfully the cats appeared unharmed. They crouched together on the floor, two oversized cotton balls, directing furious glares of disapproval at Andrew. He bit his lip, suppressing an inappropriate laugh.

A startled yelp from behind drew his attention. "Andrew? Is that you?"

He looked over his shoulder and into the surprised face of Bodoron, Queen Snow's head guard and consort. He scrambled to his feet as the barrel-chested Pisal rose from his chair and swept Andrew into a bear hug.

"What a surprise!" the Pisal said, holding him at arm's length. "You've grown taller again. You are becoming a man, Andrew."

"I've had to grow up fast, Bodoron." He brought the head guard up to date with his life above ground, and then he explained the purpose of his visit. "I'm delivering these two to the hospital in Nostalgia. They've had a peaceful, long life in disguise above ground, and now it's time for a change. Plus, I'd like to catch up with Ralph - I hope Snow's parents won't mind."

"You can do all of that after you see Snow, Andrew. She'd never forgive me if I didn't take you to her. Wait here, I'll find out where she is."

The Queen's consort disappeared into the hallway, leaving Andrew alone with the cats in what appeared to be the queen's study. The cats busied themselves with grooming, settling their fur back against the skin and deliberately ignoring Andrew. He turned away from them and studied the contents of the room.

Rich tapestries hung on the earthen walls, softly accentuated by candlelit sconces. There was a framed insignia in the shape of a crown that Andrew recognised with a shock. It was King Jarl's insignia from long ago, and it bore the words

Pax et justitia

Peace and Justice, the motto of Vellistrian. He could do with ample lashings of both at the moment, he thought. Peace of mind about his mother, and justice for the awful creature who had perpetuated the atrocity against her.

He hurried onto the next display, a recent portrait of the royal family. Snow and Bodoron stood side by side in the painting: Snow in the glittering crown passed on to her by Jarl, while Bodoron wore a thin circlet of gold atop his bare, dark head. Snow was resplendent in a golden dress with a royal blue sash slung diagonally across her body. Bodoron wore the opposite, a dark navy suit with a golden sash across his broad chest. Jarl junior stood to Snow's right. The heir apparent, already towering over his mother, but with the slenderness of youth.

In front of the queen were two more children, the twins Snow was carrying during Andrew's last visit to Vellistrian. A boy and a girl. The boy already resembled Bodoron in stature, while the girl carried Snow's pale skin, her smile, and a glint of mischief in her eye.

Andrew returned to study Jarl's face. He had the pale skin of his step-sister, reflecting the skin tone of his parents. The artist had done an excellent job of capturing the young Pisal as he faced inwards to look at his mother and her new husband. There was a turmoil of emotions not quite concealed in Jarl's eyes. Andrew saw boredom and disdain, common expressions in any teenager. But Andrew also detected something unexpected: a look of hatred directed towards his step-father.

"Andrew." Bodoron tapped him on the shoulder. "I see you've found our latest portrait."

"Oh, you're back. It's a great likeness." Andrew faced him, relieved to turn his back on Jarl's angry eyes. "What are the twins' names?"

"Our daughter is called Holly, after Snow's mother, and our son's name is Felix, after my father."

"They look like great kids."

"Looks can be deceiving. And would you believe the whole portrait had to be redone after complaints about Snow's choice of dress."

"What? Why?"

"It's yellow, Andrew. The last thing the Pisal need is a reminder of the royal sickness."

"Seriously?" He rolled his eyes. "It's a dress! No one has yellow eyes in the picture." *Just one with a death stare, that's all.*

"I know," Bodoron shrugged. "But we can't have the people being unhappy. We got the mini Pisal to photograph the painting, alter it digitally, then print it out again with a clever brush-stroke filter. You really can't tell the difference. It's in the throne room if you get a chance to look at it. Snow's dress is a ruby red, if you're wondering. Matches perfectly with those rocks in her crown.

"Now," he turned away from the painting, "speaking of the mini Pisal, Snow is in Scientia. She's attending the launch of a new technology, and a meeting afterwards on specialty crops. We've received special permission from Keenan in the Chasm - you remember him, don't you?"

Andrew's stomach shrivelled as he nodded. It would be a long time before he forgot about Keenan. "Anyway, we've got the go-ahead to grow White Fire in a controlled environment. As you know, the Pisal are a long-lived race, so we're keen to use White Fire as an end-of-life medication, to ease any pain and suffering."

Pain and suffering. Bodoron's words receded as Andrew's thoughts returned to his mother, and how Black Fire acted on humans in much the same way as White Fire acted on the Pisal. "You've given me an idea," he said. "I don't suppose you could spare some Black Fire for my mum, could you?"

The guard touched a hand to his arm, his talons thoughtfully raised to spare Andrew's skin. "Of course. If you proceed to Nostalgia first, I'll have a bag of leaves prepared for you. Padlo and Mengus will accompany you, and take you to Snow after you've seen Ralph."

CHAPTER THIRTEEN

Holly and Ashton were, as ever, gracious and accommodating. After a huge hug and doggy kiss from the now russet-coloured Ralph, Snow's parents produced an impressive spread of food and invited everyone inside. Padlo, the plumper of the two guards, glanced at the food in delight. "Always a pleasure to visit you, Ma'am and Sir!" He patted his rounded belly and grinned.

Two bowls of food were laid on the floor for Napoleon and Josephine, and the pair tucked into multi-coloured biscuits in the shape of black fire leaves. "We make these ourselves," Ashton explained. "The dogs love them, but it seems the cats are partial to them as well."

Andrew and the four Pisal squeezed around the rough wooden table, eating and catching up on events above ground, Vellistrian's progress, and Snow's children. Ralph rested his head on Andrew's knee, his emerald eyes darkening with sorrow. "I'm so sorry about your mum. You're saying the Hag did this?"

Andrew nodded. "You saw her, didn't you? The day we collected you from Mrs Bargwana."

"I saw her twice: once in the car on the way home, and once in the backyard when we were playing."

Andrew's mouth parted in surprise. He remembered that day. They'd been playing under the peppercorn tree when a pretty lady had appeared out of nowhere. Ralph's barks had alerted Mrs Jordan, who had stepped in and saved the pair from harm.

"She was frightening," Ralph continued, "one minute a pretty young lady, the next, a hideous old woman with a scar on her cheek."

"Mr Lovell gave her that scar, way back in World War One. She's been around for a long time."

"Longer than you think, Andrew." Mengus spoke up. "I've done some reading, and I believe she features in Vellistrian's history too, although she is never referred to by that name. I have a theory she introduced the yellow-eyed sickness to the royal family, but I can't prove it."

"What is your plan of attack?" Ashton turned to Andrew.

"The Seer told me about a prophecy. It mentions me and the dogs - you, Ralph, and your brothers and sisters."

"What prophecy? What's it about?" Ralph said.

"Listen to this. Tell me what you make of it."

The group listened with interest, each reacting at certain points during the recital: "The ancient three rise up - oh, that's got to be Owen, Secunda, and Torr," said Padlo.

"The hound disappears - hey, that's me!" Ralph exclaimed.

"And there are rocky times ahead," Holly observed. "That piece about Ralph's siblings: *Disperse the four others, in time, in disguise -* is this pertinent to your quest?"

"The custodian of extraordinary animals and her predecessor believe that finding Ralph's siblings is key," Andrew answered. "The Hag wanted them, now we need to know why." He turned to Ralph. "Do you know what happened to your sisters and brothers?"

Ralph's face dropped. "I wish I did. But I was the first to leave, Andy. I can't help you."

"What about the Seer?" ever-practical Mengus asked. "I assume he took the dogs and embedded them in their new lives?"

"I guess." Andrew shrugged. "Regardless, he refuses to interfere in any timeline. He provides guidance, then leaves us to figure it out. He obviously thinks we have enough information to solve this riddle."

"If we think of anything, we'll let you know," Ashton promised.

"That goes for me too," Ralph added.

Andrew rose from the table, and the cats returned to his side. "We must be off. I have to deliver these guys to the hospital."

He crouched down beside Ralph for another hug, and he sensed the dog's words in his mind: *I send all my love and strength to your mother, Andy.*

"Thank you," he whispered, blinking back tears.

Ralph faced the cats, touching each of their foreheads with his nose. "We shared good times together, friends," he said. "I wish you well on your next journey."

The foyer of Nostalgia's animal hospital was whisper quiet. Andrew strode up to the two nurses behind the admissions desk and explained the reason for his visit.

"Do they speak?" the female Pisal nurse glanced down at the cats.

"Not in this lifetime," the male cat interrupted with a distinctive Corsican accent. "Ma Chérie and I hope for more latitude in our next life."

The nurse's eyes widened. "We'll see what we can do." She led the pair down the hallway, glancing over her shoulder to Andrew. "Wait here. There'll be some paperwork to sign."

Andrew sighed. There was no escaping paperwork, not even in the chocolate box world of Nostalgia. He turned to the other admissions nurse. "Is it always like this? It's very quiet."

The nurse finished tapping away on the computer with his claws and stood up, stretching his long arms above his head. "We have peaks and troughs. There is also a procedure in place for when creatures return for reassignment. The O'Donnells' reappearance, for instance. Unexpected but necessary, thus prompting the return of Napoleon and Josephine." He leaned forward on the desk. "To tell you the truth," he lowered his voice, "I like those ones the best. They break up the monotony!" He closed a salmon-coloured eye in a wink.

"Do you get many cases like this one?"

The nurse shook his head. "Sadly, no. Although I remember one about ten years ago. Four puppies came in. Beautiful golden labradors, they were."

Andrew's ears pricked up. "Why was that so unusual?"

"Oh, it was all hush-hush." The nurse leaned towards him and lowered his voice. "No one was supposed to know anything about them and where they were going. I heard they were all sent into the past, which was quite unusual. And one even got reassigned as a cat."

"Do you know why?"

The nurse frowned. "Something about supporting a young boy. It was that long ago, I can't remember the details. It was one of the girls, I know that much. I recall thinking she was brave going to that time, as it wasn't particularly kind to cats." He rested his head on his hands, elbows propped on the desk, his long talons interlacing over the crown of his head. "The other girl was a real sweetheart. She swore black and blue she would never leave her master's side, whatever happened. I wonder how that worked out for her?" He gave Andrew a sentimental smile, then his eyes narrowed. "Hold on. You had one of the dogs too, didn't you?" The nurse straightened up, a look of keen interest on his face. "We heard about how you saved the Queen. That must have taken some courage."

Andrew blushed. It was the second time in as many hours he'd been forced to remember that moment. "It was nothing, really." He squirmed under the nurse's gaze. It *was* something, of course. As a twelve-year-old boy, Andrew had been terrified of the predicament he'd found himself in. No one had come to save him, and he'd quickly realised he would have to save himself... *and Snow... and a few others,* he added silently.

The female Pisal nurse reappeared, a sheaf of papers in her hand. Andrew signed where indicated, promising he would pass copies on to the Seer and Mrs Jordan. Thanking the nurses, he stepped into the softly lit cobblestone street.

"Andrew!" Padlo waved to catch his attention. He and Mengus were seated on the driver's box of a cockroach carriage, the preferred method of transport in Vellistrian. "Shall we go? The queen awaits your arrival in Scientia."

Chapter Fourteen

"I farewelled a boy last year, and now I welcome back a man." Snow broke away from her entourage and fluttered across the room, a dainty Pisal in a brilliant orange dress. But appearances are deceiving, and Andrew knew better. Beneath the flowing dress and behind the large, compassionate eyes lay a steely will. Snow had not been destined from birth to rule Vellistrian, but she had risen to the task. She was a fair and just ruler, and willing to do anything to defend the rights of the Pisal. She reached up to hug Andrew, her huge amethyst necklace brushing against his chest. She drew back and studied him, a concerned look on her face. "There is sadness in you, Andrew. What bothers you?"

"My mother is unwell, Snow." He was tired of explaining, and he knew Bodoron would fill in the gaps later. Looking down at the queen, he changed the subject. "You are back to being tiny after having the twins, I see. And I haven't seen you in orange before, you usually wear pink. I think orange brings out the colour in your eyes."

He meant it as a compliment, but Snow burst out laughing. "In that case, we will all be wearing orange dresses in the future, Andrew," she said, teasingly reminding him of the predominant Pisal eye colour. "But thank you for your kind words." She turned to the group of Pisal behind her. Her smile turned to a scowl as she beckoned to someone to come forward.

Jarl junior emerged from the depths of the group, a sullen expression on his face. His mother drew him aside, and Andrew heard snatches of their whispered conversation: "We've spoken about this before... the heir to Vellistrian... start acting that way!"

"Why don't you get your husband to do it... no one respects me... laughing at me, now there's two more children."

"You are my first-born!" Snow shook his arm. "Do this for your father."

The pair rejoined the group, Snow with a tight smile on her face. "You remember my son, Andrew? Jarl is here today to perform the opening ceremony in honour of his late father."

Jarl gave Andrew a moody look. "Hey."

"Hey, Jarl. Nice to see you again."

The youth retreated, mingling with a group of scientists in lab coats. Andrew raised his eyebrows but said nothing. Instead, he turned his attention to the miniature Pisal, the brains of Vellistrian. The brilliant scientists were based in Scientia, a unique town built on a monumental boulder that defied all gravity and hovered in space within a massive cavern. Andrew had visited Scientia once in the past, and the laboratory they were gathered in now was vaguely familiar to him.

The scientists stood before a machine with a fancy ribbon draped across its surface. Something about the machine tugged at Andrew's memory. It looked like an old-fashioned photo booth, where people squashed into the tiny space, posed for their pictures, then waited outside until the photos were delivered to a slot on the side of the machine.

"I remember," he snapped his fingers. "I've seen this machine before. It was when I was with Jarl senior and his brother!"

The scientists looked up from the clipboards with a frown. "Andrew, this is a brand-new machine," Snow said, a puzzled look on her face. "That's why we're here today, to mark the launch of this new technology."

Andrew stared at her. "Oh. My mistake. What does the machine do?"

I'm NOT mistaken. I was in this room. I saw that machine.

"My scientists tell me that if a DNA sample is inserted, all ancestors and present-day relatives will be identified."

Andrew sighed. He'd had this exact conversation with Jarl senior. He even remembered the comment he'd made at the time: *But in the human world, we already have DNA testing.*

And Jarl's answer: *This machine will show you where your relatives reside in the world, or any other world, for that matter. It can even take you to that place in the blink of an eye.*

"It was something Jarl tasked before he died," Snow was still speaking. "He was hopeful of tracing the royal sickness back to its roots, but sadly he didn't live long enough to see it himself."

He saw it! He showed it to me.

Now another thought arose in Andrew's mind, filling him with excitement. "Have you tested the machine yet, Snow? I have a sample you could use."

The queen tilted her head towards the scientists. They glanced at each other, shrugged their shoulders and eventually nodded. "That should be fine," she said. "Is it to help your mother?"

"In a way, yes." Andrew fished out the black, star-shaped talisman from beneath his hoodie and opened it. Curled inside was the tuft of hair Andrew collected from Ralph when he was in Germany last year. "Is this enough?"

The lead scientist stepped forward and examined the sample. "More than enough." He separated a small piece of hair from the bundle and returned it to Andrew, who put it back in the talisman and closed it. "First, though, the opening ceremony." The scientist motioned to Jarl junior to step forward. With a flourish, Jarl extended the long talon of his forefinger and cut the ribbon. Everyone cheered and applauded. Jarl smirked and quickly disappeared into the crowd.

The lead scientist placed Ralph's fur in a pull-out drawer on the side of the machine. Next, he motioned to Andrew, indicating a large green button on the panel beside the drawer. Andrew pushed the button, stood back and waited.

The machine came to life, chugging away as it processed the sample. Blue smoke emerged from outlets at the top of the apparatus, and it began to hop around the room like an overloaded washing machine. Andrew looked in alarm at the scientists. "It's quite alright," they reassured. "She's got a few teething problems, that's all." They watched as the machine settled back down, then a loud alarm sounded, followed by a final puff of smoke. "Wait for it," the lead scientist cautioned, before a neatly-folded piece of paper landed in the slot on the side of the machine. With a pair of tweezers, he lifted the paper from the machine and placed it in the queen's hands.

She smiled and handed it over to Andrew. "Go on," she encouraged. "You open it."

He nodded his thanks and unfolded the paper. At the top was a title: *The Gifted Hounds,* and underneath were four columns with the headings: *Name, Status, Location, Guardian.*

His skin prickling, Andrew scanned the list. Abi, the dogs' mother, appeared first. Her status was *Eternal, mother of all*. She was mysteriously listed as being *Off-world/Unknown,* and her guardian was *Blair*. Next was Ralph. He was listed as *Transmogrified,* living in *Nostalgia* with his guardians *Holly and Ashton*. Andrew's shoulders slumped as he saw Brianna, Pierce, and Shannon were all listed as deceased, with no further detail.

But there on the last line, Max was listed as alive. Andrew's heart pounded as his finger flew across the paper, absorbing the knowledge of the remaining dog's whereabouts. His elation was immediately overtaken by horror: Max's location was also listed as *Off-world/Unknown*. And his designated owner? None other than *The Shrew,* the name used in the prophecy to describe the Hag. His hands shaking, he crumpled the paper into a ball and shoved it in his pocket.

"Not the news you were expecting?" Snow asked.

"No. It's bad news. Awful news." Distracted, he looked away, and caught sight of Jarl junior edging away from the gathering, a sneaky look on his face. He had made it to the far side of the room and was opening a door when he met Bodoron coming the other way. They both expressed surprise, before performing a clumsy dance as they attempted to pass each other. Bodoron saw the humour of the situation, but Jarl junior remained unimpressed, his face flushed with anger. Eventually they disentangled themselves, Jarl scuttling into the next room and Bodoron striding towards them.

"Your Majesty, they're ready to start the presentation on White Fire next door." He jerked a thumb over his shoulder. Noticing Andrew, he smacked his head in annoyance. "I left the Black Fire in the other room. Hold on, I'll go back for it." He ducked away, threading his way through the crowd.

The head scientist hovered at the queen's side. "I believe that went rather well, Your Majesty," he murmured. "We should be able to move onto phase two in a couple of weeks' time."

Snow nodded. "Excellent. Make sure you have the findings to me by tomorrow afternoon."

Bodoron reappeared, carrying two paper bags. "Here you are, Andrew. This should keep your mother going for a while. And if you need any more, don't hesitate to visit us again. I hope it helps."

"Thanks. I hope it does too." He clutched the bags, feeling awkward. "I'd better get going. You have another meeting to attend."

"We do." The queen wrapped him in another embrace. "Please come back soon, Andrew. And I send my best wishes to your mother. May she rest, receive the healing of the Black Fire, and recover."

The entourage now moved as one, proceeding into the adjoining lab to discuss the benefits of White Fire. Andrew stuffed the bags down his top, grasped his talisman and thought of his mother, a big grey cat, and home.

CHAPTER FIFTEEN

Andrew lay back, staring into the darkness. It was after midnight and he couldn't sleep. His eyes moved around the room and eventually settled on a spot above his bed. After many years, the adhesive glow-in-the-dark stars on the ceiling were fading. He remembered the comfort they gave him as a young boy after his mother kissed him goodnight and shut the door behind her, leaving him alone in the dark. He'd refused to have a night light - they were for babies! - but the stars had provided a neon glow that made him feel safe and cosy in the night. They were little comfort now as he listened to his mother coughing in the room across the hallway.

On his return from Vellistrian, his father had taken him aside to tell him fluid was building up in Mrs Adler's lungs. The doctors suggested it was quite a common occurrence when the cancer spread, and she was scheduled to have the fluid removed the following morning. The treatment would coincide with a round of radiotherapy. External beam radiation therapy, his dad said. It was the next big hope for killing off the cancer. But hearing his mother cough and wheeze in the next room, Andrew wondered if finding Ralph's brothers and sisters could help. Was it just another wild goose chase?

Mrs Jordan had brought over a box of pot plants a few days ago, and they were now in position on the window ledge in his parent's room. They were all healing plants of some description, and some of them offered protection, Mrs Jordan said. He recognised a few of the plants, a maidenhair fern among them. His neighbour insisted the fern was useful against coughs, but he'd seen no evidence of this to date. Andrew also recognised some carnations and a pot of bluebell bulbs, but the remaining plants were a mystery to him.

Bodoron's bags of Black Fire leaves lay on the desk beside his computer. He was keen to reintroduce his mother to the plant to see if it had any effect. Beyond that, Andrew felt they were out of options. They were running out of time, and like the stars above his head, Mrs Adler's life was ebbing away.

"Last time, I told you about my first meeting with the Hag. That was hard enough, but today it's about my last day with Cecil." There was a slight tremble around Mr Lovell's mouth which he pressed down on, disguising it in a grimace.

The group were assembled in the old man's lounge room, and he had taken up the tale as soon as Andrew arrived home from school. They all studied their elderly friend, noting his watery eyes and shaky speech. Andrew felt the old man's pain, and wished he could say something to lighten the moment. As usual, Mrs Jordan beat him to it. "Pat, are you sure you want to do this?" she enquired softly.

"Of course." he dismissed her concern with typical gruffness. "You all need to hear it. The Seer made it quite clear Cecil couldn't die in war, so when he ended up tangled in barbed wire after going over the parapet, I did the only thing I could think of. As the bombs were raining down on us, I threw myself on top of him."

Gasps of horror filled the room. Kevin stood up in Mr Lovell's lap, and the old man ran his gnarled fingers through the cat's fur. "That was the end of me... in that timeline, anyway. I had saved Cecil, and I ended up in the Seer's cavern, disillusioned and angry. I'd gone to war to avenge the death of my brother, but I'd ended up even more bitter. I thought I knew everything about war, but boy, was I wrong." He swallowed; his hands motionless on the cat's back.

Kevin reached up and nudged against the old man's face. "Why don't we take a break, Pat?"

Mr Lovell blinked back tears. "That's a good idea."

While the humans paused for a cup of tea, Mrs Jordan pulled a bag of kangaroo mince from the fridge and fed the three cats. They devoured the food, heads pushing against each other in an attempt to grab an extra mouthful. When all three bowls were clean, Kevin threw Mrs Jordan an adoring look. "What was that? It was delicious!"

Her eyes twinkled. "Are you sure you want to know?"

"Yes, of course, Dorothy," Colleen said. "You can feed us that anytime. What was it, lamb mince? Venison?"

"Kangaroo mince, actually."

"Eeew!" The three cats howled in unison. "You could have warned us."

Mrs Jordan chuckled. "But you enjoyed it!"

Mr Lovell stuck his head around the kitchen door. "All right, you lot. Enough skylarking. There's a story to be told."

They all trooped into the lounge room and resumed their seats, Kevin leaping back onto the old man's lap, and Colleen curling up between Mrs Jordan and Andrew on the couch. Deirdre maintained an aloof distance, choosing to crouch in the doorway near Mrs Bargwana's chair, her eyes narrowed and watching.

"Before we start," Andrew said, "Can someone tell me why you all came back as cats?"

"It's quite easy when you think about it," Mrs Bargwana said. "The Hag has an affinity with dogs."

"And a hatred of cats," Deirdre added. "We had no intention of coming back as dogs and risk her acquiring us for her own purposes. We are the guardians of the guardians, young Andrew, and we have stepped forward to assist in interpreting the prophecy. You may see us as pitiful small creatures, but our connection to your guardians is a force to be reckoned with. Don't underestimate us."

"I won't, I promise." Andrew shifted uncomfortably in his seat.

"Cats can move around undetected, Andrew," Mrs Bargwana intervened, saving Andrew from Deirdre's ferocity. "No one blinks an eye at a cat leaping over a fence, or squeezing through an open window. They can come and go as they please, and that's exactly what we need."

"We'd better get the cats microchipped, Lucy." Mrs Jordan said. "We don't want them ending up in the pound."

"Already done, my dear. I have a block of microchips I pre-purchased back home in Canberra, and the cats' home addresses correspond with our own addresses."

Mrs Jordan blew her a kiss. "You think of everything."

Andrew cleared his throat. "Speaking of cats, Mrs J, I must tell you about Napoleon and Josephine—"

"Tell her later, Andrew." Mr Lovell interrupted. "I need to get on with my story."

Andrew gave him a guilty look. "Sorry."

"The Seer expressed his displeasure at my attitude by sending me forward in time to another war," the old man continued. "And by another war, I mean he threw me right into the action in World War Two. It was lucky I popped up beside another young bloke who had half a clue about what was going on."

"Who was that?" Andrew frowned.

"Angus. It was the first time we crossed paths."

"And I imagine you kept on crossing paths, didn't you, Pat?" Deirdre commented from her spot in the doorway. "It's the one way we know we're on the right path. We keep bumping into the same people, over and over again."

"Deirdre's right," the old man said. "But Angus being Angus, he disappeared when I could've done with his help. The second time I came across the Hag, for example."

The light-hearted frivolity in the room evaporated, and all eyes turned to Mr Lovell. "You saw her again?" Mrs Bargwana asked.

"Yes. She was a young woman this time round, and feeding off the attention of any soldier, sailor or airman she could get her clutches on."

"Are you sure it was her?" Andrew asked.

"There was no mistake, son. I don't know how, but she'd come into possession of my soldier doll. It was lying on the café table where she sat, faded and bloody, but without doubt the doll my own mother had made for me."

Andrew shivered. The Hag's powers were otherworldly, bordering on sinister magic involving voodoo and curses. "What did you do?" he asked.

"Do?" The old man's eyes flared with anger. "There was nothing I could do. She showed up as a warning. It was a reminder that she'd cursed me. She wanted revenge for her dog. And she got it."

"How?" Mrs Jordan asked the question they all feared.

"She got to me by hurting someone else; a dear friend. My heart still aches for him. The Seer was right, I'd been slow to learn the intricacies of war, but I was catching up, at light speed. And there were better times, of course. Don't forget I ran into you in Churchill's war rooms, lad." He beamed at Andrew.

"My point exactly, always bumping into the same people." Deirdre interjected.

Mr Lovell arched an eyebrow at the cat, annoyed by the interruption. "Not only did I meet Angus in World War Two, I came across another lovely young chap who was to have an enormous bearing on your life, Andrew."

"And that was...?"

"Your grandfather, Andreas Adler. I saved his life, and that's a case in point. All our lives are intertwined, and for good reason. We're going to need all the help we can get to defeat the Hag."

CHAPTER SIXTEEN

The house was empty when Andrew arrived home from school. He found his father's note on the kitchen table:

Don't wait for me. There's some dinner in the fridge.

He wondered how his father kept going, taking his mother to all her medical appointments, being there as her support, and maintaining a smile while she endured unimaginable pain. He knew Mr Adler wouldn't have it any other way, but it was exhausting for everyone, not just his mother.

Andrew dropped his bag in the kitchen and headed down the hallway to his bedroom. Winston greeted him, leaping off the bed and winding himself through Andrew's legs. "Do you know, I believe I'm making up for all the hours I didn't sleep when I was Prime Minister. I'm amazed at how much I can sleep in this cat body!"

"Good for you," Andrew grumbled. He yanked the tie from his neck, placed his uniform on a hanger, and changed into jeans and a long-sleeved t-shirt. "Have some sleep for me while you're at it."

Winston gazed up at him. "I'm sorry, that was insensitive. In my defence, however, I believe cats do their best work while they are sleeping."

"Oh really?" Andrew raised his eyebrows. "Impress me. What have you come up with?"

"I've decided I'll come with you when you talk to your guardians. It will keep me in the loop, and then I can better advise you."

Andrew studied the cat. "Fair enough. Are you sure this is not just a case of you wanting to revisit the past?"

Winston licked a paw and brushed it across his face. "Perhaps," he said blithely. "No doubt I am more accustomed to the times Patrick and the other cats speak of, but the more heads the better, wouldn't you agree?"

The pair headed to Mrs Jordan's house, Andrew carrying the paperwork he received from the hospital in Nostalgia. "Hello gents!" she greeted them at the doorway. "Come inside. Lucy is here as well. Andrew, you can tell us how you got on in Vellistrian."

The three humans sat around Mrs Jordan's kitchen table, while Winston engaged Colleen and Deirdre in a spirited conversation about Ireland.

"Did my babies behave when you returned them?" Mrs Jordan placed a glass of juice and a piece of cake in front on Andrew.

Andrew pictured the two white fluffballs glaring at him on arrival in Vellistrian, and he suppressed a chuckle. "You could say that, Mrs J." He patted the paperwork in front of him. "Here are the hospital details, anyway. For your records."

Mrs Jordan sniffed, and wiped a tear from the corner of her eye. "They were an arrogant pair, but I was sad to see them go." She looked down at the two tortoiseshell cats talking to Winston on the floor. "However, I'm grateful we have the O'Donnells here to help us."

"Why have they come back?" Andrew asked between mouthfuls of cake.

"We believe they're here in response to the Hag choosing another henchman," Mrs Bargwana said. "Her powers seem to peak when she has a dog. Dorothy and I got rid of one years ago, but at great cost." She rolled up the sleeve on her shirt, revealing a jagged scar on her left arm.

Andrew glanced at the ugly scar and swallowed. "One of her dogs did that?"

Mrs Bargwana rolled her sleeve back into place. "Unfortunately, yes. Trust me, Andrew, I got off lightly! Dorothy and Patrick suffered far greater sorrows." She squeezed Mrs Jordan's hand in sympathy. "As for the O'Donnell's return, why don't we get it from the horse's - oops, the cat's mouth."

The larger of the tortoiseshell cats looked up, her eyes dark with anger. "A bit of respect, Lucy. You know who we are!"

Mrs Bargwana's cheeks turned crimson. "Sorry, Deirdre."

The tortoiseshell cat climbed onto the spare seat beside Andrew. "Child, I mentioned before, we are the guardians of your guardians. Colleen spent time with young Dorothy in Tasmania; Kevin, as you know was in the war with Pat, and I was Lucy's mentor."

Andrew hid a smile at Mrs Jordan being referred to as 'young'. He nodded politely as the cat continued. "From the series of events that have occurred in recent times, I suggest to you that the prophecy is in motion. What do you say to that?"

"I'd agree with you, ma'am." Andrew had no idea why he'd called Deirdre 'ma'am', but as soon as the words crossed his lips, Mrs Bargwana groaned and buried her face in her hands.

"DON'T call me Ma'am - I work for a living!" the cat growled, her ears flattened against her head.

Andrew jerked backwards in his seat. "I-I'm sorry! I was trying to be polite."

Her tail lashing, the cat stood upright, her ears flicking back into position. "I need your full attention, Andrew, not your P's and Q's. Call me Deirdre from henceforward, if you will. Now, we have agreed that the prophecy is in motion. It's obvious we must do all we can to stop the Hag. She's had her way for far too long."

Mrs Bargwana turned to Andrew. "Our theory is that the Hag derives much of her strength from her dogs. We don't know how to get the better of her, but we do know that removing her dog sends her into hiding. And that may give us enough time to fully interpret the prophecy and end this nightmare for good."

"She won't give up, Andrew," Mrs Jordan drained her cup and fixed him with a stare. "It's an awful pill to swallow with your mother sick, but we all have to work together now. You've discovered the identity of the Hag's current dog, now we need to do something about it."

"You warned me not to do anything while Mum was sick, but I think we've done everything we can to help her," Andrew thought aloud. "She's getting the best medical attention, plus protection from the pot plants you gave her, Mrs J. I'm ready to try out the Black Fire as well." He took a deep breath and blew it out. "Let's do this. I know I have to go after Max. But there's something that's really bothering me. That line in the prophecy, about dispersing the dogs in disguise."

"Why does that worry you, child?" Deirdre asked.

Andrew shifted anxiously in his seat. "What if I get it wrong? I don't know what Max looks like, plus I bet he's smart enough to conceal himself, with the Hag's help, and pretend to be another dog, or cat, or horse..." He trailed off, his shoulders slumping.

"Don't you be getting all long in the face, Andrew!" Deirdre tutted. "All animals have a weakness, or a habit. Figure that out, and we will undo the wretched woman's schemes. The quicker the better, too, if we want to save your mother."

The words hung in the air, and Andrew looked into his empty glass. Discovering the dogs' habits sounded more elusive than finding the holy grail.

Mrs Bargwana squeezed his shoulder. "You know what pets are like, they all have that special spot where they love to be patted, or an odd behaviour. Have you ever played poker, Andy?"

It was an odd turn in the conversation, and Andrew gave her a puzzled look. "Just those online games where no money is involved. I taught myself to play on them."

"I play them myself from time to time." Mrs Bargwana said with a wink. "Face to face though, you pick up little things about each player, certain mannerisms - often inadvertent - that betray their intentions: tapping the cards, an eyebrow raise, the pull of their mouth. It's called a tell in the poker vernacular, and each of Abi's litter had a certain tell as well. Can you see where I'm heading with this, Andrew?"

"It gives away which dog is which?"

"It does, but more than that. It gives you an in. We all know animals take time to warm to strangers, but if you can go straight up and pet them in their favourite spot, you'll have them eating out of your hand."

"But who knows what each of the tells are?"

"I'd start with Ralph, and find out what he knows. However, I have a feeling only one dog knows all the tells for sure, and that's Abi."

"But Abi is with Blair!" Andrew groaned. They were going around in circles.

"I know," Mrs Bargwana agreed. "And we don't know where that is. Not yet, anyway. In the meantime, go back to Ralph and see what he has to say."

Later that day, Andrew sat outside Holly and Ashton's house with Ralph. His gaze alternated between the dog and the softly winking lights of Nostalgia as he explained the reason for his visit.

"You know I was the first of our litter to leave, Andy," Ralph said. "I loved my brothers and sisters, but they're a distant memory to me."

Andrew frowned. "There's nothing you can remember about them? A little quirk like this spot on your belly that always needs scratching?" He bent down to illustrate, and Ralph rolled over, his back legs kicking in pleasure.

"Ah, that's the spot. Thanks, Andy!" He lay on his back a moment longer, before he sat up with a shake. "Why do you think this information will lead you to Max?"

"*You* might recognise all your brothers and sisters, but I doubt I can. Plus, they've all been sent to different times and places, and some are in disguise, if we trust the words of the prophecy and the hospital nurse. I need these 'tells', as Mrs Bargwana calls them. They'll help me identify which dog is which." He rested his hand on Ralph's head, idly stroking his soft russet fur. "And I wouldn't put it past the Hag to have Max masquerading as one of his siblings. We have to break the bond between the Hag and her dog, and I'd hate to get the wrong dog."

"Why don't you go back to when we were puppies, at Mrs. Bargwana's house?" Ralph mused. "You could nip the whole thing in the bud from the start."

Andrew threw his arms around the dog. "That's a fantastic idea, Ralph! Why didn't I think of that myself?"

Ralph beamed a big doggy smile. "That's why we make a great team, we think of different things. And don't forget to ask Snow if you can use the Pisal DNA machine," he added. "Anything to get the jump on that nasty woman. I can't believe she recruited one of my brothers. What would my poor mother think?"

"I'd like to know the same thing," Andrew said. "But I don't know how to reach her. She's with Blair, the creator of Vellestrian, and Blair's Bypass."

"Hold up a minute." Ralph's emerald eyes glistened with tears. "My mother is still alive?"

Andrew clapped a hand over his mouth. "Oh, Ralph, I forgot! The DNA machine listed your mother as 'off-world', living with Blair."

Ralph's mouth parted in surprise. "When you figure out how to find her, I'm coming with you."

Andrew wrapped Ralph in an even tighter hug. "Of course. I'm doing this for Mum, so it's only right for you to see your mum as well."

Ralph snuffled against his cheek. "I like the symmetry of that, Andy. Thank you."

"Speaking of finding your mum," Andrew stood up. "I'm off to talk to Snow. Maybe the Pisal can point me in the direction of Blair. And I want to confirm if they've come across the Hag in their long history, as Mengus suggested. The more I know about her, the better."

"It's lovely to see you back again so soon, Andrew." Snow raised her teacup in his direction. "However, I'm well aware that you always visit us with something in mind," she added, her eyes twinkling. "How can we help you today?"

Andrew blushed behind his own teacup. Was he really that transparent? He'd have to factor in a visit to Vellistrian for no other reason than to spend time with Snow and her children. They always made time for him. As soon as he'd arrived, Snow and Bodoron had dropped everything and laid on an

afternoon tea in his honour, complete with the musk-flavoured chocolate chip cookies he loved so much.

But right now, he needed information, and there was no polite way
to go about it. "You know me too well, Snow. I'm hoping you or
Bodoron can point me in the direction of Blair."

They both burst out laughing, Snow shaking so much she sloshed
her tea across the crisp white tablecloth. A servant materialised and in
the blink of an eye the table was stripped bare, a starchy new tablecloth
laid and all the cups and plates returned to their original positions.

Andrew stared in bewilderment at the queen and her consort. "It
was a serious question, guys. I've seen him once before. Surely, I can
see him again? I need to speak to his dog."

Bodoron wiped his eyes with the back of his hand. "If you've seen
Blair, you're one lucky human, Andrew."

"You see, asking a Pisal where to find Blair is akin to asking a human
where to find God, Andrew," Snow added, suppressing a smile.

Andrew sighed. What remained of his patience was rapidly disappearing, and he hadn't expected to be the butt of their jokes. "Look, I
don't care if you think it's funny. I want to know if I can see him again.
Can you think of any way to do it?"

"I still believe you saw Blair in a vision," Snow said. "Remember
our discussion about you laying in a bed of White Fire, Andrew?" She
turned to Bodoron. "If we had any White Fire, we could give it to
Andrew as an experiment."

"I know." Bodoron gave her a frustrated look. "We were supposed to
have a sample for that meeting the other day, but I'm darned if I know
what happened to it."

Snow turned to Andrew. "Leave it with us," she said. "If we can
secure an amount of White Fire, for you, we'll be in contact. Perhaps
for now you could consult with the Seer?"

"He hasn't been around much." It surprised Andrew how much those words hurt. He had expected some kind of guidance from the oversized hare, but his participation to date had been sadly lacking.

"He's a slippery one. He comes and goes as he pleases, Andrew. But I'm sure he's watching on."

Andrew managed a half-hearted smile. "I guess. What about the Hag?" he asked. "Has she interfered with Vellistrian at all?"

Snow and Bodoron exchanged a guarded look. "I am too young to remember anything of note," Snow admitted, "But Bodoron recalls a few things, which, with hindsight, would suggest she played a hand in Jarl's death."

"When Jarl was still alive," Bodoron said, "He searched for a cure for Torr's madness, when Torr was quite young. I remember he was out of options, and was about to journey to see an old medicine woman, or a shrew as he called her."

"A shrew?" Andrew drew in his breath.

"It was around the same time a young human girl visited, sent by the Seer... What was her name?" Bodoron scratched his forehead with the tip of his claw.

"Dorothy?" Andrew hazarded a guess.

"Yes, that was her! Jarl was reluctant to go, he knew dealing with the medicine woman was a double-edged sword. And he was right to be worried. The shrew warned him that dabbling with herbs would lead to his undoing. I don't remember what she gave him, we'd have to consult his diaries, but she sent him away with these words: *One may mend, but two will end.*"

"And Jarl died from a deadly mix of two herbs." Snow reminded Andrew. "White Fire and Crystal Nightshade."

"But I thought Jarl's poisoning was Owen's fault!" Andrew said.

"Owen wanted Jarl dead," Bodoron said, his voice bitter. "But he enlisted the Hag's help to get the job done, we're almost certain of it."

CHAPTER SEVENTEEN

"Cecil had always insisted I visit him after the war. I didn't get that chance until World War Two ended in 1945."

Mr Lovell sat back in his chair, eyes closed as he revisited the past. Space was at a premium in the small room, as humans competed with cats for a comfortable seat. Winston resorted to sitting on Andrew's lap, while Colleen took up the middle seat on the lounge beside Mrs Jordan. Mrs Bargwana was in the remaining chair, warming her hands on the heater, while Deirdre crouched in the doorway, one ear forward and listening, the other bent towards the hallway, alert to any intruders. Outside, the bare fingers of the elderly frangipani tree shifted in the wintry wind, brushing against the window.

"Weren't you worried about a time anomaly?" Andrew spoke up. "Cecil would've been in his fifties, and I'm guessing you still looked 24!"

The old man opened his eyes, the pale blue awash with memory. "I was, Andy, but my desire to see my old mate overrode any sensibility. For the first time in 31 years, I was back in Australia, and I wanted to see a familiar face. Alas, it was not to be. When I arrived in the Northern Rivers, I found Cecil had passed away two years previously. And this news was delivered to me by none other than his beautiful daughter, Helen.

"I won't lie to you, I fell in love with Cecil's daughter in that moment. But to profess my love for her, I lied to her. She could never know I was her father's old war comrade."

"Please tell us Cecil lived a happy life after you saved him." Mrs Jordan voiced everyone's thoughts.

"He did. Like many men that came home from war, he was torn apart by memories, but there were two dogs in Cecil's life that calmed and protected him. Helen told me Cecil's first dog followed him everywhere, and even tried to stop him from joining up in 1914. Brianna was overjoyed when Cecil returned home, and slept next to her master to ease his nightmares."

"Excuse me, Patrick. You said the dog's name was Brianna?" Mrs Bargwana leaned forward in her chair, a curious expression on her face.

"Yes, it was."

"Sorry to interrupt. Please continue."

"Helen was born in 1920, and Cecil's son James came along in 1922. Brianna died of a snake bite that year, and despite his son's birth, Cecil was inconsolable. He vowed not to have another dog, and he kept that vow until 1939, when war came knocking again. He bought another labrador, this one was called Pierce, and he became Cecil's shadow."

"Just a question, Patrick." Mrs Bargwana spoke up, an edge of anxiety in her voice. "You're absolutely certain Helen said the names of the dogs were Brianna and Pierce?"

Mr Lovell blinked. "Yes, Lucy. They were strange names. I thought they had some family significance, but Helen said she had no idea where the names came from."

Andrew stared in stunned disbelief at his old neighbour. Cecil Jordan had been gifted not one, but *two* of the gifted hounds in his lifetime. Finally, he had a lead as to the whereabouts of Ralph's siblings!

The light was fading as Andrew and Winston left Mr Lovell's house. A fog was misting between the houses, and along the street, he noticed a familiar figure striding towards them, head down, hands deep in his pockets.

"Gus," Andrew called out, his voice muffled in the moist evening air.

Gus's head jerked up, and he jogged the remaining distance between the boys. "Hey, Andy. How have you been?"

"I'm okay, I guess."

"And your mum?"

"Not so good. She's just had some radiology treatment."

"Oh. Fingers crossed it works for her."

"Yeah, thanks."

It was an awkward, stilted conversation, as if their friendship was dwindling away through lack of words. Andrew decided to change the subject. "I was in Vellistrian the other day, and we found out Ralph's brother Max has joined sides with the Hag."

"I'm not surprised." Gus shrugged his shoulders.

"But Ralph had a good idea. He thought if I time-stepped back to the day I chose from all the puppies, I could intervene and change the outcome."

"It's a good theory, but it won't work," Gus shook his head.

"Why not?" Andrew said, annoyed.

"Mate, that time is blocked to us."

"What do you mean?" He didn't like Gus rejecting his idea. In fact, it seemed downright suspicious.

"We can't access it, for whatever reason. I've only come across this a couple of times before, but take my word for it. I've tried to get there myself, Andy. It's like hitting a brick wall. We can't go back there."

After imparting that intriguing nugget of information, Gus appeared in a hurry to leave. Andrew said goodbye with a mixture of emotions. He wasn't used to people dismissing his ideas, particularly Gus. It wasn't like he'd been contributing any help to Andrew of late. "Why should I believe him?" he said to Winston. "What if he's lying? He could be hiding something important from me and I'd never know."

Winston looked up at him, his eyes a glassy reflection from the street lights. "There's only one way to find out, Andrew. Go there yourself."

Andrew let himself in the back door. The house was warm from cooking, the kitchen fragrant with a soup bubbling away on the stove. Andrew's Aunt Joy was seated at the kitchen table, watching a video on her phone. She looked up as he came inside, Winston trailing behind. "Hello, Andy. Your dad asked if I wouldn't mind coming around and doing some cooking." She gave him a tired, guarded smile.

Andrew knew that look. He'd seen it on the face of every adult he'd spoken to about his mother: a grim reaction to the word cancer, and a rambling, non-committal opinion about her future. It was a different matter entirely to see the same look on his aunt's face. Aunt Joy was his mother's sister, a younger, smaller version of his mum, with the same irrepressible nature and sunny disposition. To see the spark missing in her eyes was like a punch to the stomach.

She returned to the stove to stir the soup. "It's nearly ready. It's chicken noodle. I know she likes chicken noodle. I added an egg." She skirted around the unmentionable, filling the conversation with trivial detail. "I'll get you to take a bowl in to your mum."

"Sure. I'll change out of uniform and be back." He hurried to his room, throwing the clothes on his bed. Winston leapt up beside the untidy pile. "Are you thinking what I'm thinking, Andrew? It's time to add some nourishment to your mother's meal."

"Way ahead of you." Andrew had changed into track pants and an old jumper. In his hand was a bag of leaves from Bodoron. "I think three leaves to begin with." He separated the round leaves from the vine and concealed them in the palm of his hand.

"Good show." Winston circled around and sat down on Andrew's still-warm uniform.

"Get off my clothes!" Andrew glared. "I don't need your cat fur all over them."

"Fair point," Winston conceded, leaping to his feet. "Would you fetch me some dinner when you're finished?"

"Winston… Don't try me! Your biscuits are in a bowl in the pantry, feed yourself." They left the bedroom as one, the cat bounding in front and nearly tripping him up as they entered the kitchen. Aunt Joy was ladling the soup into a bowl on a tray. "Smells delicious," he said. "How about some salt and pepper?"

His aunt whirled around to retrieve the grinder by the stove, and while her back was turned, Andrew scattered the Black Fire leaves into the soup, submerging them with the help of the soup spoon. Aunt Joy turned back and ground a decent amount of salt and pepper into the bowl. "That ought to do it!" she said brightly. "Here you go, love."

Andrew balanced the tray on one arm and made his way down the hall. He tapped on the door to his parent's room and went in. His dad was there as well, but Andrew's gaze flipped to his mother. She had lost more weight, and her eyes were sunken pools in her head. Her skin was pale, a hideous contrast to the bright pink scarf wrapped around her head. It was an outrageous burst of cheerfulness that Andrew decided he didn't like.

"Hi, Mum." He forced a smile. "Aunty Joy made you some soup. It's chicken noodle. You know what they say about chicken noodle soup!" *Now I'm doing it,* he thought. *Enough with the mindless chatter!* "Do you think you can eat some?" he asked her.

She shifted under the covers, stick-thin arms emerging to push herself upright. "Oh, I don't know, Andy. I'm quite tired."

"Just a few mouthfuls, darling," Mr Adler coaxed. "Here, I'll hold the spoon." He scooped up a spoonful, and Andrew saw a flash of black amongst the soup.

"There's some kelp in there, Dad," he explained hurriedly. "It's supposed to be good for energy."

His father gave him a bemused look. He shrugged, blew on the spoon to cool the liquid, and held it up to his wife's lips. She took a tentative sip, swallowed, and her whole face transformed. "More," she demanded. Spoonful after spoonful was devoured, and soon the bowl was empty. "Ah, that was tasty," she said, the colour returning to her cheeks. She laid back on the pillows, beaming with contentment. "Tell Joy I'll have the same again tomorrow!"

Andrew took the tray back to the kitchen. He placed a hand on his aunt's shoulder. "She loved it," he said. "A repeat order for tomorrow."

Aunt Joy flashed a rare smile, and Andrew was struck by the difference between the sisters. They had once been so alike, often mistaken for twins. But now there was little chance of confusing the two, as one bloomed with good health, while the other was a fading flower. *But Mum loved the soup,* he reminded himself. *The Black Fire gave her a spark. I can't wait to give her more tomorrow.*

For now, though, he had another task to attend to. He hurried back to his room and shut the door behind him. Winston was on the bed, seated up near his pillow, his tail neatly curled around him.

"Did you eat?" he asked the cat.

"I did. I'm not keen on those biscuits, though. They taste like cardboard!"

"How do you know what cardboard tastes like?"

"An educated guess," Winston sniffed. "So, what now? Are you going back to the day you collected Ralph?"

"I am." He sat down on the floor, his back resting against the wall beneath his window. "Make sure no one comes in while I'm gone. Create a disturbance if you have to."

"You can count on me," Winston puffed out his chest. "My speeches used to hold everyone's attention. A few well-placed meows will have them eating out of my hands... I mean, my paws."

Andrew rolled his eyes. "Whatever you say, Winston. I'll be back as soon as I get this sorted."

He pulled the black star necklace from beneath his jumper and held it in his hand. A quick glance inside confirmed that a portion of Ralph's fur was still nestled within. He snapped the locket shut and closed his eyes. "Take me back to the litter of puppies at Mrs Bargwana's house," he murmured. "Let me see with new eyes, and alter the outcome."

He was away immediately, the insides of his stomach clenching, a looping dizziness overcoming him. He dropped through time and landed on all fours with a grunt. He was in a dense shrub beside Mrs Bargwana's log cabin house. There was a sudden flurry of movement as a young goanna exploded out of the bush, startled by his sudden appearance. "Ugh!" Andrew held up his hands to protect himself from the lizard's scrabbling claws. "Settle down, lizzie. Is that you, George?" He remembered his recent visit to Mrs Bargwana, and the lumbering goanna that had taken a liking to

Leo. The creature turned; his head cocked to one side. "It *is* you. Look, be a good goanna and keep quiet, okay? I'll be out of your hair in a minute."

Visions of a goanna with a stylish brunette hairdo formed in Andrew's mind, and he stifled a nervous laugh. "Keep it together, Adler," he whispered.

In a low crouch, he crept to the side of the house and risked a glance around the corner. He was gifted a rare sight that plucked at the recesses of his mind: a mother labrador surrounded by a litter of wriggling, exuberant puppies. Pure yellow bundles of joy, clambering over each other and their mother, pulling on tails and snuffling each other's faces. He became still as he heard the mother speaking: "Brianna, leave Ralph alone! You can't follow him everywhere. Your master will appear soon, and it will be your responsibility to follow *him*, do you understand?"

The young female with a pink collar sulked, flopping against her mother's torso. "You never tell Shannon off, or Max," she said.

"Perhaps they listen more closely to what I say. Would you agree, Max?"

A puppy with a green collar somersaulted in front of her. "I listen. But I can make up my own mind as well."

That explains how we got ourselves into this mess, Andrew thought.

There was a crunch of tyres on the gravel driveway, as a car familiar to Andrew rolled to a stop near the log cabin. It was the car of his childhood, a dark red Toyota sedan. His fond memories turned to shock as his parents exited from the vehicle; young and brimming with good health. A tear slipped down his cheek as his mother released his younger self from the child's seat in the rear of the car. Her golden hair, her sparkling eyes, her kind touch.

Now the little boy sprang from the car, yelling "Where are the puppies?" The boy's face was hidden from Andrew. He had seen this phenomenon before and was unsurprised. It was an effect that protected the time stepper from the dangers of any time anomalies, as the Seer had explained when his stepping first began.

Mrs Adler took young Andrew by the hand, and the trio started towards the house. The front door opened, and an equally young Mrs Bargwana emerged, her honey-blonde ponytail halfway down her back. The adults spoke for a few minutes before Mrs Bargwana led them around the back towards the puppies.

It's now or never, Andrew thought, standing up. He wondered if any of the adults would recognise him, or try to stop him from taking the puppy with the green collar. He wasn't sure what he'd do once the puppy was in his hands, but he had to try something.

He burst around the corner, relying on the element of surprise. Mrs Bargwana glanced in his direction then looked away, as if distracted by a bird flying past. His parents had their backs to him and did not see him. Andrew continued towards the group before he encountered an odd resistance. There was a spongy, invisible barrier preventing him from going any further. He pressed against the barrier but it was like pushing against a trampoline. "What's going on?" Andrew muttered. He strode forward, and immediately bounced backwards. Inside the invisible bubble, he saw young Andrew choose Ralph, and the adults' delighted reaction.

Mrs Bargwana turned his way, looking at him. Through him. She stepped through the barrier and headed into the house, reappearing moments later with puppy toys, a blanket, and some paperwork. Once again, she passed cleanly through the barrier and proceeded to discuss the finer details of dog ownership with his parents.

"This is garbage!" Andrew fumed. "There must be some way to get through." He went up to the barrier and felt his way around it with his hands. Any entrance point evaded him; his only success was in feeling like a cheap imitation of Marcel Marceau, the famous mime artist. "I'm going back. I'll try again, ask for a slightly different time."

He clutched his talisman and thought of home. The next thing he knew he was back in his bedroom, landing heavily on the floor. Winston rocketed off the bed into the air, his tail puffed to twice its normal size. "Could you possibly warn me next time?" the cat cried, his eyes like saucers. "I'm not a young man, I have to look after my heart."

"I'm sorry, but I'm not hanging around," Andrew replied. "My first attempt didn't work. I want to try something different." He formed a new request in his mind, and he was away. He arrived in the driveway, just in time to witness Mrs Bargwana waving the red Toyota out of sight. Andrew kicked the gravel with the toe of his boot and swore.

Winston eyed him warily as he reappeared in the bedroom. "You weren't gone long. What happened?"

"Nothing. I can't get the timing right. I'll give it one more try." His brow furrowed in concentration, he disappeared from the room.

A light rain was now falling at Mrs Bargwana's house, and Andrew was unsure if he'd arrived too early or too late. He rushed around the corner of the house, and ran smack-bang into a tall and clearly unimpressed hare. "Seer? What are you doing here?"

"I may well ask you the same question, Andrew." The Seer's voice was cool. "Were you not told that this time was blocked to you?"

A blush of anger crept up Andrew's cheeks. He stared at the Seer's t-shirt, white with a red traffic sign on the chest that read:

Wrong Way
Go Back

"I was," he answered. "But I wanted to see for myself. Can you blame me?" He raised his chin in defiance.

"I blame you for nothing. I do wonder why you would not believe the words of a friend and guardian."

"Sure, Angus is a guardian, but is he a friend?" Andrew's eyes shone with hurt. "He's been avoiding me ever since Mum got sick. You tell me, would a friend do that?"

"You don't know the full story." The Seer gestured to Andrew and they moved onto the verandah, out of the rain. "While some answers lie in the past, this particular moment was too precious to allow anyone to tamper with it."

Andrew said nothing. Through the window of the log cabin, he could see the young Mrs Bargwana in the kitchen, measuring out food for an adoring group of creatures gathered at her feet.

"This moment was the obvious choice for a time stepper." The Seer's face softened as he continued. "And that's why I added my protection to it. The irresistible convergence of you and Ralph, the remaining gifted puppies, and the all-powerful mother Abi. What a tempting prospect for anyone with less than honourable intentions." He gave Andrew a keen look.

"My intentions were good, you know that!"

"There are others with dishonourable intentions, the Hag included."

"Tell me about her," Andrew pleaded. "It's obvious you and the Hag have been enemies for a long time."

"Adversaries. Not enemies."

Andrew frowned. "What's the difference?"

"An enemy would imply a hatred for the other. I do not hate the Hag, I balance her. We are combatants in the battle of dark and light, night and day."

Andrew considered the hare's comment. "How did it all start? What happened?"

The Seer's face was unreadable, but for a brief moment Andrew swore he detected a look of pain in the hare's eyes.

"The story is old, and our history is long. One day, when you are ready, it will be revealed."

"I'm ready now!" Andrew retorted. "I need to know. Who is this person that gave my mother cancer?" His voice caught in his throat.

"No." The Seer's tone was forceful. "You need time. You react from a place of hurt, of anger. And that is natural." His voice softened as he leaned forward, paws on his haunches. "But one day - and soon, I promise you -

the story will float to you on a breeze of understanding, and all will be made clear."

Andrew sighed. He knew from past experience he could not change the Seer's mind. "Okay, I get it, all in *time*. But let me ask you this: the Hag, she can shape-shift. One minute she's old and haggard, the next she is a beautiful young woman. Why don't you change? It doesn't seem like a fair contest."

The Seer closed one eye in a sly wink. "Perhaps I *do* change, Andrew. For now, though, follow the path of the puppies. You already know Cecil had two of the dogs. Use the Pisal machine if you have to. Or find another way. I know how ingenious you are."

The hare was fading from sight. "Wait!" Andrew called to him, "I need more information." But it was too late, the Seer was gone. Andrew swore under his breath. He was annoyed with himself for trying to access this time, and embarrassed at being caught out. He now understood his presence in this time was undetectable to all but his clever mentor, the creator of this protected scene.

He watched the pack of animals through the window, yipping and meowing at the prospect of food. Mrs Bargwana was busy filling bowls with food and water, oblivious to his presence. There was nothing left for him in this time. Andrew took hold of his talisman and disappeared.

CHAPTER EIGHTEEN

Andrew arrived home from soccer practice in time to prepare dinner. He hadn't attended practice for the last month, and two days ago the coach asked if he needed to give Andrew some time away from the game. The suggestion was well-intentioned, but Andrew was devastated. He'd forfeited so much in recent times; he didn't want to lose sport as well. Soccer was the one thing that kept him sane. Out on the field, he was in the moment and he could tune out the voices in his head that whispered those negative words about his mother.

But getting to and from training had been impossible, and initially, he requested a ride home with Gus. To Andrew's surprise, Gus had made some lame excuse about going elsewhere immediately after training. He was sorry, but Andrew would need to secure a ride with someone else.

At wits' end, Andrew asked Mrs Jordan for help. "Of course, Andy-Pandy!" She studied him, her eyes narrowed. "Have you been missing training because there was no one to take you?"

He dropped his eyes.

"Andrew!" She put her hands on her hips. "For crying out loud! I'm your guardian. Nothing is too much trouble." She reiterated that statement when she picked him up after training that afternoon. "As your guardian, I'm more than happy to help out."

"Wish I could say the same about Gus," Andrew mumbled as he threw his sports gear on the back seat of the Volvo.

"What was that?" Mrs Jordan turned the engine over.

"Nothing. Let's go home, Mrs J. I've got more Black Fire to feed to Mum."

Now in the kitchen, he pulled the large pot of soup his aunt had prepared from the fridge. In the absence of his father, Andrew ladled some of the liquid into a bowl and warmed it in the microwave oven. He added a few more of the shiny black leaves to his mother's bowl and took it to her room.

"Here you are, Mum! As requested, the same yummy food as last night."

Mrs Adler ate the whole bowl of soup unaided. "Marvellous!" She grinned at him, a feverish light in her eyes. "Now, I really must get up. I've been lying around in bed for far too long. I can't imagine how dirty the kitchen is."

"What?" Andrew blanched. "No, Mum. You have to rest!"

"Nonsense." She swung herself out from under the covers and stood up, her legs swaying. "I'll knock this cleaning over, and then we can talk about the washing."

"Mum, please! You're not well enough." He blocked her path. "Come on, lie back down."

He raised his hands to guide her back to bed, but she swooped under his arms. Full of bravado, she tottered into the hallway. "Let me guess, my interfering sister has rearranged the entire house, hasn't she?"

Andrew caught her up as she reached the kitchen. "I'm not joking, Mum. I gave you that food to make you feel better, not for anything else!"

She turned on him, her face flushed with anger. "I've had enough of people telling me what to do! Get out of my way." She tossed aside her bright headwrap, and began to search under the sink for her cleaning gear.

Andrew clutched his head in dismay. His mother was digging deeper in the cupboard, her pale, bald head bobbing around in the darkness for a favoured cloth. At a complete loss, he pulled out his phone and sent a message to his father:

Where are you? Mum is out of bed and being difficult. I need help!

He winced as he read the reply:

You've got to be kidding me. I'm in the supermarket. You're almost six feet tall and your mother is tiny. You'd better have her back in bed by the time I get home.

Behind him, Mrs Adler uttered a small cry of triumph. She emerged from the cupboard with a microfibre cloth in one hand and a spray bottle in the other. Steadying herself on the cupboards, she stood up. But while her brain was still surging on Black Fire, the physical effect had worn off. Like a weightlifter pushing an impossible weight, she was on her feet for a matter of seconds before her legs gave way. Andrew heard a dull thud as his mother's head met with the edge of the sink. A surprised "Oh!" escaped her lips as she slumped onto the tiles.

"MUM!" Andrew shoved his phone in his pocket and ran to her. "Mum, are you okay?" He cradled her in his arms and searched for injuries. An egg-shaped lump was already forming on her forehead, but there was no blood. He stood up and lifted her into his arms, angrily dismissing the voice in his head that observed how light she was. He carried her down the hallway and tucked her into bed. She murmured a weak protest, but the herb's effect had worn off and the fire was gone from her.

Back in the kitchen, he stowed the cleaning gear and retrieved his mother's headscarf. Returning to the bedroom, he made a makeshift turban, disguising the tell-tale bump on her forehead. She burrowed under the covers, her breathing heavy and rhythmic as she dropped into a deep sleep.

Andrew dashed to the kitchen, eager to clean the incriminating bowl before his father arrived home. He was drying the bowl with a tea towel when he heard the car in the driveway.

His father came in through the back door, dumping several bags of groceries on the floor. "Your mother? You got her back to bed?"

Andrew nodded. "She knocked her head on the sink. Apart from that, she seems to be okay. She's asleep now."

Mr Adler ran a hand through his hair. "What happened? What made her get out of bed?"

Andrew shrugged. "I've got no idea, Dad," he lied. "She wanted to get up, and she pushed me out of the way."

His father's lips pressed into a thin line. "I'll go in and check on her. Be more careful next time, Andy. You know how fragile her bones are. Would you mind taking care of these groceries for me?"

Andrew spent the next few minutes sorting the groceries and putting them away before retreating to his room. "I don't know why I thought Black Fire would work," he confessed to Winston as he perched on the bed. "I forgot about the crazy side effects."

"Don't be too hard on yourself," the cat replied. "If you hadn't tried, you'd still be wondering. It was worth a try, for your mum's sake."

"True, but now she's got a massive bump on the head for her troubles. I hope she didn't injure anything else."

He snatched up the two bags of Black Fire from his desk. "I have to get rid of these. I can't risk Dad finding it. I refuse to go through that madness again." He tiptoed down the hallway and headed outside to the garage. Using the light on his phone, he found a spade and dug a hole under the branches of a tall grevillea near the fence. He tipped the contents of the first bag in, but when he opened the second bag, a phosphorescent glow lit up his face. Puzzled, he plunged his hand into the bag, and pulled out a handful of round, pure white leaves.

White Fire.

Andrew reflected on his recent trips to Vellistrian. The pomp and ceremony in Scientia, and a belligerent young Jarl, reluctant to step into the role of son and heir. And later on, Jarl skulking away to the adjoining room, clearly up to no good. Had he orchestrated this switcheroo for his own purposes? "Quite possibly," Andrew murmured. The young Pisal was unhappy. He could have stolen the leaves from the White Fire meeting in a bid to forget his destiny and responsibilities. Or had he stolen the leaves in the hope of making Bodoron look bad? Either way, his plot had failed, because Bodoron had taken the leaves under the assumption they were all Black Fire.

The words of Snow and Bodoron filled Andrew's mind:

I still believe you saw Blair in a vision.

If we had any White Fire, we could give it to Andrew as an experiment.

We were supposed to have a sample for that meeting the other day, but I'm darned if I know what happened to it.

By some small miracle, the magical white leaves had ended up in Andrew's possession. He folded the bag over and put it in his pocket. Then he shovelled dirt back over the hole, tamped it down with the spade, and returned the tool to the garage. Back inside, he showed the leaves to Winston.

"Look. This could help us locate Blair and Abi!"

The following morning, Andrew tapped on Mrs Jordan's front door. He wanted to ask her advice before proceeding with the White Fire experiment. There was no answer, so he leapt the fence to his own house and proceeded over the next fence to Mr Lovell's. Mrs Jordan answered the door. "Good morning, Andy! I popped in to see how Pat was going. He wants to tell the next part of his story."

"Great. Can I ask you a question about something?" He followed her into the lounge room. "Morning, Mr Lovell, Mrs Bargwana. Morning, O'Donnells." He waved to the humans and the three cats.

Mrs Jordan patted his arm. "If it's not too important, let's wait until Mr Lovell is finished, dear."

Everyone sat down, and Mr Lovell picked up from where he had left off. "As you know, Helen and I were 'going steady', as we used to call it. She told me about her upbringing, and little by little, I built a picture of Cecil and his life after the war.

"Cecil yearned for the quiet life, and his dogs were there to protect him. With the benefit of hindsight, and after what happened to us in World War One, I wondered if that protection was enough. He'd always put faith in his good-luck necklace, but I didn't trust it, beautiful piece of jewellery that it was. Helen ended up with it, and its delicacy suited her far better. Anyway, I'm rambling. My worst fears were confirmed when Helen told me how Cecil died. He was alone in one of the paddocks with Pierce. Helen's brother James found them. Cecil and Pierce lay side by side in death, apparently bitten by a deadly snake. James never found the snake, but he saw a vulture sitting nearby, ready to move in on the bodies."

Mrs Bargwana gasped. "A vulture? Oh, no. The cunning old crone. A vulture visited me the day Andrew's family came to collect Ralph."

"What?" Andrew spun around in his seat. "You've never mentioned this before!"

Mrs Bargwana grimaced. "I hadn't made the connection. I'd presumed it was one of her evil cronies, but no, the coincidence is too great. It was *her*, spying on proceedings."

"And she kept on spying, Lucy, even after Helen and I moved into this house in 1946. In 1948, Helen gave me the greatest news of my life. We were going to have a child! After the pain of two wars, I was overcome with joy.

"That joy was obliterated when I returned home from work one day and found my doll in the kitchen. Mr Ruggles had returned as a warning. I resolved to get rid of the doll, once and for all. I took it to the park, and threw it down one of the big storm drains. I was so happy to see it go that I paid no attention to the old woman leaving our house as I came home."

Andrew drew in his breath. "Oh, no. Not again."

Mr Lovell swallowed. "My beloved Helen - and our baby - were taken from me soon after. And it broke me. I ended up peering into the bottom of several bottles of alcohol in a cheap Melbourne hotel. I wanted to end it all, but the Seer had other plans."

"What happened?" Mrs Jordan asked.

"I made a deal with him. War was all I knew. I begged him to send me away to war again. I told him if I saved one more person, then I was his to do with as he pleased. And that's how I ended up in Vietnam."

CHAPTER NINETEEN

Another week passed. Andrew went through the motions of school, homework, soccer training, and cleaning duties at home. His mother's adventure with Black Fire marked a turning point in her health. Mrs Adler lost her way after the accident in the kitchen, descending into the depths of the sickness. She ate less and slept more. Her pain levels increased, and it soon became apparent that she required around-the-clock care. Andrew and his father drove Mrs Adler back to the hospital, with the promise they would visit her each day. She offered them a weak smile as they waved goodbye.

The car felt empty as the pair drove home. "She'll be okay, won't she?" Andrew asked.

"She'll be fine." His father kept his eyes on the road. "It's the best place for her."

Andrew desperately wanted those words to be true, but the torment in Mr Adler's eyes told him otherwise.

As they pulled into the driveway, his father said, "What do you feel like for dinner?"

Andrew gave him a bleak look. "I'm not really hungry, Dad."

"Good. Neither am I." Mr Adler parked the car and pulled on the handbrake. "Have you done your homework?"

"Most of it. I thought I'd drop next door and catch up on Mr Lovell's life story."

His father whistled. "You should feel privileged! I haven't even heard that myself. Has he mentioned my father yet? Mum always reminded us how much Mr Lovell did for us. He's a real trooper, Andy. Go and listen, it will take your mind off things."

That night, Andrew heard how Mr Lovell jumped forward in time to another war: Vietnam. And once again, it was an experience the old man shared with Gus. Andrew was in turn amazed and horrified at the sequence of events as the story unfolded. Mr Lovell described the reappearance of his childhood doll, patrolling through the hot and humid jungle, and a serious injury that was his ticket home from the war.

Later on, Andrew slipped beneath his warm doona. He was tired, but his brain refused to rest. Stories of war, the wickedness of the Hag, and a lingering, deep sadness for his mother competed for space in his mind. The war stories and the Hag soon evaporated, but the sadness remained, dancing in a relentless circle while the old nursery rhyme *Ring a Ring o'Roses* provided disturbing background music:

> *A pocketful o'posies*
> *A-tishoo, a-tishoo*
> *We all fall down*

After his soccer game on Saturday, Andrew dropped by Mr Lovell's house. At long last, they had reached the end of his epic story. Mrs Bargwana had driven up from Canberra, and the group heard of Mr Lovell's return home, and his surprise at learning Andrew's grandfather was his next-door neighbour.

"It was both a blessing and a curse that your grandfather had combat fatigue," the old man told Andrew. "A blessing, because I should've been another twenty years older than I was. And a curse, because he was struggling. I worried my appearance would add to his mental anguish."

"Why wasn't I told about this?" Andrew asked, his face white. "Why didn't Dad tell me?"

"Back then, people didn't talk about such things," Mr Lovell said. "Picture this, Andrew: a fine, strapping lad like your grandfather goes off to war. He's bright, he's strong, he's proud to fight for his country. A few short years later, he's back home. He's broken. One minute he's yelling the house down, the next he's cowering in a corner, paralysed by a plane flying overhead."

"You're saying he was a coward," Andrew accused.

There was an abrupt intake of breath around the room, and the women glanced at Andrew in dismay.

"I'm saying nothing of the sort," the old man answered. "And I'm a little disappointed you would think so, Andrew. Your grandfather was a sensitive man, ill-suited to war. He'd been through the wringer and was effectively abandoned by his platoon when I rescued him. On the outside, he appeared fine. But inside, it was a different matter altogether. He held himself together for as long as he could. And when he no longer could, your father found me."

"He found you?" Andrew frowned.

"He poked his head through the hedge one day, and we got talking. He was a good kid. And I was concerned about him growing up without a male influence. We played cricket together in the backyard, and later on, I taught him how to drive."

"Is that why you were always calling me Peter?"

"No, I was just doing that to pull your leg," the old man grinned. His smile faded as he continued. "In the end, I arranged for your grandfather to be placed in full-time care. But there was little help, and even less understanding of his condition. After a long battle, your grandfather passed away in 1978, Andrew. Your father was 16 years old."

Sixteen years old, Andrew thought. *The same age as me.* He stood up, went over to Mr Lovell and gave him a hug. "I didn't know any of this," he said, his voice catching in his throat. "Thank you for looking after him. Thank you for looking after my family."

The old man brushed away a tear. "It was the least I could do, Andy. No one wants to see a broken man."

After a short break to collect himself, Mr Lovell told the end of his story. He spoke of another visit from the Seer, how the prophecy was revealed, and his next responsibility. "War prepared me for my greatest role of all: being Andrew's guardian. Through war, I learned to trust my gut, and my mantra became 'If it's to be, it's up to me.'" He tapped the framed quote beside his chair. "That self-sufficiency stood me in good stead, and I can see you've taken that message onboard too, young man."

Andrew nodded. "You guys understand what I'm going through. No one else does, not even Leo."

"That's why we're here, Andy-Pandy!" Mrs Jordan ruffled his hair. "We've all been through the grinder, we know how you feel."

"And I've been here to witness most of it," the old man said. "I watched out the window as your parents brought you home from hospital, Andrew.

A tiny bundle swaddled against the cold May winds. As soon as I met you, I knew. My gut instinct told me you were the one spoken of in the prophecy. But as we all know, it's a rocky road, and we still have some way to go. Nonetheless, we've reached the end of my story." He rose to his feet, his legs shaky. "I'm glad it's been told, it's a relief to have it off my chest."

Andrew checked his watch and whistled. "I'd better get going. Dad will be leaving for the hospital shortly." He stood and hugged the old man.

"Give my love to your mother," Mr Lovell said. "Oh, and one more thing." He fossicked in his pocket, and pressed a piece of jewellery into Andrew's hands. "This is yours, now. Guard it well."

"Oh, Mr Lovell, I couldn't!" Andrew protested.

"You can, and you will," the old man answered, his voice gruff. "It's meant for you; I feel it in my bones."

"Thank you." Andrew held the silver filigree necklace up to the light, the same necklace that once belonged to Cecil Jordan and his daughter Helen. "That's some amazing work," he said. "Look at those round leaves! They look a little like Black Fire leaves." *Or White Fire, for that matter. I still haven't mentioned those leaves to Mrs Jordan.*

He put the chain over his head and tucked the silver ball beneath his shirt. "Thank you again, Mr Lovell." He glanced around the group, and met Mrs Jordan's eyes. "I need to talk to you about something, Mrs J, but I don't have time now."

She gave his arm a reassuring pat. "Come and see me when you get home from the hospital."

"I will." Andrew waved goodbye to the group. As he leapt the fence into their front yard, he experienced a sudden sense of foreboding. He paused, wondering if there was more to this odd feeling coursing through him. Was it a warning about his mother, or something else? He shook himself, but the pit in his stomach remained.

His father emerged from the house, shoulders hunched, his arms thrust deep into the pockets of his jacket. "Oh, there you are. We have to go." There was a grim look on his face, and he didn't quite look at his son.

Andrew heard the reluctance in his voice and he felt another odd shudder of premonition. Was this the last time they would make this trip? His feet dragged as he got into the car. "Did you get an update from the hospital?"

His father started the car and looked over his shoulder as he reversed down the driveway. "They called twenty minutes ago. They suggested we come in. She's slipping in and out of consciousness, and they've increased her medication."

"Oh." A cold fear rushed through Andrew. He searched for words to respond to his father's comment and none came. He swallowed, aware of the savage pounding of his heart.

It began to rain, a sharp, spring shower that appeared out of nowhere, and the swish of the windscreen wipers masked the pair's silence as they made the short trip to the hospital. Mr Adler drove into the car park but as expected, the electronic sign above the entry indicated there was only a handful of spaces left. He sighed and turned to Andrew. "No point in us both driving round and round. You go in and I'll catch you up."

CHAPTER TWENTY

Mrs Adler was sleeping when Andrew entered the room, and he took a seat by the bed. She was hidden beneath a snarl of white blankets, a mere sliver of the woman he knew and loved. The cancer had ravaged her small frame, and now all that remained was a papery husk, clinging on against the final gust of wind.

He hid his face in his hands, tears slipping through his fingers. A small noise distracted him, and he wiped furiously at his face as a nurse approached his mother's bed. "Has she eaten today?" he asked, his cheeks flushed.

"No." The nurse paused, weighing her words carefully. "It's getting close now. You know that, don't you?"

He looked away. "Yes."

"Keep talking to her, she can still hear you," the nurse continued. "It's the last thing to go." She placed a comforting hand on his arm and left the room.

The nurse left, and Andrew glanced up at the oversized hare who had materialised by his side. "Please," he murmured. "Can't you do something? Anything, I'm begging you." The words caught in his throat.

The hare's eyes were dark with sorrow. "This path has been decided, Andrew. I can no more stop your mother's sickness than I can stop the sun from rising. The world turns, our loved ones pass onto the earth... and off. Your mother's time nears."

They were interrupted as Mrs Adler stirred in her bed. She lifted a waxen hand and pointed to a corner of the room. "Look, it's my mother," she said, her voice a dry whisper. "She's come through that door over there... Hello, Mum! You look lovely... so young."

The hairs raised on Andrew's arms as he turned his head. There was no door in the corner of the room, and Mrs Adler's mother had been dead for nearly twenty years. The Seer touched his shoulder and dissolved from sight as Mr Adler entered the room. Mrs Adler abandoned her brief conversation, dropping into a gurgling snore.

Andrew stood and drew his father aside. "She's seeing things. Her mother. And she hasn't eaten."

Mr Adler's face paled, and he pulled out his phone. "Joy? You'd better come."

Andrew's wild imagination had conjured a tumultuous night as his mother passed from the earthly realm and into the next. The wind howling outside, candlelight flickering up the walls, and banshees wailing in the shadows.

The reality was altogether worse. Aunt Joy sat on the broad window ledge, singing along to Michael Bublé's *I Wanna Go Home*, while a pale springtime sun emerged after the rain, splashing a weak puddle of light at his feet. His father paced, unable to sit still. "Joy, will you switch that off!"

He glared at his sister-in-law. She blushed, and turned off the music on her phone.

Andrew remained frozen, perched on the edge of an oversized hospital chair. He wished he could shrivel into a ball and roll away. Far away from this nightmare, to another world where his vibrant mother still possessed her beautiful smile, her irrepressible energy.

Surrounding them, dozens of cards proclaimed well-meant but trite messages. Not *Get Well Soon,* because no one dared to say that when cancer was involved. Instead, smug messages disguised in flowery script that said: *Thinking of You, Hope is the Best Medicine,* and one card that was a bizarre attempt at humour: *It's only a flesh wound,* a reference from a Monty Python movie, his father had explained.

The flowers took up any remaining space in the room. Boxes and vases squashed onto the bedside cabinet, a further cabinet borrowed from the empty bed beside his mother's, and still more crowded on the windowsill. Their scent merged to form a cloying smell that only added to Andrew's nausea.

Aunt Joy rose and placed a soft kiss on her sister's forehead. She turned to Andrew. "Why don't we go downstairs to the food hall and get a bite to eat?"

"I'm not hungry." He knew he sounded sullen, but he didn't care.

"I'm not either, but we should try. Come on, let's get a warm drink, I'm feeling chilly." She extended her hand towards him.

"Go on, Andrew," his father encouraged. "You need a break. We've been here for ages."

"Okay." He took his aunt's hand, and she helped him up. Another little bird that was stronger than him, and in that moment, he detested his weakness, detested the fact that all he wanted to do was crawl into a hole and bawl his eyes out.

How do they do this? She's still here. She hasn't gone, but I'm paralysed with grief. How do they keep going? Talking? Smiling? I can barely move.

He brushed away a tear and allowed his aunt to lead him from the room, leaving his father alone with his mother.

Peter Adler sat beside his wife and took her hand in his own. He stroked the papery skin and listened to the rattle of her breath. After a few minutes, he leaned in and whispered, "Helen, it's me. Can you hear me? Don't hold on, darling. Andrew and Joy are downstairs ordering a coffee. You can go if you want to. I know you dreaded leaving while Andrew was in the room." He attempted a smile, and failed. "I love you so much, Helen. Rest now."

Blinded by tears, he stepped into the small bathroom to splash water on his face. When he returned, Helen Adler drew her last breath.

In a corner of the room, the Seer watched on. A single tear passed his whiskers, alighting on the star talisman at his chest. A blinding prism of light shot from the jewel, and for a moment, a rainbow touched Helen Adler's face, now serene in death. Peter Adler bent over the bed and cried.

In the background, the large hare bowed his head and slipped away.

CHAPTER TWENTY-ONE

Gentle classical music played at the edge of Andrew's thoughts. From time to time, he heard the respectful murmur of people filing into the small chapel. There was a faint perfume from the flower arrangements dotted around the room and the huge arrangement on the white coffin at the front of the room. More than the perfume, it was the coffin that overwhelmed Andrew's senses. Such a tiny box. How could it possibly contain his beautiful mother?

Her smile was larger than that coffin.

Andrew's father sat to his left on the pew, and Aunt Joy to his right. Besides his aunt, there was no joy in the chapel, just a forced cheerfulness and the empty words of the funeral director who hovered near his father's elbow.

She would've loved those flowers, Andrew thought, glassy eyes fixed on the roses and irises, their bright colours contrasting with the sterility of the coffin. *Why do we shower dead people with flowers? They're not here to appreciate them, and no one else is in the mood to enjoy them.*

He looked over his shoulder to the pew behind him. Aunt Irene, his dad's older sister, and her husband Martin had arrived from Melbourne yesterday. Uncle Martin was a gentle giant of a man, with a pink, balding head and a hearty laugh. Today he was more subdued, giving Andrew's shoulder a reassuring squeeze as he turned around. Aunt Irene was kind but unpredictable: his father had always said she was just as likely to give you a dressing down as she was to wrap you in a hug. Mr Adler admitted she'd done both at once on a number of occasions, confounding everyone. His dad was certainly more easy-going than his sister, and Andrew wondered how they had turned out so differently. Today there was nothing but compassion on Aunt Irene's face as she leaned towards her brother, her salt and pepper curls merging with Mr Adler's greys as she whispered a word of encouragement to him.

Leo, Gus, and Teresa sat on the pew behind Andrew's aunt and uncle. Leo and Teresa looked distinctly uncomfortable: Leo in a baggy grey suit, tugging at the tie around his neck. Teresa wore a long-sleeved bottle green dress, and her red curls were tamed into a simple ponytail. Both gave him a tentative smile and quickly looked away.

Gus appeared much more at ease. He was dressed smartly in a charcoal suit, and he nodded and smiled at Andrew, as if to say, *you can do this*. He nodded back. *I bet Gus would know about the flowers... he must have seen a few funerals in his time.*

A hush fell over the room, and the director made his way to the lectern at the front. "Thank you, everyone, for coming today, as we celebrate the life of Helen Adler..."

Aunt Joy's hand slipped into his. She smiled at him through her tears, the skin around her nostrils red from blowing her nose. He swallowed and turned to his father, but Mr Adler was faring no better. Silent tears ran down his father's face, prompting a sudden epiphany in Andrew. His dad had sat through a similar agony when he lost his father at sixteen. The sorrowful looks they'd exchanged in the five days since Helen Adler's death took on a new poignancy.

The director's words washed over Andrew, a monotone speech his foggy mind refused to interpret. He scanned the chapel for familiar faces. There was Mrs Jordan, a few rows back behind his friends. She wore a black suit, and without her usual brightly coloured clothes she looked rather washed out. But in true Mrs Jordan style, she spurned the solid black funeral uniform and wore a violet scarf tied around her head. She caught Andrew's eye and gave him a sad smile and a wave. He waved back and continued his scan of the room.

He'd expected to see Mr Lovell and Mrs Bargwana, but he couldn't find the pair in the small chapel. This raised an unexpected panic in Andrew. He was reminded of the strange twinge he'd felt as he hurried away from Mr Lovell's house after the old man finished his life story. Where were they? Fear clutched at his stomach. *Don't tell me the Hag has gotten to them as well?*

He twisted around to look at Mrs Jordan, the question in his eyes. She gave a brief shake of her head, *not now.* Her eyes flicked to the front of the chapel, a delicate reminder for him to focus.

Andrew turned back, the beat of his heart merging with a dull throb across his forehead. They were playing a video now, a photo montage of Mrs Adler's life. Pictures of his mother as a little girl, his parent's wedding, the day he was born, photos with Ralph. Andrew and his mother playing in a pile of autumn leaves. A vivid spark of memory: a trip to the Southern Highlands when he was eight. His mother pressing a perfect leaf into his hands. Flame orange, the same rich hue as the roses on her coffin.

"It's a pin oak leaf, Andrew," she had said, her lovely face leaning towards him. "Aren't they beautiful?" He'd held onto the leaf all the way home, only to have it torn from his little fingers when he leapt from the car in the driveway. Memories pressing down on him. Memories no longer wanted because she, too, had been ripped from his grasp.

Mr Adler stepped up to the lectern for his eulogy. His emotions under tight control, he recounted a number of stories, including one where he'd visited the library every day for two weeks in the hope of wooing Mrs Adler. "And it took her the full two weeks to even notice me," Mr Adler said with a laugh. "I guess I was Helen's second love - after books." A titter of laughter spread through the room, adding to Andrew's distress. *Stop this. We shouldn't be laughing. Mum is dead, and Mr Lovell and Mrs Bargwana are missing!*

His father signalled to him as *Time to Say Goodbye* began to play. Two other pallbearers materialised to help Andrew and his father shoulder the coffin and carry Mrs Adler on her final earthly journey. The men stepped in unison down the aisle. Andrea Bocelli's voice soared, and Andrew caught sight of Teresa and Leo, both in tears. Gus remained ramrod straight in his seat, his lips a thin line, his eyes far away. Further along the aisle, Mrs Jordan sobbed into a purple handkerchief.

Andrew blinked back his own tears. *Just a few more steps*, he told himself as the coffin pressed down on his shoulder. He could almost fool himself into thinking he was carrying a heavy box and nothing more.

But the constant denial was too much to bear. His brave façade dissolved, and he cried as they left the chapel and approached the hearse. He'd always been frightened of hearses, they radiated a deep sadness with their gleaming, smug appearance. *We always win,* Andrew imagined the elongated vehicle saying. *We envelop your loved one in a dark embrace, one last velvet kiss before their final destination...*

"Andrew?" A flushed face appeared to his right as the white coffin slid into the hearse.

Mrs Bargwana. He brushed at his face and attempted to make sense of her words.

"I'm sorry I couldn't make it earlier," she said. "But Patrick needed my help. We need to have a group meeting - as soon as possible."

CHAPTER TWENTY-TWO

There was a wake at the house after the funeral. Mourners floated through the hallway and lounge room, black shrouds with paper plates of chicken and lettuce sandwiches. Others stood together in awkward clumps, clutching a beer or a glass of wine, silently toasting the life of Helen Adler.

Andrew kept himself busy, circulating the crowd and removing empty plates and glasses. He searched the room for a familiar face but his friends were gone, preferring the safe routine of school. Aunt Irene and Uncle Martin were flipping through a photo album of memories left on one of the coffee tables. They looked up and gave him a wave as he collected another glass.

Inside the mercifully empty kitchen he spied a half empty bottle of beer. In a moment of desperation, he stole a swig of alcohol, telling himself he needed something to calm his racing thoughts.

"I've told you before." A voice spoke behind him, and he jumped. "Champagne is by far the best drink. Madame Bollinger once said she drank it when she was happy *and* when she was sad." Winston nudged against his knee.

"I don't think Dad bought champagne for today," Andrew murmured with a frown. "And if you want to talk, let's go to my bedroom." He headed down the hallway, ripping off the blue tie he and his father had worn for the funeral. It was Helen Adler's favourite colour, and the ties had matched the irises in the flower arrangements. His librarian mother would have loved their eye for detail. She had taken great pride in producing engaging book displays. She once assembled a clever library collection with an explanatory sign: *I can't remember the name of the book, but the cover was blue.*

Winston slipped through the door as Andrew closed it and leapt onto the bed. "How are you bearing up, m'boy?"

Andrew sank down beside him. He was stiff, and his shoulders felt like they were up around his ears. "I'm not great, to be honest," he said. He stroked the cat's fur, soothed by the soft, thick coat. "I don't know how to go forward from here. There's this gaping hole inside me." The words stuck in his throat.

Winston head-butted his arm and climbed onto his lap. "I remember when my mother died. It was in June, 1921. I didn't always agree with the way she lived her life, Andy. But when she died, it left a huge hole in my heart that not even my darling Clementine could fill." His bright orange eyes glowed with emotion. "But in time, the searing pain lessens. Oh, you still love this person more than life itself, but the grief fades. A sword in the heart becomes a knife in the stomach, then a slash to the leg. Eventually the pain is a pin-prick on your arm." He flexed a claw into Andrew's forearm to demonstrate. "It has not disappeared, you can still feel it, still recognise it. But it does not render you weak; you no longer collapse in misery, or hide away in fear. Life goes on, Andy, and your mother would have you remember that."

Andrew gazed into his cat's eyes, and he felt the world shift around him. A cat was seated on his lap, speaking his wisdom on grief. But inside the cat body resided a brilliant and famous man, and today this made little sense. His head began to throb again, the tears bubbling beneath the surface.

"I'm tired, Winston. Only a few months ago, I could go to Mum and tell her how I was feeling, and she'd put her arms around me and give me a whole new perspective on things. I can't do that anymore! And I can't go to Dad, he's barely coping." He pushed the cat off his lap and leaned back on his pillow. "I'm not strong enough to go after the Hag. Hunting her down won't bring Mum back."

The cat clambered onto his chest and glared at him. "Balderdash. Success is not final, failure is not fatal. It is the courage to continue that counts. Besides, you have to find out what's happening with Lucy Bargwana and Patrick." He glanced away to the window, distracted by a sudden movement. "There's someone here to see you," he said as a large ginger cat alighted on the window ledge. "You'd better let him in."

Andrew sighed and sat up. "It's Kevin. They want me next door for their council of war." He opened the window and let the cat inside.

"Andrew?" Kevin spoke in his lilting Irish accent. "They sent me to collect you. Can you spare us some time?"

"Sure," he answered. "But you can't expect me to go after the Hag. I don't care anymore. Mum's gone." A muscle twitched in his jaw.

"I understand. But from what I've heard, it's more involved than that. If you won't do it for yourself, at least do it for Patrick."

A cold weight settled on Andrew's chest. "What's happened to Mr Lovell?"

"Lucy can tell you more about that. Come to Dorothy's as soon as you can." Kevin leapt through the window and disappeared.

Andrew looked at Winston and sighed. "You're right, it looks like I have no choice." He changed out of his suit, favouring the comfort of jeans and a hooded sweatshirt. "I'll help Dad clean up and then I'll head next door."

"Shall I come with you?" Winston offered. 'I'd like to hear about Patrick too."

"Would you? I'd really like that." Andrew smiled, and for the first time since his mother's death, his smile was genuine.

Andrew finished loading the dishwasher with glasses and side plates. He straightened up as his father entered the kitchen. In an eerie repeat of the day Andrew learned of his mum's sickness, Mr Adler reached into the cupboard above the fridge for the bottle of scotch. He poured himself a shot and sat at the table, his blue tie askew, shirt sleeves rolled up to the elbows. He threw his head back and swallowed the drink in one gulp. Grimacing, he stared at Andrew. "You're a good kid, Andy. I don't know what I would've done without you."

A lump rose in Andrew's throat. "I'd do it all again, just to have her back."

Mr Adler rested his forehead on his fingers, his thumb massaging his right temple. "Joy's coming over tomorrow. We're going to start sorting through your mother's things. You've got the rest of the week off from school, if you need time. I spoke to your principal yesterday. She said you can go back when you're ready."

"Thanks, Dad. I might stay out of your hair tomorrow. I think Mrs Jordan wants to take me under her wing." It was a partial truth, but it also gave him time to discuss the latest developments with his guardians.

"Dorothy's got a heart of gold. Same as Pat. We couldn't ask for better neighbours, Andy." Mr Adler unscrewed the cap on the bottle and poured himself another shot. "Is there anything I can get you, son? Are you okay?" He looked up from his drink, tired concern etched on his face.

Andrew threw an arm around his shoulders and hugged him. "I'm as good as I can be, Dad. I promised Mrs Jordan I'd see her, so I'll run next door for a minute. Will you be all right on your own?"

"Irene and Martin went back to the hotel to get changed," he said. "They're picking up a pizza and then they're coming back. I'm exhausted, Andy." He stood and walked into the lounge room, Andrew following. "I'm going to stretch out on the couch, talk to my sis and brother-in-law, and remember your mum."

Andrew nodded. "Okay. I'll be back soon."

CHAPTER TWENTY-THREE

They were all waiting when Andrew and Winston arrived: Mrs Jordan, Mrs Bargwana, and the three O'Donnell cats. Even Gus was propped awkwardly against the sunroom wall, but there was still no sign of Mr Lovell.

"Where is he?" Andrew scanned the faces of the adults.

Everyone turned to Mrs Bargwana. She flicked her long ponytail over her shoulder and cleared her throat. "He's in Nostalgia, at the animal hospital. After Pat finished his story, Dorothy and I were on our way home when we came across another cat, a male black and white tuxedo. I sensed he had a connection to Pat, and I was right. It was his brother, pushed through time to re-forge their bond. And not a moment too soon! As I went to give Patrick the good news, I found him unconscious on the floor, and that hideous soldier doll was sitting on the windowsill in Pat's kitchen.

"I didn't know what to do, so I followed Dorothy's lead when she saved my life all those years ago. I scooped him into my arms, and I asked to be taken to Nostalgia. At the last minute, Pat's brother jumped into the embrace, and we all ended up in the foyer of the hospital."

"I didn't know you could do that, Lucy," Mrs Jordan said.

"Neither did I, but desperate times call for desperate measures."

"You'll find the Seer played a hand in that transportation," Deirdre spoke up. "As custodians, Lucy and I had little need to time step on our own, as the animals were always delivered to us. But we both developed a feel for requesting help when it was needed, and bless him, the Seer never let us down."

"That's all well and good," Andrew said, "But is Mr Lovell still in hospital? It's been a week since he finished his story. Mum was still alive when he, when he..." he trailed off, his fists clenching and unclenching by his side. "And is that awful doll still in his house?"

"I got rid of the doll," Gus said.

"How can you be sure?" Andrew said. "It's turned up that many times I swear it's attached to a boomerang."

"True," Gus agreed. "But I know a thing or two about how to get rid of curses."

"You do?" Andrew stared at him.

"That may be a good thing," Mrs Bargwana interrupted. "Pat's in the safest place for now, in the hospital in Nostalgia."

"Is he okay?"

"The medical staff in Nostalgia appear to know what they're doing, but I wondered if his sickness has something to do with the Hag's curse on Patrick back in World War One." Mrs Bargwana turned to Gus. "If that's the case, we'll need your help removing it, Angus."

"Of course," Gus answered. "I'm a little rusty, but you know I'd do anything for Pat."

"Great. I'll need you to visit him in hospital tomorrow," she said.

"Will do," Gus nodded. "I'll be off then. I need to prepare a few things before I leave. Goodnight, everyone."

"Goodbye, Angus," Mrs Jordan said. "Now, Andrew." She turned to him. "We know this is an awful moment for you, but I need you to focus your energies on bringing down the woman - the creature - that did this to your mother."

Andrew rubbed his eyes. He was well past the tired stage and was now entering the realm of jitteriness. "Mrs J, it's been a long day. Can we talk about this tomorrow?"

He stood up and she swept him into a hug. "I'd like that very much. You need to get some rest. And Andrew..." She held him at arm's length, her dark eyes bright with unshed tears. "I'm so proud of you, how you've gotten through these past few weeks. Your mother would be proud of you too."

He smiled at her through his tears.

It was early evening in Nostalgia's Animal hospital, and a group of Pisal doctors were conferring in the hallway outside Patrick Lovell's room. "Let's be honest with ourselves," a female doctor addressed her colleagues. "We've tried a number of remedies, but we still don't know what we're dealing with. If it's an infection brought on by another creature, we can heal it."

"But it could be a curse," a thin male doctor with eyes the colour of ruby grapefruit spoke up. "That's what the Custodian of Extraordinary Animals suggested."

"I wonder if it's a bit of both," a third doctor said. He was an older Pisal, with sooty grey skin and intelligent, peach-coloured eyes. "We know The Hag played a role in Mr Lovell's sickness, and we know she is at her strongest when she has a dog at her side. Is there any chance her dog did this?"

"Not that we're aware of," the female doctor replied. "We have Mr Lovell's brother Andrew with us, in cat form. He was on the spot almost immediately, and he didn't mention a dog."

"I remember the brother's case!" The thin doctor interrupted. "He'd made a promise to Mr Lovell as a young boy, and it took him years to fulfil it. I heard Blair himself became personally involved." He lowered his voice at the mention of Blair.

"What? Why didn't you say something?" the older doctor frowned. "If Blair is taking a personal interest in the case, we'd better come up with a solution quick-smart."

"Doctors, excuse me." A voice came from behind them. "There's someone here to see you." A Pisal nurse stood with a young human man. He strode towards the trio, arm outstretched. "I'm Angus Walker, an old friend of Patrick's. I may be able to help with your predicament. Is it possible to see him?"

The doctors swallowed their surprise and shook hands with the visitor. After a brief chat, they ushered Gus into Mr Lovell's room and retreated.

Gus shut the door behind him, pulled up a chair and sat by the bed. He studied the old man, and a ripple of fear ran through him. "Oh, Pat. What's become of you?"

The old man was connected to a number of machines that monitored his condition. Mr Lovell lay on his back, mouth open, a random snuffle and snore escaping from his lips. A black and white tuxedo cat was curled against his thighs, keeping a close eye on proceedings. Gus touched the cat on the head by way of greeting. "So, you're the famed Andrew, Pat's older brother. I'm glad you two finally reconnected. I just wish it was under better circumstances."

The cat blinked in acknowledgement. "I agree. I had no idea how much time had passed, and by the time I returned, Paddy was an old man." He paused to glance at his brother's aged face. "You know Patrick. Has he lived a good life?"

"He has lived a hard life, my friend. I've been with him for much of the journey, through tricks of time. He's experienced much heartache, and has lived under the shadow of a curse for too long. But he always had the courage to go on. I admire your brother enormously for that."

The cat's eyes gleamed. "Then this makes my decision all the easier."

"Your decision?" Gus looked puzzled.

"Yes," the cat nodded. "But that's between me and Paddy. Problem is, he hasn't spoken a word since we found him." He nudged his brother's leg.

"That's about to change." Gus stood up and emptied the contents of his pockets onto the bed. "I'm here to break the curse on Patrick. I was too naïve, I thought he'd beaten the old bat."

"You can remove curses?"

Gus paused. "I can. But I promised many years ago to hide my skills for fear of reprisal. This will be the first spell I have cast in hundreds of years. I hope it works."

The cat's eyes narrowed. "So do I."

Gus lit a black candle and placed it on Mr Lovell's bedside cabinet. He glanced over his shoulder to the closed door. "If you see anyone coming, distract them. I don't want the Pisal nurses interrupting."

He took a purple stone off the bed and placed it on the pillow above the old man's head. "Amethyst," he explained. "It protects and dispels." Next, he placed a jet-black stone in each of Mr Lovell's hands. "Black tourmaline, for shielding." He held a neatly-trussed bunch of dried herbs by the stem and lit them. Once they began to smoke, Gus extinguished the flame and paced around the bed, waving the smoke above the still-sleeping Mr Lovell. "White sage and bay leaf. To purify and remove negativity."

"Am I in the way?" the cat asked.

"No, stay where you are. You're a part of this." Gus placed the smudge stick on a saucer beside the candle and sorted through the pile of items on the bed. "Here." He handed Andrew a striped ochre and gold stone shot through with a beautiful metallic sheen. "It's called tiger's eye. Put it between your paws while I perform the ceremony."

Gus moved two additional bunches of herbs to the base of the bed, and took up position near Mr Lovell's feet. He drew a deep breath. "We're ready. Let's begin."

His eyes closed; Gus called out in a loud voice:

I see it
I name it
I call it into the light
This curse on Patrick Lovell
Ends here tonight

He raised the herbs above his head, a collection of fiercely sharp spines in his left hand, and a bundle of dried leaves in the other:

By Blackthorn spine
And leaf of Rue
I remove this curse
And return it to you
Hear me, Hag
And hear me well
We reclaim our Patrick
And bid you farewell

As Gus uttered the final words of the spell, the candle flickered and went out. The hospital lights faded, and an unnatural darkness filled the room. The machines attached to Mr Lovell stuttered, and the steady beep of his heart monitor accelerated.

Gus held his breath, waiting. Above his head, a large pair of electric blue eyes took shape in the blackness. The eyes filled Gus with an old, familiar dread. *She's here,* he thought, a tingle running down his spine. *I knew she would come.*

The eyes hovered above the old man, casting an icy glow over the bed. Static crackled through the malfunctioning machines, eventually separating from the racing beeps and building into the mocking voice of the Hag: "I walked the earth long before you, Angus. I know you. I know *all* of you, but you know nothing of me or my origins. Your silly little spell won't dismiss me."

"Then why did you come, Hag? Were you scared?" Gus stared into the huge blue eyes.

The eyes flashed with anger, transforming the sheets into a neon blue "You always did have an ego, Angus. The curse is gone, but only because *I* removed it. He'll die anyway. The old fool should never have scarred me. Remember... I know *everything* about you, Angus the ageless. You are limited by your own contradiction. No one will listen to a man trapped inside a 16-year-old body. Not now, not ever!"

One of the eyes closed in a sinister wink, and then they were gone. The hospital machines resumed their monotonous beat, and the lights came back on, revealing a small, tight smile on Gus's face that disappeared as quickly as it appeared.

The cat gave him a worried glance. "Is what she said true?"

"Some of it. And if some of it is true, it stands that some of it is *untrue,* so hold onto hope, my friend. Patrick still lives." He returned to the side of the bed, removing the crystals from Mr Lovell's hands and above his head. He tucked the candle and smudge stick into a paper bag and stashed it inside his jacket. He wrapped the herbs in a wad of tissues and threw them into the garbage bin. "Don't touch them," he warned the cat. "The spines are highly poisonous."

He sat down in the chair and took Mr Lovell's hand in his own. "Pat? PAT! Wake up, you old fossil! Who said you could have a rest?" He gave the old man a gentle shake.

Mr Lovell's eyes fluttered open, and Gus jerked back in surprise. The pale blue eyes were gone, replaced by a rich emerald green that looked out of place in the old man's face. Mr Lovell was equally surprised. "Is that you, Angus?" he said. "What in the devil are you doing here?" He glanced around the hospital room. "*And where is here?*" His voice rose in panic. "And what's this cat doing on my bed?"

Gus smiled. "Welcome back, old friend. You had us worried!" Truth be told, Gus was still worried. Now that Mr Lovell was awake, it was clear he had suffered at the hands of the Hag. The old man had shrivelled away, like a deflated party balloon. His fiery spirit remained, but his body was fading.

Hiding his concern, Gus picked up the cat and placed him in the crook of Mr Lovell's arm. "Here. This is your brother Andrew. He fought through time to see you again, but you had to go and be all melodramatic and end up in hospital."

"Wait." The old man's gaze swivelled between Gus and the cat. "The last thing I remember is seeing the doll." He clutched Gus's arm. "Tell me it's gone!" The heart monitor quickened as he grew agitated.

"Pat, calm down. It's okay. I took care of it. I was a fool – I made light of the connection she had with you. I should've taken care of it much sooner." Gus gave the old man's arm a reassuring squeeze. Patting his pockets to make sure he had everything, he rose to his feet. "I'm going to tell the doctors you're awake and lucid. In the meantime, catch up with your brother. He has a proposal to put to you. Take care, gents," he addressed them both. "I'll see you on the other side, back at home."

CHAPTER TWENTY-FOUR

"What part of the assignment are you having trouble with, Teresa?"

Despite Gus's best efforts, his red-headed friend was off-topic again, using every delaying tactic in the book to prolong his visit. To be honest, his mind was elsewhere. Time had been wonky during his visit to Nostalgia. He had left in the morning and arrived at the hospital in the early evening. Now he was back, and it was late morning. Was the Hag meddling with time from afar? He bit his lip and dragged his thoughts back to the present.

He'd promised to help Teresa with her history assignment, but after an hour, the schoolbooks still laid untouched on the floor. He sighed. He picked up the history textbook and opened it to the section on the Vietnam war.

Teresa turned to him, her eyelids fluttering. "I'm sorry. I got distracted." She pulled herself upright, her fingers twirling a ringlet of red hair. "Why was the war so unpopular? I'm trying to understand. Wasn't it a good thing to push back Communism?"

Gus closed his eyes. He remembered the slogans of the time, *All the Way with LBJ,* and American President Johnston visiting Australia and stirring the population into a frenzy about the war. And then there were the protestors with their placards and buttons:

Draft Beer NOT BOYS, and
Make Love Not War

For Gus, they were dark days, the remorse and cynicism weighing as heavily as the act of war itself, and he had little desire to revisit that moment in time. But there was a greater purpose at stake, and that was keeping Teresa safe while Andrew pursued the Hag. *It was your idea to be the decoy,* he reminded himself.

"It wasn't as simple as that," he said aloud. "Vietnam was a country desperate for its own sovereignty, and in 1968 the Viet Cong launched an offensive that took everyone by surprise."

"The Tet Offensive?"

Gus nodded. "It shifted perceptions about the war, and why we were involved." *Although I'd already left the war in 1968,* he thought as his hand strayed to his left collarbone, the site of an old war wound.

Teresa followed his hand, and she let out a surprised exclamation. "Where's that pretty blue necklace you always wear?"

"I gave it away."

"Oh," she pouted. "You could've given it to me. I loved that colour."

Over my dead body, Gus thought.

She leaned closer, examining the spot Gus had touched below his collarbone. "Is that a scar? Oh, you poor thing, what happened to you?" She placed a hand on his chest, her chin tilting upwards, her eyes firmly fixed on his lips as she drew nearer.

Gus leaned away. He gently removed her hand and stood up. "Teresa, I like you, but as a friend, okay?"

Her cheeks flaming, she jerked away and leapt to her feet. "I... I thought—"

Gus raised his eyebrows. "And I thought you liked Andrew."

"Well, I did, Gus, but you told me to stay away from him!"

The morning after the funeral, Andrew awoke to blazing sunshine in his room. He rolled over and checked the clock on his phone. It was 10:00am. He wondered why his father hadn't woken him. He got his answer in the kitchen, with a note propped against the fruit bowl on the table:

Out with Irene and Martin. Thought you could do with some rest. We'll bring dinner home x

"Excellent," he said. He put some bread in the toaster and grabbed a plate from the cupboard. Winston appeared, and he filled a small bowl of meat for him. He buttered his toast and put a thin smear of peanut butter over the top. The pair ate in silence, each absorbed in their own thoughts.

Once they were done, Andrew washed up and left the dishes to dry on the rack. Then he had a long shower, washing away the stress of the last few days.

"Are you going to start looking for the dogs?" Winston asked.

"Not today. I thought I'd visit my friends and thank them for coming to Mum's..." He trailed off, reluctant to say the 'f' word.

"That's thoughtful of you, Andrew," Winston said. "They'll appreciate you making that effort." His tail swishing, he sauntered into the hallway. "I'll see you later on. I'm going to chat with the O'Donnells and reminisce about old times."

Andrew was greeted at the front door of Teresa's house by her father. The tall, sandy-haired man seemed uncharacteristically pleased to see him. "Well, well. Look who's here."

"Mr McKenzie." Andrew's tone was stiff. "I came to thank Teresa for coming to the f-funeral."

Mr McKenzie's smile vanished, replaced by a look of remorse. "Of course. I'm so sorry about Helen. Your mother was a lovely lady. Come on, I'll take you down to Teresa."

Andrew followed the tall man down the hallway, arriving at Teresa's bedroom in time to hear a familiar voice say, "And I thought you liked Andrew."

And Teresa's reply: "Well, I did, Gus, but you told me to stay away from him!"

Andrew burst into the room. Gus and Teresa stood a suspicious distance apart, both crimson-faced at his sudden appearance. Mr McKenzie had a sudden change of heart and decided to stay. He propped himself against the doorframe, a look of ghoulish interest on his face.

"I did not say that!" Gus retorted. "I said for you to stay away while Andrew's mother was sick."

The words hung in the air, and Teresa shot Andrew a guilty look. "I didn't know you were coming over."

Andrew stared at her, wishing he could redo this scene from the beginning. "It was a spur-of-the-moment thing. I wanted to thank you for coming to Mum's funeral." He dropped his eyes. "You too, Gus."

Mr McKenzie was by Gus's side in an instant, casually draping an arm across the young man's shoulders. "Gus is a great guy, isn't he? He's been a terrific help to Teresa lately. If he hangs around any longer, I'll have to recruit him into the Navy."

"I'm sure Gus would love that." Andrew's reply was laced with sarcasm. He turned on his heel and strode down the hallway. He refused to stay and listen to Mr McKenzie extol Gus's virtues. There was simply no way he could compete with the boy who had lived for hundreds of years. He slammed the front door behind him, feeling a mixture of anger, betrayal, and humiliation. He turned in the direction of Leo's house. He knew the welcome there would be much warmer than the McKenzie household.

After Andrew's hasty retreat, Gus stared at Teresa's father with a quiet fury. "While I appreciate your glowing endorsement, Mr McKenzie, I don't appreciate you doing it at Andrew's expense. He's a good friend of mine, and he's just lost his mother."

Mr McKenzie drew back in surprise. "I... I meant nothing of it."

"I expected you to show some compassion!" Gus turned his back on Mr McKenzie, speaking to Teresa. "I hope I gave you enough pointers for your assignment. Let me know if you need anything else. I'll see you back at school." He collected his books, pushed past Teresa's father and left.

Mr McKenzie blew out a gust of air. "Wow, he's got some nerve, stripping me down like that! But I've got to admit, there's something about that young man, Teresa. He'd make an excellent naval officer."

"I don't think he's too keen on the military, Dad."

Mr McKenzie tutted. "His parents must be hippies. I can tell you now, joining the military would be the making of that boy."

CHAPTER TWENTY-FIVE

"They said what?" Leo exploded.

The two boys were in Leo's bedroom, Andrew stretched out on the bed, Leo reclining in his office chair. At the latest news about Teresa and Gus, he catapulted forward in his seat, hands clutching his head.

"I was outside in the hallway when I heard it." Andrew closed his eyes as he remembered, his cheeks still hot with embarrassment. "She said she liked me, but Gus warned her to stay away because my mum was sick."

"That's garbage," Leo said. "And it doesn't make any sense. Why would he say that?"

"I don't know!" Andrew rubbed a hand across his forehead. "Because he's jealous? Because he wanted Teresa for himself? When I burst into the room, I swear they were about kiss. They had that awkward, guilty look—"

"Yes." Leo nodded. "Like one of them had just farted!"

"What is it about you and farts?" Andrew wrinkled his nose. "No, it was like they'd been caught out. And then Mr McKenzie was carrying on in the background, saying how much he liked Gus and that he was going to join him up to the Navy."

Leo roared with laughter. "Mr McKenzie thinks he can teach Gus a thing or two about the military? I'd love to be a fly on the wall for that conversation!" He wiped tears from his eyes. "Give it time, Andy. Mr

McKenzie will lose his cool about Gus as well, just you wait and see. The only thing Teresa will end up being married to is the Navy. Mr McKenzie will see to that."

"You're probably right," Andrew sighed. "I have to concentrate on finding out more about Ralph's siblings. I need to get to Abi, the mother of the dogs, and ask her some questions." He swung his legs onto the floor and sat upright. "Problem is, I don't know *how* to get to her. I've got the White Fire leaves, but I don't know if they'll work. Abi is 'off-world' with Blair, whatever off-world means."

"You got to Blair in a dream state, didn't you?" Leo tilted back in his office chair, hands behind his head.

"I'm not sure how I got there."

"Snow said you fell asleep in a bed of White Fire," Leo persisted. "What if it was as simple as that? Use the White Fire, enter a dream state, and go looking for Blair."

"But that would involve me being in control of my dream. I don't know about you, Leo, but when I dream, I'm just along for the ride."

His friend grinned. He leant forward, elbows on his knees. "It doesn't have to be that way. It's even been proven by science."

"What has?" Andrew saw the joy on Leo's face and realised he was in for a science lesson. He groaned inwardly, but he was too tired to voice a protest.

"Lucid dreaming. It's when you're 'awake' in the dream - you realise it's a dream but you can control your actions. Recent research proved that deliberate control is possible in about a third of lucid dreams. It's worth a shot, Andy. We could do it in a controlled environment. I could sit with you and take notes. Heck, if we had continued access to White Fire, we could do a few experiments. I could even write a scientific paper on the topic!"

Andrew stared at him. "By George, Lambie, I think you're onto something."

"Thank you." A flush of pleasure appeared on Leo's cheeks. "And don't call me Lambie."

Andrew ignored him, his chin resting on a fist, deep in thought. "I was going to ask Mrs Jordan about this, but I forgot when Mum... when she..."

"It's okay, Andy," Leo stopped him. "You don't have to say it."

"I still can't believe it." He swallowed the lump in his throat.

"Give yourself time. Everyone says you have to grieve in your own way. For some it may take a few weeks or months, for others it may take years."

Andrew shook his head in wonder. "You continually amaze me, Lambie. When did you become so smart *and* compassionate?"

Leo laughed. "I think it was after I was with Einstein. I was frightened I would never see my family again, and when I did, I vowed I would never take any relationship for granted. You included, Andy-Pandy." He clapped his friend on the back. "So, what are we going to do about this White Fire experiment?"

Andrew's face brightened. "First of all, I want to ask Mrs Jordan some questions. She knows heaps about herbs, so maybe she can help us with a recommended dosage. I've been meaning to ask her for ages, but things kept getting in the way." He pulled his friend to his feet and swept him into a hug. "Thanks, man. For everything. I don't know what I'd do without you." He darted out the door, leaving behind a bewildered Leo.

Andrew knocked on Mrs Jordan's front door. He rested against the bricks, taking a few deep breaths. After the thrill of Leo's suggestion, he'd run all the way down Constitution Hill to home.

A moment later, his neighbour threw the door open. Kevin and Colleen were twined around Mrs Jordan's legs, their noses lifted to catch a sniff of the great outdoors. "Hello, Andy," she greeted him. "It's warmer today. Spring is on its way."

"Good." He flicked his fringe off his sweaty brow. "It's been a lousy winter."

Her eyes saddened. "That it has, my dear. Come inside, we'll have a drink."

Over a cup of tea, Andrew described his latest embarrassment with Teresa. "I think she likes me, Mrs J, but it seems every time I get close to her, Gus is in the way. What's his game? Do you know if he's interested in her?"

Mrs Jordan's brow furrowed. "It's trickier than it looks, Andy-Pandy."

"You *know* something! Tell me what's going on," he begged.

She blushed and shook her head. "It's not my story to tell. All I can say is that Angus will tell you when he's ready."

"Oh, that's convenient. It sounds like the Seer's favourite saying, 'It will all happen in time.'"

"I promised, Andrew." Her eyes pleaded with him. "I know you've been through hell, and none of this makes sense, but please, just focus on what you can control."

"Sure. I'll add it to the pile of things I don't want to think about. It's growing bigger by the minute." He took a sip of his tea. "Any news on Mr Lovell?"

"Angus visited him. He said it went well, but the hospital is crossing their T's and dotting their I's before they release him."

"I hope he's home soon. I miss him."

Mrs Jordan gave a brief nod. "He is a special human being, Andy. He's seen so much, and that's why I value his observations. I'll be glad to have him back - we could do with another guardian around, what with you going off to find Ralph's brothers and sisters."

Andrew drained his cup. "Speaking of which, I went to Leo's after Teresa, and he had a great idea. He suggested using White Fire to get to Blair. I've wanted to talk to you about it, but there's been a lot going on." His mouth pushed down in a sad smile. "Anyway, Leo thought I could do something called lucid dreaming."

Mrs Jordan's eyebrows skyrocketed. "Good heavens. Scientific Leo suggested that? What's gotten into him?"

"I have no idea, but what do you think? I've got the White Fire leaves. Last time I fell asleep in the plant, so how much do you think I'd need this time round?"

Mrs Jordan took off her glasses and studied them, her mind deep in thought. "I have no idea how these things get so dirty!" She blew on the glass and cleaned them with a soft cloth she drew from the pocket of her lavender cardigan. "Andy, you ate White Fire when you were imprisoned in Vellistrian, didn't you? That was what enabled you to see Owen and Secunda in their true form."

Andrew nodded. "Ralph and I shared a small sprig. No more than a couple of tiny leaves each."

Mrs Jordan put her glasses on and peered at him. "Much better, I can see you now. My guess is that you'll need half a dozen to send you into that dream state. Oh, what's that, Colleen?" The tortoiseshell cat appeared on the seat beside her, nudging her arm.

"Add some mugwort for good measure," the cat said. "It's renowned for improving dream quality and recall."

Mrs Jordan paused, a hand over her mouth. "I've got some in the pantry, from memory. We'll add it to the mix. Thank you, Colleen."

Andrew gave the pair a bewildered look. "You two should compare notes with Leo. I know nothing at all about lucid dreaming, but I'm willing to give it a try. If anyone can solve this mess, it's Abi the mother dog."

"Well, what are you waiting for?" Mrs Jordan prodded him. "Go next door and get the White Fire, and I'll dig out the mugwort. See you back here in five minutes."

"We're doing this now?" His eyes widened.

"Why not, Mr Impatient?" she teased him. "I'll watch over you, and I'm sure Colleen and Kevin would be keen to help out too."

"Leo wanted to be in on this as well, Mrs J. He'll be disappointed if he misses out on some major scientific discovery."

Mrs Jordan laughed. "Call him up. The more the merrier, I say."

Half an hour later, three humans and two cats crowded into Mrs Jordan's spare bedroom. Andrew was stretched out on the single bed, his bare feet dangling over the end. Kevin and Colleen took up residence at the foot of the bed, one on either side of Andrew's legs. Leo had dragged two kitchen chairs into the room, and now he and Mrs Jordan were squashed side by side in the remaining space. Leo had a small notepad on his legs, and he was firing questions at Andrew and jotting down the answers. "How many White Fire leaves did you take?"

"Six."

"And how much mugwort?" Leo asked Mrs Jordan.

"He took a teaspoonful in a cup of tea at 12:45pm," she said, checking the time on her phone. "It's one o'clock now, I expect we'll see some changes in the next 30 minutes." She unlocked the phone, and pulled up a playlist. "Andrew, this will help you slip into the lucid dream state, it's a playlist designed by neuroscientists for that express purpose." She hit play, and the room was filled with gentle classical piano music.

"They have playlists for this?" Andrew shifted onto his side, and Kevin moved up the bed, settling in the crook of his legs.

"Oh yes, it's quite commonplace," Mrs Jordan said. "I searched for one as soon as you mentioned lucid dreaming. Leo, you'll want to record what song is playing when Andrew falls asleep."

"Of course," Leo muttered, scratching his head with the lid of his pen. "Although we haven't established a baseline. For scientific purposes, we should have tested Andrew with the mugwort alone to begin with, and then factor in White Fire's effect. I'll also need to know how much water he's drunk, when he last went to the toilet—"

"Shh, don't stress." Mrs Jordan raised a finger to her lips. "It will all work out. Give it time."

Andrew shifted position on the bed again. He felt a little silly with an audience waiting around for him to fall asleep. Kevin protested at his restlessness, standing and circling before claiming a warm patch of bedding. There was something pushing into the back of Andrew's neck. He reached around, freeing his tangled necklaces and resting them on top of his shirt.

Leo noticed them and let out an exclamation. "Two necklaces? What is it with you? You're like a walking jewellery store these days!"

"The silver one is from Mr Lovell. It was Cecil's good luck charm."

Leo looked doubtful. "Okaaay. Well, I hope it brings you some luck too."

"It will. These two want to be together, they have an almost magnetic attraction to each other." He tucked them out of sight, and the group lapsed into silence. Andrew could feel his body relaxing, the tension of the past few weeks slipping away. "I hadn't realised how tired I was," he said, his eyelids fluttering. "Can't keep my eyes open..." His head dropped to one side of the pillow, a gentle sigh escaping his mouth.

Leo seized the phone. "The current song is Mermaid, by Sade." He wrote down the details, noting the time. "Nice work, Mrs Jordan! He went under quickly."

"I think that's the White Fire more than anything, Leo," she murmured. "From what Andrew told me, that's more than three times the amount he ate in Vellistrian. Now we must wait."

CHAPTER TWENTY-SIX

D rifting.

Andrew floats away on a gossamer cloud, above the house, above the city, and beyond. He merges with a bank of clouds, rolling across the sky in a storm. Bolts of lightning shoot tremors through Andrew's weightless form.

Rocketing downwards, quicksilver propelled. Slicing through the soil, severing stone, and piercing the lid of the sky above another vast world. Andrew sleeps on. There is no resistance, only forward movement.

He is lost in the cloud. He is the cloud. He glides.

There is an excited flutter beside him, a flurry of wings. Andrew feels the wind in his face and awakens. A troupe of green, bat-sized butterflies accompany him on his flight, and a thrill of wonder rushes through him.

The butterflies stir a memory, and he recognises the landscape he is flying over. A vivid green countryside, comprised entirely of crystals. Dark crystal forests, apple-green crystal fields. He spies a breathtaking piazza below, and a crystal lounge situated beside a fountain in the centre of the piazza. *I remember now. This is Vertis.* The thought collides with his body, a gentle nudge to proceed in this new direction.

He begins to descend. The cloud dissipates, and Andrew finds himself sitting comfortably on the lounge. A strong hand grips his in welcome. "Yes! You made it back to Vertis. Greetings, old friend."

Andrew feels a joy exploding inside him, a desire to laugh hysterically. *I did it! I'm here, in Vertis with Blair.* He turns to the ageless man beside him, and drinks in his long limbs and startling orange eyes. They radiate with kindness as a smile creases Blair's bearded face. Andrew decides there is no need for words, and he forms a question in his mind:

Abi. May I meet with her? I wish to learn about her puppies.

You may, Blair answers. *As a great poet once said, we are in the forest primeval. Bearded with moss, and in garments green. We must journey further, to the heart of the heart. Come.*

Blair unfolds himself from the lounge and stands. He is unusually tall, and his white garments glow in the soft green light. A serpent is emblazoned across the chest of the man's tunic. Andrew watches, mesmerised, as the snake comes to life. It rears backwards, then shoots forward to strike, stopping millimetres before his face. The serpent smiles, its tongue flickering past his jaw:

I sss-see you, Andrew. What do you sss-see?

Everything, he says. *I see with new eyes.*

The snake slithers back into place on Blair's tunic, one ruby red eye closing in a wink.

Blair beckons to Andrew, and the pair begin to walk. Crystals crunch beneath their feet, and the air sparkles around them. They pass through the forest, the trees forming a canopy over their heads. Gentle birdsong envelops them, and Andrew's mouth parts in wonder as the butterflies return, their antennae vibrating in song.

Blair does not speak. A path opens up for him as they walk, shrubs and flowers parting in reverence, the ground crystals sparking like fireworks beneath his feet. Andrew follows, awake but asleep, attuning himself to this unique landscape.

The lush forest gives way to open green plains. Blair walks on, occasionally glancing over his shoulder to smile at Andrew. A group of hills rear up from the earth, and Blair produces a staff as the terrain grows rocky. He is nimble, and climbs with no sign of tiring. At one point he extends the staff behind him for Andrew to steady himself on. The staff is scaly, and in the half light, Andrew notices the serpent has departed Blair's tunic, transforming itself into a sturdy walking stick. The snake's tongue flicks across Andrew's hand as he pulls himself onto a ledge.

In the side of the hill is an opening to a cave. Crystalline flowers are dotted around the entrance, and a heady perfume fills the air. *We are here,* Blair announces. *The heart of my home, the Heart of the Heart.* A golden labrador trots out to greet them, and Andrew's heart stutters. He bends on one knee and bows his head. This is Abi, the mother of his beloved Ralph, the mother of the gifted puppies.

We meet again, Andrew. Abi touches her muzzle to his forehead. *Welcome, to the place where only truths are told.*

Inside the cave, Andrew is stunned. Huge beams of rose quartz crystals jut from the ground and soar above his head to form a cathedral-like vault. Beneath the huge crystals lay smaller outcrops that over time have worn down into seats and tables, archways and doors. There is a warmth in the heart of hearts, a feeling unlike any Andrew has experienced before. There is peace, contentment, and acceptance. But like the Tardis in Doctor Who, the heart represents something bigger. Dozens of identical rose quartz tunnels radiate outwards from the pink centre. It is a glittering hall of mirrors, an alluring maze. *What lies beyond these tunnels?* Andrew wonders.

More than you can possibly imagine, Blair answers. *Arleigh's Passage, Blair's Bypass, they are all here, along with many others.*

Blair reclines on a low crystal settee, and the mother dog leans against his legs. The man places a comforting hand on her flank, and she gazes up at him in adoration.

Andrew takes a seat nearby. *Abi, I'm after your help,* he begins. *I request knowledge of your children, to help me identify Max.*

For what purpose do you seek Max? Abi turns her intelligent eyes onto Andrew.

He has aligned himself with the Hag. This has caused untold grief for me and for those I love.

Ah, but she is the grief-bringer, not my son, the dog answers.

This is true, Andrew says, *but she feeds off Max's power. Abi, please! You are a mother. I lost my mother because the Hag interfered. With your help, I can stop this.*

The labrador gives him a sorrowful glance. *I grieve for your loss, Andrew. But as a mother, I cannot betray my children, regardless of who they align themselves with. Max was always strong-willed... Perhaps this is the only clue you need.*

Andrew accepts Abi's response without query. The heart of hearts has a purity that cannot be questioned, and while Andrew hoped for a clue, the dog's response is both fitting and reasonable. He stands to leave, but a movement in one of the hallways catches his attention. He turns to see his mother waving to him.

She is radiant, her cheeks the same rosy colour as the crystals around her. There is no trace of illness. She smiles, and mouths the words *I love you,* before disappearing around a corner.

The heavy stone of grief weighs on Andrew's heart, and tears form behind his eyes. *Mum, wait!* He rises to follow her, but a hand grips his arm and pulls him back.

There are many arteries in this heart, Andrew. They represent the choices we make in life, and the paths we choose to take. Blair grasps Andrew's shoulders, his orange eyes glowing with emotion. *We are not meant to traverse every pathway. Each artery leads to a junction, which leads to another choice, another decision. Even Abi's refusal today has set you onto another path. Choosing poorly leads to heartache. Choosing wisely will return you to the heart, to this primeval forest. Remember this above all, and trust that one day you and your mother will meet again.*

Blair places his hand on Andrew's head. Pursing his lips, the tall man blows a gentle breath into his face. Andrew rises off the cave floor and floats through the opening into Vertis. His cloud is there, waiting to envelop him. They lift above the green landscape, passing up through the sky and into Andrew's home world.

He sleeps.

CHAPTER TWENTY-SEVEN

"Welcome back, sleepyhead."

Andrew lifted his head. Mrs Jordan and Leo were smiling down at him, but he detected a hint of anxiety behind their eyes. Colleen and Kevin remained on the bed, and another had joined the party. Winston leapt up beside Andrew's shoulders. "You had us all worried," he growled. "You were out for nearly four hours!"

"What?" Andrew's eyes darted to the window. The light had gone out of the day, and deep shadows were falling across Mrs Jordan's backyard. "Garbage! It only seemed like an hour, maybe less."

Leo held up Mrs Jordan's phone. "See the time? It's ten past five. You were gone for so long we ran out of music."

"How did you get on, Andy-Pandy?" Mrs Jordan interrupted. "Did you get there? Did Abi tell you anything?"

Andrew sat up on the bed, hugging his knees to his chest. "Yes, I made it back to Vertis, back to Blair. It was incredible, that feeling of being in a dream, but being fully aware. And Abi *could* have told me something, but she didn't. She wouldn't betray her children, even if one of them had gone over to the dark side."

Leo sighed. "The lucid dreaming worked, but we're no further along. What now?"

"Blair said something about a primeval forest," Andrew said. "I've got no idea what it means. Was he talking about Vertis, or something else?"

"There's a famous poem about a forest primeval." Winston paused to scratch behind his ear. "It's called Evangeline, by American poet Henry Wadsworth Longfellow. It speaks of murmuring pines bearded with moss, and standing like druids. Does that sound like the landscape you walked through?"

"In a way, but I think he wanted to draw my attention to something else." Andrew swung his legs onto the floor. "Can I get a drink? I'm a bit dry."

They moved into the kitchen. Mrs Jordan busied herself feeding the cats, while Leo filled the kettle and prepared three cups of tea.

Mrs Jordan watched the cats devour their food with a bemused grin. "I don't want to hear a peep out of you cats about roo meat again," she said. "You're eating me out of house and home!"

"In our defence," Winston mumbled between a mouthful, "we haven't eaten since this morning. I thought we were supposed to get three square meals a day."

"Not if you're lazing around on beds for half of it." Mrs Jordan winked. "Now, let's discuss your journey, Andrew. You said Abi would not reveal any of Max's traits?" She joined the boys at the kitchen table.

"Nope," Andrew said. "The only thing she mentioned was that he was strong-willed."

"Maybe she was hinting at Max's owner," Leo said. "That he'd need to be strong to keep Max in check."

"Maybe it's the opposite," Mrs Jordan mused. "Maybe Max chose his owner to give him strength when needed."

"Stop it, you're confusing me!" Andrew interrupted. "The only way through this is for me to visit Brianna and Pierce. We know they were both Cecil's dogs, and we know *when* they were with him. But I'm still wondering about the forest primeval."

"I have a theory." Winston jumped onto Andrew's lap. "What does Blair look like? Who is he, and where did he come from?"

"It's all a bit sketchy, Winny."

"Winny?" The cat glared at him. "Who said you could call me that?"

"Sorry." Andrew grinned as he stroked Winston's soft fur. "I thought it suited your new form."

"Winston will do just fine," he sniffed. "Now, about Blair?"

"Most of what I know comes from the Pisal. Their homeland was originally built by large moles. Apparently, there was a devastating land slip and Blair stepped in and saved the lives of hundreds of moles. He used Blair's Bypass to transport them to safety, moments before the land gave way beneath his own feet. In a gesture of gratitude, the moles gifted their land to the Pisal."

"What is this Blair's Bypass you mentioned?"

"It's a really cool way of getting from one place to another, especially if you're in a hurry. I've only done it once."

"Not to be confused with time stepping, I assume?" Winston asked.

"Completely different. Blair's Bypass gets you from one place to another in the same timeline, while Arleigh's Passage will transport you through time."

The cat turned a circle and sat down in Andrew's lap. "This Blair sounds quite capable. Is he a tall man?"

"Yes. Tall and thin, tanned skin. Ageless. Salt and pepper hair and beard. And orange eyes. Each time I've seen him, he's worn a white tunic with a snake across the chest."

"I knew it!" Winston exclaimed, leaping to his feet. "The poem refers to *him* as much as the land he lives in. He's a druid!"

Andrew gave him a quizzical look. "How do you know that?"

Winston drew himself up. "I'll have you know I joined the Albion Lodge of the ancient order of the Druids in 1908!"

Andrew shook his head in wonder. "Is there anything you haven't done, Winston? Why do you think Blair is a druid? Because he has a long beard?"

Leo snorted with laughter, and Winston gave him a disapproving look. "Of course not. I'm more interested in the myth of Blair, and what he wore on his tunic. Snakes hold incredible significance to the druids, boys. Have you heard the legend of Saint Patrick driving the snakes out of Ireland in the 5th century? Many believe the snakes were a metaphor for druids."

"But what has this got to do with us?" Andrew asked. He was growing tired and irritable. He failed to see how snakes and Druids would help locate Max and his otherworldly mistress.

"You have a powerful ally, Andrew. Druids are renowned for their magical abilities. You said he saved a world and its inhabitants from destruction. That's no small feat. I imagine he's keeping a very close eye on you."

"Oh, great," Andrew moaned. "Just what I need, someone else waiting to see if I mess things up."

"You're looking at it all wrong, Andy," Leo said. "Blair is someone you can call on if it all starts getting ugly. He gave you a riddle to solve with his true identity hidden within, and you figured it out. I think that's a sure sign you have his support."

"Maybe he can help me extract some information from Brianna."

"You don't need any help," Mrs Jordan said. "It's clear that Brianna's tell is loyalty, she followed Cecil everywhere. That should be enough to sway her in your favour, Andy-Pandy."

"I hope so," he sighed.

"Your visit could be two-fold. From what Pat told us, Brianna very nearly stopped Cecil from joining up to go to war. If I were you, I'd time step to 1914. Aim for the outbreak of war in August, otherwise no one will have a clue what you're talking about! It's not like today, when we hear news instantaneously. Australia was thousands of miles from the action and didn't care much about anything until the ball was fully rolling. Find out Pierce's tell, if you can, and make sure Cecil joins up."

He nodded. "I'll get onto it tomorrow. Strangely enough, I'm exhausted after the lucid dreaming."

The group stood and made their way to the front door. "One last thing," Mrs Jordan said. "Keep your eyes on the prize, Andrew. You're doing this to find Max, the dog who betrayed his family - and yours. Find him, break the bond between him and the Hag, and we have half a chance of ending this madness, once and for all. Please..." She clutched his arm, her eyes glistening with tears, "do this for all of us."

CHAPTER TWENTY-EIGHT

After a good night's sleep, Andrew bolted back some breakfast and prepared himself to time step. He revisited everything Mr Lovell had said about Cecil: his home in the Northern Rivers of New South Wales, his zest for life, and above all, his love of animals. He recalled Cecil and his father were on their way to Tweed Heads on the day Australia declared war on Germany. With that in mind, Andrew sat on the floor of his bedroom, clutched his two necklaces in his hand and willed himself away.

He arrived in the back of a moving horse-driven cart, his head bouncing off one of the metal milk canisters lined up behind the driver and his passenger. A golden labrador stood above him, teeth bared and a low growl emanating from its throat. There was an odd leap in Andrew's chest, fear mixed with recognition, quickly followed by a dull realisation. *It's not Ralph. This is his sister.*

He scrambled upright. The dog maintained her aggressive stance, a paw on either side of Andrew's legs, her muzzle inches from his face. "Brianna, please!" he said, his palms up. "I'm sorry to surprise you, but I need your help. Do you remember me? My name is Andrew. I chose your brother Ralph, many years ago."

Her ears pricked up at the mention of Ralph's name. She backed away, her head cocked to one side, attentive but suspicious.

The threat of attack dissipating, Andrew risked a glance over his shoulder. A golden-haired young man sat up front with the driver; an older, bearded man with a battered hat shoved low over his face to shield his eyes from the sun. The young man was only a few years older than Andrew, and oblivious to the new passenger in the rear. He chatted with his father, his dark blue eyes flashing with excitement. Andrew caught snatches of conversation over the drum of the horses' hooves and the creak of the carriage: *war... Europe... enlist,* and he was rapt to learn he had arrived on 4 August, 1914, the day Australia discovered it was at war with Germany.

He turned back to Brianna. "I know you have no reason to trust me, but I can prove myself. Your owner's name is Cecil, right? And you sleep next to him every night, don't you? You'd be in the front with him now if Cecil's father hadn't shooed you into the back here. Oh, and lastly," he leaned forward, his voice a whisper, "I know you can talk, but only if it's an emergency. Do you think me being here is an emergency, Brianna?"

The dog sat back on her haunches, her eyes wide with shock. She swallowed, then cleared her throat. "You were little, and you had long hair that was almost white," she said, her voice cracked and dry. "I envied the immediate bond between you and Ralph, and I dreamed of the day I would experience the same with my own master. And then I found Cecil, and I was delivered into his arms." She glanced at her owner, an adoring look on her face. "He is special, he needs my protection. But now he speaks of going away, to fight in some battle across the seas. I have to stop him."

"No, you can't!" The words burst out of him.

"Don't underestimate me, human." Her eyes glinted with menace. "I've already worked it out. I can bite him on the leg, injure him. He won't be going anywhere."

"Brianna, I'm sure you *can* stop him, but you mustn't. Cecil going off to war sets in motion a whole chain of events that we must not interfere with."

"Is that why you're here, to stop me?"

Andrew sighed, his patience waning. "No. Well, yes, if you're that intent on stopping him. Cecil *has* to leave. He has to meet his friend Patrick. Patrick saves Cecil, and Cecil saves Patrick." He mentally slapped himself, annoyed at disclosing future events.

"My master becomes a hero?" Brianna cast another besotted look over Andrew's shoulder to Cecil.

"Among other things, yes."

She relaxed onto the wooden floor of the cart. "I had this awful feeling he was going to die! I guess I was wrong."

"I guess you were." Andrew's cheeks burned. "Look, I need to ask you something, and I don't have much time."

Metal struck metal as the horses' hooves clattered across a railway line. They were on the outskirts of a town, and traffic was building. Andrew knew from Mr Lovell's story that Cecil and his father were on their way to view a new land release in Tweed Heads. Cecil had seized the opportunity to sign up with the Queensland contingent while visiting the border town. There was nowhere to hide in the back of the buggy. As soon as they reached the town, Andrew would be discovered. He needed information from Ralph's sister, and now.

"How can I help you, human?"

"Your brothers and sisters, do you remember any special traits they possessed? For example, Ralph has a certain spot on his tummy that makes his hind legs kick. And you, you're the loyal one, you're always by Cecil's side. Is there something you can remember about any of the others?"

Brianna tilted her head back and closed her eyes. "I have glimpses of memories. My beautiful mother, singing to us. Ralph was clever, he and Max picked up our lessons so quickly. But Ralph was kinder, he stood up for me if I made a mistake."

The cart was slowing now, and the hubbub of town infiltrated the buggy. A paperboy stood on a corner, proclaiming: *AUSTRALIA AT WAR! Special edition out NOW*

Dozens of men loitered in the streets, eager to hear the latest news. Random cheers rippled up and down the street, and Cecil became swept up in the excitement. "YES!" he roared, his hands raised in fists. "We're going to war!"

Andrew flinched and sank lower in the cart. "Brianna, please! What about Shannon? And Pierce?"

The dog frowned, deep in thought. "Shannon struggled with our lessons. She was really sweet, but I can't remember any one thing about her. Pierce was like me. He took the idea of protecting our master seriously."

"Come on! There must be something."

Andrew risked another glance to the front and saw Cecil's father pulling back on the reins. The man turned to his son, a doubtful look on his face. "Are you sure you want to do this, Cecil?"

"Yes, of course I am, Pa!" Cecil beamed at his father. "It'll be over by Christmas, so if I don't sign up now, I'll miss out! Besides, I'll have my good luck charm with me." The young man pulled a silver filigree necklace from beneath his shirt, and under Andrew's top, the same necklace floated upwards of its own accord, keen to meld with its past self.

Andrew squashed the necklace against his chest and turned to Brianna. "Well?"

"I remember something! Pierce loved eating grass, and Mum was always telling him off about it. She was convinced he was going to swallow fertiliser, or weed killer." Her eyes shone at the memory.

The buggy rolled to a halt, and Cecil jumped to the ground. "Come on, Brianna, I'm off to sign up!"

The dog crouched back on her haunches, ready to leap after her master. Andrew pointed a finger at her. "Don't you stop him."

The dog gave him a contemptuous look. "I will accompany him while I can, and you can't do a thing about it." She flew over the side and trotted after Cecil.

Andrew rolled his eyes. Now Cecil's father was shifting off his seat, stepping to the ground, reins in hand. Andrew ducked out of sight, lying flat in the tray. As he grasped the two necklaces in his hand, the sky above him blurred. A moment later, he was rolling through time, back to the present day.

CHAPTER TWENTY-NINE

Andrew arrived back in his bedroom feeling the worse for wear. There was a bump on the left side of his head from a milk canister, and his mind strayed to his mother's accident in the kitchen after taking Black Fire. He immediately squashed the memory before the waves of grief overcame him.

After a quick trip to the toilet, he encountered Winston in the hallway. "Your father was looking for you. He's on his way to the airport with your aunt and uncle."

Andrew slapped his forehead with his palm. "Oh, I was supposed to go with them." He pulled out his phone and sent his dad a quick message:

Sorry. I got stuck in the past. Some bad memories resurfaced. Please say goodbye to Aunty Irene and Uncle Martin for me.

Every word in the message was true, but his father would put his own connotation on them. He received a short message back:

I understand. Waving them goodbye now.

Winston glanced up. "Is everything all right, Andrew?"

Andrew scooped the cat into his arms and retreated to his room. He dropped onto the bed, placing Winston beside him. "I think so. My mind is all over the place. Memories of Mum, tracking down the dogs for more information, the business with Mr Lovell..."

Winston became alert. "Where is he? Is the curse gone?

"He's still in hospital. I'll find out more after I do this second time step."

"Do you need any assistance getting there? Any special knowledge from a particular era?"

"I should be okay, Winny. Mr Lovell said Cecil chose Pierce as his dog in 1939. I'll aim to arrive towards the end of the year."

The cat scowled. "I'm not sure I like this new nickname, Andrew. Clementine used to call me Pug."

Andrew chuckled. "I can't call you that! You'd be a cat with a dog's name. Far too confusing. Anyway, keep an eye on things while I get myself to 1939."

Winston nodded. "Be careful, Andrew. It was a hard year, full of fear and uncertainty."

Andrew sat on the floor, his back against the wall. "I'll be on my guard," he promised. "See you soon."

Churning through time was not the easiest of pastimes, Andrew decided as he landed on a hill a short distance away from a sprawling country homestead. His head ached from the bump he'd received in 1914, and now he had an upset stomach to go with it. He shook himself. "Get a grip, Adler. Look at the big picture and stop feeling sorry for yourself."

He stood up and scanned his surroundings. The large home sat in the lee of a hill, and across the driveway from the house was a long, low building which Andrew assumed was the milking shed. Further down the hill, he spotted a herd of black and white cows, calmly feeding on the grass near a dam covered by waterlilies.

It was around midday, the sun high in the sky. Andrew caught the smell of a roast drifting on the breeze. "Everyone is inside eating lunch. Everyone except the dog," he said, as a labrador stuck its head around the corner of the house. The dog spotted him and galloped across the grass barking a warning.

Andrew held his hands in front of him as the dog approached. "I mean you no harm. Can you please be quiet, Pierce?"

The dog halted at the sound of his name, and seizing the opportunity, Andrew went on. "Pierce. It *is* you, isn't it? Do you remember me? I chose your brother Ralph, many years ago."

Pierce tilted his head to one side, an action reminiscent of Brianna in the back of the cart in 1914. He lifted a paw, as if to say, *follow me*. The dog walked away from the house, towards a stand of eucalyptus trees further up the hill. He paused to make sure Andrew was following, then he slipped in amongst the trees, out of sight of the homestead.

Andrew caught the dog up. "There's more I need to tell you. I've just been into the past, to see your sister Brianna. She told me that your mother Abi was always concerned about you eating grass. Is that right, Pierce?"

"Tell me," The dog spoke in a raspy voice. "What do you know about vultures?"

Andrew was taken aback. "I beg your pardon?"

"Vultures." Pierce sat down at the base of a tree. "I thought they didn't exist in Australia. Until I saw one."

Andrew took a seat in the dirt, his legs splayed out in front of him. "I heard Helen saw a vulture hanging around on a couple of occasions. Mrs Bargwana has seen one too. Do you remember her? She was the lady that cared for you as puppies, before you were separated."

"I remember," the dog nodded. "Have *you* seen any, time stepper? They've got to be an omen. Helen warned Cecil about them, but he wouldn't listen. He's in his own world. I have to keep a close eye on him."

"I haven't seen one, Pierce. But I believe you."

"And you should!" The dog turned his large, melancholy eyes onto Andrew. "My poor sister died defending Cecil from a snake. But this snake was no ordinary snake. It did the bidding of a large vulture."

Andrew blew out a surprised breath. "Who told you that?"

"Cecil did. Not directly, of course - he often talks to himself in his room and I listen. Losing Brianna weighed heavily on him. He kept saying, 'I must be going mad. I saw that snake sitting right beside the bird, and the next thing I knew, it was coming for me. And Brianna, leaping between me and snake. I *am* going mad,' he said, 'because I heard Brianna say she would save me.'

"Poor Cecil. Is he better now?"

Pierce brightened. "I think so. He felt guilty about Brianna for years, and he didn't want another dog until now. But he loves me, and I him. Brianna and I were lucky to share the same master."

"I'm curious, Pierce," Andrew frowned. "How did that come about? What do you know of your siblings?"

The dog lifted his muzzle and gazed into the distance. "We were all together in an animal hospital. I remember seeing many creatures with rusty-red fur and bright green eyes. One day they gathered us together to watch a movie. Our new owners were projected onto a screen of some sort. We saw a young man with a vivid blue stone at his chest—"

Andrew was dumbfounded. "Pardon?"

"A boy with a necklace." Pierce repeated. "A bright blue stone necklace. Do you know this person?"

"I think I might," Andrew nodded. "Go on."

"There was a slightly older man with bright blond hair who worked with dairy cows. Brianna and I both felt a pull towards this man, so they allowed each of us to serve him, at different moments in time."

"Since you came later," Andrew said, "did you have to wait around?"

"You are a time stepper," Pierce said. "You know time is relative. I waited a minute or two longer. But it was enough."

"Enough for what?"

"To see my siblings choose their masters."

"Hold up." Andrew froze. "What exactly did you see?"

"There was another man who appeared on the screen, he was older than the others, and well-dressed. I looked at Max, and I could tell he preferred this person. Max was a cunning one, he had a good sense of smell, and I wondered if he was sniffing out money when he saw that man."

"He liked money?"

"He liked to feel special," Pierce replied. "Humans with money pamper their pets. I think that's what Max was after."

"So poor Shannon, she chose no one."

Pierce cocked his head to one side. "I wouldn't be so sure, time stepper. The boy with the blue stone necklace, he was like a deer in the headlights. Nervous, frightened, or both. I took one look at Shannon and I knew. She was quite prepared to transform into a cat and go into the dark past to serve him. I think she knew what she was getting into, and she went regardless."

"The dark past. What do you mean by that, Pierce?"

"Shannon went way back in time, further than any of us."

"How do you know this?"

The dog appeared confused. "Didn't I mention? Not only did we see our masters on the movie screen, we also saw the year we were delivered to them."

"And you remember all this?" Andrew was incredulous.

"To me, it is a recent memory." Pierce smiled. "And I loved my brothers and sisters. I couldn't go with them, but that didn't stop me from noticing where they were headed, and when. Shannon went to 1597. Brianna went to 1913. I came to 1939, and so did Max."

Andrew felt a tingle run down his spine. "Pierce, you're amazing. Thanks for sharing your memories with me."

The dog's tail thumped at Andrew's praise. "You're welcome. Will you visit Shannon? You must promise to do something for me."

"Of course."

"Give her a strong pat on her rump. A few hard thumps, and run your fingers the wrong way through her hair. She used to love that."

Pierce had unwittingly revealed Shannon's tell to Andrew, although he couldn't help but wonder if his actions would be met with delight or contempt.

"Can you tell me," Pierce interrupted his thoughts, "how my own life turns out?"

"You made Cecil proud," Andrew answered. "You protected him. No owner could ask for more."

Pierce grinned. "See? Mum didn't have to worry about me eating grass! And what about Ralph? How is he?"

"He's great. Those creatures you mentioned, with the russet fur and green, green eyes. Ralph has joined their forces."

Andrew landed on the floor of his bedroom with a grunt. He immediately checked the clock on his phone. A mere five minutes had passed since he left, and he gave himself a mental pat on the back. "Not bad, Adler! Keep up the good work."

"Are you talking to yourself, Andrew?" Winston looked down at him from his spot on the bed.

"I am. At least I get intelligent conversation." He gave Winston a cheeky wink and stood up. "I've got news. I'm off to 1597. Shannon's master was none other than Angus."

"I beg your pardon?" Winston spluttered.

"That's what I said. I'm going to bolt next door and tell Mrs Jordan."

His father still on the way back from the airport, Andrew locked the house and hurdled the side fence. Within minutes, he was inside Mrs Jordan's kitchen, explaining his find to his neighbour and Mrs Bargwana. There was a stunned silence around the table.

"Goodness," Mrs Jordan breathed, "this is not something we knew at all! Angus would have been quite young at that stage."

"And they were dangerous times," Mrs Bargwana added. "Perhaps that's why Shannon was assigned to Angus."

"Lucy's got a point." Mrs Jordan clutched Andrew's arm. "Will you be safe?" She looked down at the sibling cats on the floor. "Have you three studied this era? Is there anything you can think of?"

"You said 1597, didn't you?" Colleen queried. "I believe that's when the witch trials happened up north in Scotland. Andrew, if I were you, I would not interact with Angus at all."

"Why not, Colleen? He won't know me."

"If I'm right, Shannon went into the past with a good understanding of her fate. She was the only one transformed into a cat, and we all know how cats were viewed in that time. They were the familiars of witches, frightful and devious creatures. Don't be seen talking to Shannon, either, or there'll be trouble."

The group was distracted by a sudden movement outside the kitchen window. Andrew glanced up and did a double take. "Am I hallucinating? I just saw a dragon, and I can't even blame it on White Fire!"

Mrs Jordan followed his gaze. A miniature, indigo blue dragon with a golden belly hovered outside the window, a small vial in its talons. "I felt the same way the first time I saw Nostradamus," she chuckled. "I must say he's looking good. He hasn't aged a day since I saw him back in 1982."

"Nostradamus. THE Nostradamus." Andrew sounded dubious.

"Yes. One and the same. He visits Lucy and passes on information to her."

Andrew shook his head in disbelief. "Of course he does. I'd expect nothing less."

Mrs Bargwana opened the window, and the small dragon fluttered inside and landed on her outstretched hand. She bent her head towards the creature, listening intently. She nodded in reply, murmured a few words and nodded again. The dragon released the vial, launched off Mrs Bargwana's hand and flew out through the window.

Mrs Bargwana turned to Andrew. "Right, that was Nostradamus." She smiled apologetically. "He doesn't hang around for long, he normally drops in, imparts some wisdom and leaves. He used to stay longer, but I made a joke one time." She paused, her cheeks reddening at the memory. "I told him a dragon would never explode, but a dino might. Do you get it?"

Andrew guffawed. "That's terrible."

Mrs Bargwana giggled. "I know, but it tickled Nostradamus's funny bone. He laughed so much he snorted, and… well, I ended up with a burnt hand." She rolled her eyes. "Anyway, he had some advice for you, Andrew. We know you have to time step to 1597. Nostradamus lived in the 16th century, so he thought he'd throw his two cents' worth in. You're going to Aberdeen, in Scotland, and he suggested you use the Pisal machine to get there. It's a long way back in time, and you don't want to mess it up. People weren't particularly understanding back then. And," she held up the vial, "he's provided a super-concentrated shot of thyme tea to take when you arrive."

Andrew frowned. "Do I really need that?"

"Absolutely," Mrs Jordan chimed in. "This will be your third time step in a short period of time. Do you remember what I told you last year? We have to be mindful of exhaustion or sickness, and of creating anomalies. The machine will smooth that path for you, and the thyme concentrate will soothe your stomach."

Andrew took the vial and shoved it in his pocket. "Okay, I'm going tonight, after I've had dinner. Is there any more news about Mr Lovell?"

An uneasy look passed between the two ladies. "He's coming home, Andy," Mrs Jordan said.

"But he'll need some rest," Mrs Bargwana added, "so you can catch up with him after your time step."

Andrew's eyes darted between the pair. It was obvious they knew more about Mr Lovell than they were letting on, but they were reluctant to share any detail. He'd find out more after he returned from Vellistrian. It was time to go home, eat some dinner and be on his way.

CHAPTER THIRTY

"Oh, Andrew, thank goodness you're here!" Snow appeared before him in a flurry of green taffeta. "We've lost Jarl junior."

Andrew closed his eyes, inwardly groaning. He had arrived in Vellistrian hoping for an easy passage to Scientia and the machine. He didn't want to answer questions, and he certainly didn't want to become embroiled in a family drama. Besides, he'd only eaten one hot dog sausage and nothing else before leaving. Time was ticking and his stomach was growling.

"Hi, Snow. What's happened to him? Has he gone off by himself without telling anyone?" *Knowing Jarl,* he thought, *that's exactly what he did, the ungrateful little—*

"He was here this morning," Snow lifted her tear-stained face to Andrew. "He was in a foul mood, and Bodoron had words with him."

That wouldn't have helped, Andrew mused. *I have a feeling Jarl doesn't like Bodoron.* "Have you used the Scientia machine to find him? That's actually why I came to visit, I've figured out the location of Ralph's sister."

Snow threw her arms around him. "Why didn't I think of that? Let's go there now. Bodoron! Summon my carriage."

With a speed that is only afforded to royalty, Snow and Andrew were whisked away to the floating town of Scientia. The miniature Pisal scientists followed in Snow's wake as she swept into the lab, calling for answers.

She carried the discarded casing of one of Jarl junior's talons, and she passed this to her head scientist. "My son is missing," she announced. "Find him!"

"Right away, your Majesty." He placed the DNA sample in the drawer of the machine and hit the start button. Some improvements had been made since the initial test, and the machine now hummed smoothly as it processed the sample.

Almost immediately, a piece of paper appeared in the slot, and Snow snatched it up. "It says he's here!" she cried. "Here in Vellistrian. How can that be? He hasn't responded to any of our calls." She scrunched the paper into a ball and threw it away in disgust.

"Maybe he visited your parents?" Andrew hazarded a guess. "Or is it possible he called upon the Seer?"

"Why would he ask the Seer for help?" Snow's tone was scornful. "He has everything he needs right here in Vellistrian. He's royalty, or have you forgotten?"

"It was only a suggestion." Andrew's cheeks burned.

"Keep them to yourself! You don't know my son like I do."

"I'm sorry, Snow. I was only trying to help."

"You can help me by staying out of the way. I'll find him, even if I have to look for him myself." Snow had worked herself into a state, refusing to listen to anyone. She bustled out of the lab, her guards rushing to keep up.

Andrew and the scientists exchanged an awkward look. "I'm sure he'll turn up," he said, breaking the silence. "Teenagers. We're all the same, getting up to things we don't want our parents to know about." His comment was tongue-in-cheek, but the scientists nodded, a couple of them rolling their eyes from personal experience. "Anyway," Andrew continued, "now that the Queen is gone, could I bother you to flash up the machine again? I need to go to Aberdeen in 1597." He opened his locket and pulled out a few strands of Ralph's fur.

By no means an expert at time stepping, Andrew had, however, experienced two different methods of travelling through time: Arleigh's Passage, the Seer's preferred medium, and the shocking, instantaneous travel afforded by Gus's blue necklace.

Now he was adding a third to his repertoire. He stepped into the small machine and sat down, his knees grazing the front wall of the Pisal invention. *Certainly not the Tardis,* he thought. *It's small on the outside and the inside.* There were handles on either side of the seat, and he grasped hold of them. "Is this all there is to stop me falling out? A set of handles?"

The scientist gave him a patronising look. "You're going to 1597, we'll do you the courtesy of shutting the door." He reached behind Andrew and pulled a metal door out of a narrow recess. "It's made of titanium, so you should be safe."

"I *should* be safe?"

The scientist's eyes darted left and right. He leaned towards Andrew and lowered his voice. "We didn't mention it to the queen, but we've had more than a few teething problems with this one. Evelyn's been a bit cheeky of late, acting up. Time machines can be temperamental at the best of times – they're the prima-donnas of the machine world."

Andrew gave him a wild look. "What do you mean? It's just a machine, isn't it?"

"Evelyn's much more than just a machine. That's why she has such a posh name, isn't that right, Evelyn?" The scientist gave the machine an affectionate pat. "Time machines are special, and they know it. Fingers crossed she'll have more respect for you, being a human. Watch out for her though, she's a flirty, mischievous one."

"Really?" A flirty, mischievous time machine called Evelyn? What he had gotten himself into? Andrew loosened his hold on the handles and folded his hands primly in his lap.

The scientist tutted. "No, no, you must hold on. There are sensors in the handles, and Evelyn regulates the temperature and oxygen levels as you go along. Anyway, we'd better get you going, we don't want her getting impatient. Time to send you forth into the unknown."

"Hey, I know where I'm going," Andrew said.

"Yes, but can we be sure Evelyn does?" The scientist handed him a small remote control. "Type in the code 8988 when you want to come back," he said. "Evelyn will lock onto your location and grab you." He waved cheerfully, then slammed the metal door shut. "Happy travels!"

The machine purred into life, and Andrew's heart began to pound. He wasn't sure what to expect. In fact, he wondered if someone was going to appear and yell, *ENERGISE!* like they did in Star Trek before the crew were beamed away. Instead, he had the disconcerting sensation of the machine - Evelyn - tipping on her head, and him with it. He gripped the handles on each side of his seat and prayed it would soon be over. The machine righted itself, and he drew a sigh of relief.

His relief was premature, as without warning, Evelyn launched herself forward at warp speed. The next moment, the entire machine disintegrated around him, and Andrew could have sworn he heard a giggle of excitement in his ear.

Wherever he was, he was now plummeting at breakneck speed through the night sky. A babble of panicked thoughts invaded his brain: *Is this supposed to be happening? This can't be happening! I'M FALLING, how do I stop this? HELP!*

He saw a moonlit town below, and he briefly wondered if he would crash into the roof of someone's home, a time traveller who was out of time and out of luck. Or perhaps he'd end up splattered on the street, just another sad statistic from an unforgiving era. Carriage wheels would roll over him, unaware that the flattened object on the road originated in the 21st century.

"EVELYN!" Andrew screamed. "If I ever see you again, I'll take a sledge-hammer to you, do you hear me?" His words apparently had some effect on the wayward machine, as he heard a sound in his ear, an annoyed whisper that sounded remarkably like *killjoy.*

His downward trajectory slowed, and he landed with all the grace of a ballet dancer in a dark alleyway. He leaned against a beer barrel and heaved the contents of his stomach onto the ground. He noticed the remains of the hotdog he'd eaten for dinner, and he suppressed a manic laugh. *After that ride, I wish I'd eaten nothing. Evelyn, you can keep your version of time travel. I am never stepping inside your doors again.*

He remembered the vial of concentrated thyme tea in his pocket. He removed the cork and took a sip of the liquid. His churning stomach settled, and a few moments later he was standing upright again. His clothes had morphed into leather breeches, a scratchy linen shirt, and a leather jerkin. His feet were clad in leather boots, and he wore a simple cap on his head. *At least I blend in,* he thought. *Now, to find Shannon.*

He stepped out into the street. It was marginally brighter than the alleyway, thanks to a crescent moon emerging from behind fingers of clouds. Bawdy laughter echoed down the cobblestone street, most likely emanating from one of the taverns, Andrew thought. He headed towards the noise, while a 21st century memory tossed about in his mind: weren't women the original brewsters? Their calling cards a tall hat, a broom to signify domestic trade, a cauldron in which to brew the ale, and cats to scare away the mice. It was only after the church became involved that the women were viewed as something sinister. In a cruel twist, they were paint-ed as devil worshippers, handing their substantial beer-making income to men, while they were forced to answer serious charges.

Perhaps someone in the tavern could point him in the right direction. He continued down the street, the moonlight casting silvery outlines on the cobblestones. As he approached the inn, the door flew open and a robust woman appeared, dragging a bearded man by his ear. "That'll do, Dougall," she bellowed at the man. "I'll be having none of yer nonsense, ye hear me? Dinna mix yer wee drams of whisky with ale, it always ends in tears!"

"But Mary!" Dougall wailed as he was hauled out the door, "I'm just back from fishin', and I was pining for yer... Yer such a bonny lass..."

Mary pushed him away but he toppled against her, squashing her arm against the doorframe. "Aye, and that will be leaving a bruise, yer clumsy oaf." She rubbed her injured arm. "Go on, go home, while yer still can!" Her accent was thick, and to Andrew's ears, she was saying, "Goo on, goo horm." She left the fisherman propped against the building and turned to go back inside.

"Miss?" Andrew stepped into the pool of light in the doorway. "Miss, can you help me?"

She turned in surprise, brushing a stray auburn curl off her face. "What is it, lad? Have ye come to walk Dougall home?"

"If it were a paying job, aye," he answered, adopting the woman's lilting manner of speech. "I've come looking for work."

"I'd be thinking Dougall won't be too able come the morrow," Mary said, flashing the drunk man a cruel smile. "You could stand in for him... or were yer thinking of something other than fishing?"

"Would ye be needing help around the inn? I'm a strong lad, and willing."

Mary looked him up and down. "Aye, that ye are, but me and Janet took on a fella nigh on two months ago, so we won't be needin' another. 'Twas a good find, was Angus. He brought along a cat, so the mousing is taken care of as well."

Andrew's ears pricked up. Angus was here! He stifled his excitement. "Did you say Janet?" he enquired politely, eager to keep the woman talking.

"Aye, that's me sister. She works with the herbs and such. She puts the flavour into the ale, and good folk come from many a mile around to sup of it." Mary's lips curled upwards into an odd smile. "Some even say the brew has a touch of magic to it."

"Magic..." Dougall repeated, before dropping into a snore, his head lolling onto his chest.

Mary shook him awake. "Be off with yer, Dougall! Go home and sleep off yer liquor." She turned back to Andrew. "I can't offer yer a job, laddie, but there's a barn out the back where ye can rest yer head for the night. Be on yer way by the morrow, mind." She pushed another curl off her face, fixed him with a hard stare, and went back inside, leaving Andrew alone with the drunkard.

Dougall stretched his arms above his head and yawned. "Ye all right, lad?" he asked, his voice remarkably sober.

"Yes, I'll be heading off to bed now. And you? Will you be fit to find your way home?"

"Of course!" Dougall gave him a wink. "I acted tipsy tonight, to throw her off the scent. Can't have my Mary being suspicious. I'll have her one day, I will!"

Andrew frowned. He was tempted to ask why Dougall needed to throw Mary off the scent, but he thought better of it. "So, your heart is set on Mary, despite Janet's talent for brewing beer?"

Dougall's face underwent a rapid transformation, his smile disappearing, thick eyebrows pushing together in a scowl. "Aye, Mary has the business brain, all she needs is a strong man by her side. Janet's meddlin' in things she shouldn't meddle in. You heard about the business in North Berwick, with the king? They said it was witchcraft! It's never been the same since, people talking behind backs, spreading rumours. Blasted fools," he grunted in disgust.

Andrew murmured an agreement, secretly keen to hear this man's opinion.

"Mud sticks, in this day and age." Dougall leaned in close, his voice a confidential whisper. "Too many are jealous of the sisters' beer and their success... In my eyes, Mary's done all the hard work, while Janet only lifts a finger to prepare the herbs... and who knows what else." He shook his head, and crossed himself. "Best be on your way by the morrow, lad. There's trouble comin' and you'd be wise to stay ahead of it."

The older man trudged down the street, his gait unhurried, his path straight and sure. Whatever Dougall was, he was not a drunkard. His view of the world was similarly sober, with a touch of cunning thrown in for good measure.

Andrew picked his way along the dark lane beside the tavern, and found the barn at the rear. Stepping inside, his nose was assaulted by a mixture of horse urine, manure and straw. There were two horses in the stalls; one stamped its foot as Andrew passed, the other whickered softly in the hope of food. He favoured the friendly horse with a pat, running his hand down the white star on its forehead. "I'm sorry, I don't have anything for you."

He retreated to the end of the barn, where he found a pile of freshly-cut hay. He threw himself into it, pushing the sharp ends away from his face, and patting down the straw to form a nest. He curled into a ball and turned his head away from the moonlight streaming through the open doorway. He was close to Angus and Shannon, but he could do nothing more until the sun rose.

Andrew awoke a few hours later, startled by the touch of a paw on his face. "Wake up, human!" An urgent, silky voice in his ear.

He wiped the sleep from his eyes and sat up. The moon had disappeared, and tendrils of fog slipped through the open doorway and into the barn. "Who's there?" he asked, his voice low. "Do I know you?"

"I should think so!" Andrew felt a press on his thighs as a cat leapt onto him, its whiskers brushing against his face. "I was there when you chose my brother Ralph as your companion. My name is Shannon."

"How do I know that for sure?" Andrew frowned. "Here you are, in the body of a cat. What was your previous form, Shannon?"

"I was a golden labrador, we all were," she said. "But we were separated, some of us hidden in time, some in disguise. For me, it was both."

Remembering Shannon's tell, Andrew began to pat the cat vigorously on her rump. She purred in delight, and head-butted his chest. Now he rubbed her fur the wrong way, an action that would typically draw a hiss or a swipe with claws, but Shannon only purred louder. "Thank you, human. You have the magic touch. I relished the pats I received as a dog, and I miss them."

"Speaking of magic, Shannon, do you know why you ended up in this time?" Andrew went back to patting the base of her tail.

"I am here to support my master Angus. He will be a strong man one day, a man that will help many others. His talisman proves this, he would not have had this gift bestowed on him unless he were a great man."

"And do you know what is about to happen in this timeline, Shannon?" he asked. The cat became visible as the darkness faded, and her green eyes shone in the pre-dawn light.

"I know my time is short. I have passed on my knowledge, but Angus is young. He believes he has to protect me... but it was always the other way 'round. Will you pass on one last warning for me?"

"Of course."

The cat held his gaze, her face solemn. "Tell him to stay away from the woman with the cornflower-blue eyes. She is a glamour, and hides a great secret. To avoid heartache - heartbreak - he must protect himself from her."

"And does she have a name, this woman?"

"She does, but we do not speak it. To say her name is to summon her, and there is enough evil in this world without adding hers to it."

A rooster crowed outside, and Shannon twitched in surprise. "I must go. Promise me you will pass on my message."

"I promise," Andrew vowed.

"And whatever happens today, young human, you must not intervene, do you understand?"

"But if it means I could save you—"

"You cannot," Shannon cut him off. "Are you not aware of the prophecy? We must each play our role, and it is my turn to step onto the stage today. I presume you have searched for all of my brothers and sisters?"

"I have, and I've found all bar one."

"Let me guess," her eyes narrowed in suspicion. "You seek Max. He was always the troubled one. I loved him, but he was far too clever for his own good. Look for him in your history; he too will be in disguise. You will recognise him by his love of strawberries, he could not resist eating them."

She slunk towards the barn door, her inky coat merging with the shadows. "Wait!" Andrew called after her. "Who was his master?"

Shannon looked over her shoulder. "I know not his name, but he was clever. Max and I were the last to be assigned to our humans. We both knew that one path would lead to a premature death, while the other would be one of luxury with a wealthy, animal-loving man. Max chose first, and he chose luxury. As the man lifted Max into his arms, I heard him whisper these words: "The price of greatness is responsibility, my little friend. Always remember that."

"I don't understand. What does that mean?"

Shannon bent in an elegant stretch. "You will understand in time. There is no more to tell. Farewell, human. Give my love to Ralph when you see him." She slipped through the doorway and was gone.

CHAPTER THIRTY-ONE

The townsfolk were stirring, and Andrew accepted he would get no further sleep. His straw nest had done little to stem the moisture from the stone floor leaching into his body. He stood and stretched, his back and shoulders aching from his unnatural sleeping position. He pulled a few pieces of straw from his hair, replaced his cap and wandered outside.

A misty morning greeted him; the sounds of the village softened by a heavy fog. He located the rear entry to the tavern and found himself in the main hall, dimly lit and smelling of beer from the previous evening. Two men were seated at a table, deep in conversation, while others scurried to and fro, sweeping out the old straw on the floor and replacing it with a fresh supply. An older woman in long skirts and an apron stood before the huge stone hearth, stirring a cauldron suspended above a fire. She offered Andrew a cup of broth and a chunk of bread, which he took to the next table over from the two men.

The men had almost finished their broth and were preparing to leave. They wore fine clothes, richly coloured, with lacy ruff collars. Heavy cloaks were draped across the table. "The others will be here soon," said one of the men, who had a thin face and an enormous nose, somewhat offset by a waxed moustache and pointed beard. "I suppose we could start the proceedings by arresting the boy and the cat."

Andrew paled. He turned his head to the side, tilting an ear towards the conversation.

"We need to round up the ringleaders first, Charles," his companion said, a ruddy-faced man with a luxurious ginger beard that cascaded over his ruffled collar. "And where is Dougall? We came early to establish the lay of the land, and he was supposed to help us."

"He won't meet us here," the large-nosed man scoffed. He stood and threw his cloak about his shoulders. "Have you forgotten, Ian? His sweetheart runs this tawdry establishment."

Ian rose from the table and fastened his cloak about his neck, taking a moment to reposition his flowing beard. "I have not. I am merely frustrated, Charles, and the stench of fish in this godforsaken town has left me in a bother." He paused to stare pointedly at his friend's nose. "In fact, I'm surprised *you* haven't noticed it! The sooner we finish this business, the sooner we get back to Edinburgh."

He drew a small box from a pocket, took a pinch of the contents and inhaled deeply through his nose, first one nostril, then the other. He returned the box of snuff to his pocket and pulled on a pair of gloves. "One of these women will know where Janet lives. I shall interrogate – I mean, enquire - now."

Andrew risked a quick glance at the two men: the large-nosed Charles hastened outside to check on the arrival of their colleagues, while Ian stood over the woman by the hearth, questioning her in a fierce whisper. A moment later, he strode outside, calling to Charles: "Come, she is but two doors away."

"Hark!" Charles raised a hand. "The others are coming!"

The muted silence was shattered by the thunder of hooves on the cobblestones. Andrew threw back his broth and scuttled outside. A group of horsemen emerged from the fog at the gallop, slowing to a trot as they neared the tavern.

The men on horseback dismounted and handed their reins to the tavern groom, who led the steaming horses away to the stables. The new arrivals conferred with Charles and Ian, while villagers filled the streets, curious about the early morning disturbance.

Andrew noticed a familiar figure sidling up to the gentrified group. Dougall, the drunkard from the previous night, tapped the men on the shoulder and began a hushed conversation. His dark eyes darted around the gathering as he spoke. They rested on one particular woman, who he surreptitiously pointed out to Charles and Ian. A bag of coins exchanged hands, and the fisherman's face filled with glee.

Now Ian looked up, a ruthless smile on his face as Dougall retired to the rear of the gathering. He raised his hands to silence the crowd. "By Royal Decree: I, Sir Ian Hogg, accuse Janet Finlay of witchcraft!" There were cries of shock, and a ripple of unease passed through the townspeople. "You are accused of bringing down a cursed sickness on your neighbour, Lorna Baines."

Lorna Baines was brought forward as evidence. She was middle-aged but feeble, supported on either side by two young children. Andrew recognised the woman's yellowed skin, the pain etched into her drawn features and he looked away, his stomach clenching. *It's cancer, not a curse! She looks just like Mum did.*

Janet Finlay was hauled into the centre of the crowd, despite loud protestations from her sister Mary. "Strip her," Ian commanded two of his recently-arrived men. "Search for the devil's mark."

Janet began to scream as the clothes were ripped from her body, and the townsfolk leaned forward with ghoulish interest. Soon enough, one of the men yelled in triumph as he removed Janet's cap and pointed to a blemish on the back of her neck.

"Look again!" Mary pleaded with the men. "'Tis but an insect bite, nothing more!"

"And what is your name?" Sir Ian asked of her.

Mary jutted her chin. "I am Mary Finlay, sister of Janet and proprietor of the tavern you stand before."

Sir Ian's eyes narrowed. "And you had no knowledge of your sister's devilish activities? I find that difficult to believe. Bring her forward, and search her for the devil's mark as well."

"NO," Dougall bellowed from the back of the crowd. "That was nae part o' the deal!"

"Silence!" Sir Ian ordered.

Another two men dragged Mary into the circle, and almost immediately they found a bruise on her forearm, the result of last night's scuffle with Dougall. "Oh, Mary!" the fisherman groaned, pushing his way through the crowd to the front. "Sir Ian, I beg of ye, 'tis but a bruise! We were horsing around, 'tis my fault."

Sir Ian fixed him with a cool stare. "It's *your* fault this woman has the mark of a witch?"

Dougall hesitated, and a hush dropped over the gathering. "Nae, that's not what I meant at all!" The colour drained from his face as he realised he had been outsmarted.

"Then step to the rear, man, and let us do God's duty." Sir Ian dismissed the anguished Dougall and turned back to the half-naked woman. "Janet Finlay, there is one further accusation you must answer, namely that of using a nightmare cat to inflict cursed dreams on others. Bring forth the cat and its owner."

"No!" Janet writhed in the grip of her captors. "He's a bairn, he's done nothing wrong."

"He has too!" A voice in the crowd spoke up, and Andrew recognised the wrinkled face of the woman who served him broth in the tavern. "I seen Angus talking to the cat, as I live and breathe!"

"And did the cat answer, fair lady?" Sir Ian asked her.

The woman blushed at being called a lady and began to nod, when she caught herself. "Can't say I heard anything," she said, a sly look on her face.

"I thought as much, lest you yourself wish to be accused of witchcraft," Sir Ian replied.

The old woman reeled backwards, uttering a yelp of terror. Regretting her foolish outburst, she picked up her skirts and fled through the crowd.

By now the henchmen had located Angus and Shannon and drawn the pair forward to join Janet and Mary. Accepting of her fate, the cat walked calmly into the spotlight, sat down on the cobblestones and began to groom herself. In contrast, Angus had the bewildered look of a person who had been completely blindsided.

Andrew stared at his friend in fascination. He had none of the worldly weariness the modern-day Gus carried. He was new on the earth, fresh-faced and naive, unaware his life was about to change forever. Shannon finished her grooming, and scanning the crowd, found Andrew amongst the sea of faces. She nodded in his direction, her sharp eyes reminding him to stay back, to remain anonymous. He tore his gaze away. He could not bear to watch this circus any longer, with its inevitable, brutal ending.

A watery sun burst through the fog, casting an eerie pallor over the agitated villagers. The scene closed in on Andrew, the screams and shouts a muted roar. He turned his head to look at Sir Ian, and he saw the man's outstretched hand, frozen in mid-air. Puzzled, he watched all but one of Sir Ian's fingers curl slowly into a fist, the forefinger creeping outwards to point in slow-motion at Janet.

Andrew glanced around the crowd. He found Dougall, the picture of agony as he considered the price of his greed. He saw Charles at the rear of the gathering, a snarl on his face as he stirred up the onlookers. There was Gus, his lips parted in shock as he rolled a blue-stone necklace in his fingers. Shannon at his feet, her eyes still fixed on Andrew, begging him to leave. And all around him, the audience of villagers. The emotions of outrage, disgust, and surprise frozen on their faces as they became a collective beast hungry for retribution.

Now Andrew understood: time had slowed, and there was an important piece of information to be gleaned before he could leave. What could he take from this moment? The horror, the conviction of belief, the innocent parties accused of wrongdoing? No, witchcraft had been examined countless times on television and in the history books. As appalling as this moment was, he was not here to alter the course of history.

He would have to dig deeper. What had Shannon told him? *He believes he has to protect me... but it was always the other way 'round.* It was true, Gus had a habit of assuming responsibility on most occasions, whether it was his fault or not. Andrew would store Shannon's words away and share them at a later time.

But it was Shannon's final words that stuck in Andrew's mind. *We both knew that one path would lead to a premature death.*

And to punctuate that, the words of the Pisal nurse in Nostalgia: *I recall thinking she was brave going to that time, as it wasn't particularly kind to cats.*

Shannon had been courageous from the start, allowing Max to choose a pampered existence while she went to an early death. Max's love of strawberries was indulged by a wealthy master who nonetheless reminded his new charge that the price of greatness was responsibility.

Andrew nodded. The cogs were clicking into place as he formed a theory about Max's owner. To confirm his thoughts, the noise of the gathering grew louder, as if someone was increasing the volume on the TV. Now Andrew's legs began to work, and he backed away from the jeering crowd, retracing his steps down the lane beside the tavern.

Sir Ian's voice rose above the babble: "Take them to St Mary's Chapel, while we prepare the ordeal by water."

At the rear of the tavern, Andrew made a quick decision, trusting his own talisman over the remote control and Evelyn's mischievous antics. He took another quick swig of the thyme concentrate, then focussed his thoughts on returning to the present day. "Please, get me away from here and back home, away from this madness," he said as a tear slipped down his face. "Goodbye Shannon."

Chapter Thirty-Two

After Andrew returned home, he made a beeline for the kitchen, bumping into his father on the way.

"You startled me, Andy!" Mr Adler said. "I thought you were at Dorothy's."

"I was. I've just gotten back. I'm getting some food, you want something?"

"No. Irene and Martin and I had dinner before they jumped on the plane."

The plane, Andrew remembered. In the foggy depths of his mind, it felt like a week had passed since he'd sent the text to his father, apologising for his absence. "They got away okay? I'm sorry I missed them."

"The plane was delayed, but they boarded around 7pm." Mr Adler paused, studying his son. "Are you all right? You said you were having problems."

"I'm okay. Lots of emotions coming and going." *Lots of coming and going in general,* he thought. *In the space of a day, I've been to 1914, 1939, and 1597.*

"Just take it easy." His father placed a hand on his shoulder. "Get some rest after you've eaten."

"I will," he said, remembering Mrs Jordan's warning about the effects of time stepping. "Trust me, Dad, I will."

Andrew awoke early the next morning, feeling groggy after yesterday's travels. The house was quiet. Winston stared at him from the bottom of the bed, his orange eyes watchful. "Good morning. How is the time stepper today?"

"I slept okay but I have a headache. Guess that's a time stepping hangover." He sat up in bed. "I need to talk to Gus, and set him straight about Shannon." He swung his legs out of bed and went to the toilet. He could hear his father snoring in the next room, so he dressed quickly, fed Winston, and headed down the street to Gus's house. Passing the driveway, he caught sight of him out the back of the house. He sat motionless on a garden bench, his back straight and eyes closed. One eye cracked open as Andrew approached. "Hey. How are you doing, Andy?"

"I'm okay. Did I interrupt something?"

"I was meditating. I find it helps these days. The longer I live, the more my head is stuffed full of things." He studied his friend's face. "You looked wrecked. Are you okay?"

Andrew shrugged. "I'm all right. I've been time stepping. I used a new Pisal machine called Evelyn that was supposed to make the whole process easier. It didn't."

"Where did you go?"

"1597."

Pain flashed across Gus's face. "Why?"

Andrew sat down on the bench. "I could ask you the same question. Why didn't you volunteer this information to me? Why didn't you tell me you had one of Ralph's siblings?"

"It's not something I like to remember or talk about, Andrew."

"What happened?"

Gus shifted in his seat. "I was with Shannon for a sum total of two months before we were rounded up on suspicion of witchcraft. She was executed. They weighed her down with rocks and threw her in the sea. They made me watch."

Andrew put a hand over his mouth. "Oh, Gus, that's awful. I'm so sorry."

"I was sorry too. They were going to hang me, but I used my talisman and got away. It was the first time I used it to escape. I knew it was special, but I had no idea how powerful it was. Because if I *had* known, I would have saved her. All these years, Andrew." He stared at his friend, his eyes haunted. "I've lived with the knowledge that I had all the tools to save her, but I didn't. I couldn't protect her. She died because of me!" He put his head in his hands.

"No, that's not true! She was sent to watch over you, she told me."

"What?" Gus lifted his head.

"The dogs chose their masters. They were in the hospital in Nostalgia, and they were shown potential matchups. She saw you, and she intuitively knew you needed help. In Shannon's mind, she was sent to protect you, not the other way 'round! Don't carry the guilt of her death, Gus. She knew what she was going into, and she didn't flinch."

Gus took a deep breath. "I mourned her death for years, wishing I could've done something different. But now you tell me she was aware of her fate?"

"Yep, without question. She was clever and fearless, more concerned for your life than hers. Oh, and she gave me a message for you."

"She did?"

"Yep. She said, 'tell him to stay away from the woman with the corn-flower-blue eyes. She is a glamour, and hides a great secret'." Andrew stared at his friend, watching for a reaction, but Gus's face was a mask. "Is this about the Hag? And is that why you've been avoiding me?"

"Look, I've tried to keep you out if it," Gus snapped, "I've tried to keep you safe. She knows me, knows me all too well, so Shannon's warning comes a couple of hundred years too late."

Andrew stiffened. "What do you mean, 'keep me safe'?"

"She knows me, don't you get it?" Gus pounded the arm of the bench. "Did Pat tell you about the woman in the French village in World War Two? Men fell at her feet, Andy, her power was immense. And before that time - a long time before - she did the same thing to me. She can tap into me, anytime she likes, and harvest all the knowledge I have about you, and what you've been up to. That's why I've been keeping my distance! I didn't want to know what you were doing, just in case she found out... through me."

"She can do that?" Andrew paled.

"She's like a bloody parasite. She feeds off things - people, animals, you name it. It fuels her desire for revenge."

"But what revenge is she seeking? And why is she coming after all of us?"

"If we knew that, we'd be able to stop it. Don't you think I've asked myself these same questions?" Gus asked, his tone bitter. "I've had a little time to ponder the way she operates."

Andrew opened his mouth, then closed it. Knowing Gus, he hadn't stopped thinking about it.

"So next time," Gus continued, "ask me before you go digging around in my past. I could've saved you the agony of witnessing that witch-hunting mania."

Andrew heard the pain in his voice. "I left before it got too ugly," he admitted. "But I had no choice. Pierce didn't know about Max's tell. I had to find out if Shannon did."

Gus nodded. "I remember we used to talk about sweetmeats and other goodies back then, and Shannon mentioned one of her brothers used to like eating strawberries. I said his master must be quite wealthy to afford strawberries for his pet."

"And he was a man who told Max that the price of greatness is responsibility." Andrew stared at Gus, his eyes gleaming. "I have a theory. I wonder if it's possible?" He pulled out his phone and typed the quote into Google. As the results flashed up on the screen, Andrew wordlessly handed the phone to Gus.

"Well, would you look at that," Gus said, shaking his head in amused disbelief. "I think it's time you went home and had a chat with your cat."

"I think you're right. And Gus..."

"Yes?"

"I-I'm sorry I doubted you. I should have trusted you, right from the beginning."

"It's okay, Andy." Gus patted his shoulder. "You've had a lot to deal with. Just remember I've always got your best interests at heart." He looked past his hand, to the vee of his friend's shirt, where Andrew's two necklaces were visible. He choked back a cry and snatched up the silver ball necklace. "Where... where did you get this from?"

"Easy, mate, don't strangle me." Andrew leaned forward and reclaimed the necklace, tucking it beneath his top. "Mr Lovell gave it to me. It originally belonged to his war mate Cecil. Cecil called it his good luck charm. After he died, it was handed down to Helen, Mr Lovell's wife."

"He never mentioned it," Gus muttered. "Not once in all this time."

Andrew frowned. "Have you seen this necklace before?"

Gus swallowed. "Not for many years. The last time I saw it, I was in Scotland. It belonged to someone very dear to me."

Andrew took the silver necklace off and handed it to Gus. "Here. You have it. You don't have your talisman any more, this will replace it."

Gus held up his hands. "No! I can never wear it. I can't figure out how it came to be in Cecil's hands, but that story will have to wait for another time. You need to talk to Winston."

CHAPTER THIRTY-THREE

Andrew received a message from his father as he arrived home:

Joy and I have finished sorting your mum's clothes. We're on our way to the charity shop in Parramatta, then we're grabbing some Chinese takeaway and heading back to Joy's house. Join us if you want to.

With a twinge of guilt, he sent his father a reply:

Thanks, but I've got some stuff to do. Say hi to Aunty Joy.

A part of him wanted to spend time with his dad and his aunt, to honour his mum. But he was struggling to face his own sadness, let alone the sadness of others. Right now, there were other conversations to be had, and in particular, one with his cat.

"Winston?" He called out as he came in through the front door. "We need to talk."

The big grey cat appeared in the hallway. "That sounds ominous," he said. "What are we discussing, Andrew? Diplomacy in modern Europe? The fine art of Cuban cigar making? The intricacies of champagne?"

"What? No!" Andrew looked down at his cat, hands on his hips. "You're a *cat*, Winston. A special one, for sure, but a cat. All that stuff is no longer relevant to you. No, I want to talk to you about your dog." He headed into the kitchen. "Are you hungry? Do you want something before I start asking questions?"

"Roo meat, since you're offering."

Andrew smirked. "How quickly you've changed, Winston. A few short weeks ago you were horrified about eating kangaroo." He pulled the bag of meat from the fridge and put some in a bowl. He filled a glass with lemonade and drank it at the table while Winston ate. "You need to tell me about Rufus. That was his name, wasn't it? I remember him bursting into the war rooms when I time stepped in World War Two."

Winston looked up from his bowl. "I had two dogs called Rufus. I lost the first one in tragic circumstances."

Andrew's ears pricked up. "Can you tell me what happened?"

Winston finished his meal and leapt onto the seat beside Andrew. "Rufus was an intelligent chap. The day I collected him from the breeder, I told him that the price of greatness is responsibility. He never forgot my words. He used to visit me every morning when I had breakfast in bed, and I would feed him strawberries."

Andrew stifled a shout of triumph. "How fascinating. Go on."

Winston crouched on the chair, deep in his memory. "As time went on," he continued, "Rufus refused to behave while I was away. He loved me and wanted to be with me! Perhaps he felt he could contribute something to my strategic meetings and political summits. One afternoon, I was returning home to Chartwell. Rufus heard my voice and broke away from the maid, and in his eagerness, he ran under the wheels of the car..." Winston trailed off. "After that, I didn't want another dog. A few years later I relented, and Rufus the second came along."

"I'm sorry, Winston." Andrew patted the cat's head, scratching him behind the ears. "I know how hard it is to lose a special dog."

"Thank you. As you know, the grief of losing a pet is somewhat lessened by the arrival of another."

Andrew nodded. "Rufus was a poodle, wasn't he? Not a labrador?"

"He was a poodle," Winston said. "But why the interest? You could've established these facts by reading a history book."

Andrew lowered his face to look Winston in the eye. "Your dog was *very* special, as you always suspected. Your dog was Max, Winston! The last of the special dogs, chosen to comfort you during Britain's darkest hours in World War Two."

Winston's mouth dropped open in surprise. "Really?"

"Really. Your story about him eating strawberries was the clincher. That was Max's tell. If I'm not wrong, the Hag chose Max's moment of death to steal him away from you."

Winston's ears twitched backwards in irritation. "I once owned a talking animal but was completely unaware. Now I've become a talking animal, helping you locate all the talking dogs, not realising I used to own one. Oh, the bitter irony!"

"True, but you weren't to know," Andrew said. "We can fix this. Winston, what year did you lose Rufus? I'll have to visit that time and see if I can alter events."

"It was July 1947, Andrew. I don't remember the date, I cast it from my mind."

"That should be enough. Fingers crossed I can stop the Hag, once and for all."

Andrew rested against the bedroom wall, forming a picture of Winston's country home in his mind. He had time stepped to Chartwell on two occasions, and now he recalled the tall red-brick building nestled in the rolling Kent countryside. "Take me to Chartwell," he said aloud. "Let me see the lead up to Max's death in July 1947."

As soon as Andrew arrived, his finely-tuned time stepping senses detected an anomaly in the timeline. There was a sense of 'wrongness' to the atmosphere that he now associated with the presence of other time steppers... or something more sinister.

He remembered his failed time step on the day the puppies were separated, and how the scene had been protected from outside intrusion. Once again, he was outside the bubble and looking in, powerless to intervene.

Andrew watched as a small group of people gathered outside Chartwell's front door: his wife Clementine, immaculate in a blue and white polka dot dress, her signature pearls around her neck. Churchill's servants stood waiting, and beside Mrs Churchill was a young woman in a maid's outfit, her hand fiercely gripping the lead of a rusty-brown toy poodle. A car rolled up the driveway, and from within, Winston Churchill wound down the window and called to his wife and dog. At the sound of his voice, the small poodle began to bark and pull against the maid. He broke free, his lead dragging behind him as he ran towards the car.

Amidst cries of dismay, the dog ran in the path of the vehicle, and at that point, time slowed. Andrew watched in horror as a stooped old woman in a cloak appeared by the frozen dog's side. Looking over her shoulder, she offered Andrew a mocking smile, the scar puckering her lips.

She turned away, fixing her attention on the fluffy brown dog at her feet. Max was in disguise and in the past, but the Hag had still managed to locate him. Andrew knew with sudden clarity there was a rat in their midst. A loyal supporter of the Hag's, embedded in Nostalgia's animal hospital, and passing on priceless secrets. He would have to share this knowledge with Snow.

Now the Hag bent down, her movements slow and deliberate. She scooped the dog into her arms, and Max yelped in surprise. The old woman shushed the dog and tucked him under her arm. As time began to speed up again, the Hag produced the limp body of another animal and threw it under the wheel of the car. Wrapping herself in her cloak, she disappeared from sight.

Andrew groaned in frustration and looked away. He had no desire to see the accident, pretend or otherwise, so he held the necklaces in his hand and thought of home.

He arrived back on the floor of his bedroom, feeling dizzy and disappointed.

"What happened?" Winston tapped his shoulder with a paw.

"I was right," he replied. "I wish I'd been wrong." He rubbed his forehead to ease the dizziness. "Now I don't know what to do."

Chapter Thirty-Four

"Pat, I'm beyond relieved to have you home!" Mrs Jordan touched the arm of her old friend as he lay in his bed. "And a big thank you to your brother Andrew for letting me know you were back." She patted the head of the tuxedo cat on the bed and paused, distracted. "How *did* you get home, exactly?"

The old man's chuckle became a wheeze. "Through Blair's Bypass. They were reluctant to send us, let me tell you. Thought I was too frail. I told them I wasn't going to die without saying goodbye to my friends, and so here we are."

Mrs Jordan's hands flew to her mouth. "Oh, Patrick! Don't say that. You've got plenty of years left in you!" She wagged her finger at him.

"Perhaps. Did you send that paperwork off to my lawyer?"

"I did." Mrs Jordan nodded. "Although I don't see what the rush is, Pat. You'll be on the mend in no time. Now, I'm off to make us a cup of tea."

She bustled out of the room, and Mr Lovell glanced at his brother. "Do you see what I mean? I've been around for that long, they can't even contemplate a scenario where I don't exist."

The cat lifted his head. "Then it's only right to do what I suggested. I died a long time ago, Paddy. My greatest desire was to see you one last time, and now I have." He walked up the bed and nestled beside his brother's arm. "But you, you have so much more to do! You are part of something much bigger, and that's why I want us to swap. I will take on your fading body, and you can make yourself comfortable in cat form. No, I won't hear your arguments, Pat!" He lifted a paw as his brother protested. "I'm older than you. Plus, I made a promise to you once that I couldn't keep, so let's even up the ledger. Tell your friends and let's prepare. We don't want you dying while you're still in this damaged body."

Andrew's time stepping disappointment was abruptly brushed aside by a loud knock at the front door. "Hang on," he yelled. "I'm coming!"

He stood up too fast, and his head spun. He staggered out of the bedroom; his arms outstretched for balance. He reached the front door and opened it, his legs swaying.

"Thank goodness you're here." A white-faced Mrs Jordan greeted him. "We need you. Patrick is back home."

"Finally, some good news!" Andrew said. "I'll grab a glass of water and come over."

Mrs Jordan shook her head. "You have to come now. He's about to make an announcement, and he wants us all to be there."

"I'm a little dizzy, Mrs J. I just got back from 1947."

She gave him a sympathetic smile as she gripped his arm. "Not to worry, I've got you."

The pair took the long route, avoiding the tricky leap over the picket fence between Andrew's house and Mr Lovell's. Once inside, Andrew's mouth dropped open at the number of humans and cats in Mr Lovell's bedroom. "Can someone please tell me what's going on?" He leaned against the wall, his head still spinning. "I went to a faulty timeline, and I'm not feeling too great."

"Welcome to my world," Gus muttered under his breath, and Mrs Jordan frowned in his direction.

Deirdre cleared her throat. "I'll explain. We all hoped that Patrick would be healed by the doctors in Nostalgia, but they could only do so much. Patrick was carrying a curse, and whilst *he* remains full of verve and vigour, his body doesn't."

Andrew scratched his head. "But Mr Lovell has always looked this way. Perhaps he's a little older—"

"You're missing the point, Andrew." Deirdre cut him off. "It's the end of the road for Patrick's body. But with the Hag sticking her nose into everything, we need Patrick's spirit more than ever, and his dear brother knows it. He has kindly offered to switch places with Patrick."

Andrew's mouth sagged open. "Whaa-t?"

Deirdre's eyes flashed. "Manners, please. Say pardon!"

"Sorry, Deirdre. You're saying that Mr Lovell will become a cat, and his brother will - *somehow* - transfer into Mr Lovell's dying body? Sure, that sounds like a piece of cake."

"It's *not* a piece of cake, and we don't have time for your sarcasm. If you weren't so dizzy, I'd have you out searching for the Guardians' wood, but I can see I'll have to do it myself!" The tortoiseshell cat leapt onto the windowsill. "Lucy, open this for me!"

"Deirdre, are you sure?" Mrs Bargwana placed a hand on the cat's back. "I could ask Nostradamus to collect what we need…"

"Summon him," Deirdre answered. "His dragon energy will be welcome as we conduct the swap. Unless he's got his head in a book like usual. Get him to bring some mistletoe, the European variety, please." She pushed through the open window and bounded off.

"Mistletoe?" Andrew exploded. "Are we going to kiss and pretend it's Christmas?" He ran his hand through his hair. "Will someone help me out here? Mr Lovell, surely you can't think this is a good idea?" He was on the verge of tears, and he hoped his anger would disguise the fact.

"The mistletoe is a sacred, protective plant." Gus moved across the room and placed his hands on his friend's shoulders. "Look at me, Andy." He met Andrew's tear-filled eyes. "We all love Pat, but his physical body has carried him far beyond the life span of any average human being. And now his brother has offered us the ultimate solution. There is no greater love, and it's not up to us to question it. Do you understand that?"

Andrew's shoulders shook. "I understand. Doesn't mean I like it." His voice was thick with emotion. "I've only just said goodbye to Mum!"

"I'm not going anywhere, son." Mr Lovell spoke up. "You'll have to look for me in a different body, that's all."

The group turned to the window as Deirdre scrambled back inside, three sticks of wood in her mouth. She dumped them on the floor at Gus's feet. "Here they are. Hawthorn, Elder, and Birch. You know what to do with them, I assume?"

Gus scooped the small branches into his hands. "Of course. Birch for me, the Elder for Dorothy, and Pat needs the Hawthorn."

"Actually," Colleen corrected, "Patrick's brother must hold the Hawthorn. The Guardians will claim their wood, and in this way, Patrick will be guided towards his new body."

Andrew sighed. "Anyone care to explain this gobbledygook?"

Gus clapped him on the back. "Think of them as wands - like the ones in Harry Potter. Each wood has a different trait, but when these three get together, they form a powerful trinity the Druids called the Guardians. The Hawthorn is the father, the Elder is the mother," he pointed to Mrs Jordan, "and the Birch represents the child, or me." He patted his chest and grinned. "Together, the three trees represent the preservation of health, something we must ensure as we embark on Pat's transformation. Are we clear?"

"Clear as mud," Andrew said. He went over to the bed and clasped Mr Lovell's waxen hand in his own. "This is going to break my dad's heart. You did so much for him!"

Mr Lovell placed his other hand over the top of Andrew's. "Son, I love your dad, and you. And that's why you're both in my will. I won't be needing my earthly possessions after this, so it's all bequeathed to you and Peter. The house will be in your name, - we all know how hard it is to save for a deposit these days. All I ask in return is that you or Dorothy care for me in my new form."

Mrs Jordan's eyes filled with tears. "Of course, Patrick. That goes without saying."

"I second that." Andrew's voice shook. "I can't thank you enough, for your wisdom, and humour, and—"

"Andrew." The old man's eyes were suspiciously watery. "It's all right. Now everyone: clear out as I say goodbye to my wonderful brother, and then we can begin the ceremony."

Deirdre stood at the bedroom door, directing everyone to their places. "Dorothy, to Patrick's right, please. And you, Angus, to his left. Andrew the cat will remain on the bed, while Andrew the human and Lucy will both stand at the base of the bed. Lucy, you're to the left and Andrew to the right as you face Patrick." She glanced at her siblings. "I think it best we sit together on Patrick's tall boy, so we can watch over the proceedings... Oh, and you, Nostradamus." Deirdre looked up as the miniature dragon fluttered onto the windowsill with a piece of mistletoe dangling from his talons. "You can stay where you are until things get going. You'll know what to do."

"Would you like me to start?" Colleen said. "I've prepared a poem."

"Thank you, Colleen." Dorothy threw her a grateful look. "You were always so good with words."

While the humans assembled around Mr Lovell's bed, hands joined, the cat lifted up her head and began to speak.

We gather now
In reverence, in unity
With sacred bonds
The trees of Trinity
Hawthorn, Elder, and Birch
The Guardian trees
A forest of strength
A woodland of dreams
Patrick Lovell
And Andrew his brother
Have agreed on a switch
From one to the other
Now raise the three woods
And cross at their peak
The magic will start
As I cease to speak

In silent agreement, Mrs Jordan, Angus, and Andrew the cat lifted their wooden branches. The cat quickly realised his branch would not intersect with the other two, so he leapt onto Mrs Bargwana's shoulder, the Hawthorn stick jutting from his mouth and angled towards the centre of the bed.

The three branches touched above Mr Lovell's body, their union creating a steeple that pointed to the heavens. Nostradamus flew above them, alighting on the peak, the mistletoe binding the three woods together. The dragon remained in place as Andrew heard the first whispers of a song.

It's the branches, Andrew thought, his skin prickling as the sound washed over him. *They're singing.* The haunting melody twisted through the gathering, unlocking memories and laying them bare. Through song, the woods spoke for all, paying tribute to Patrick Lovell's remarkable life as a guardian.

The sound filled the room, and beneath the union of wood, Patrick's body began to flicker. The vision of a blond-headed child overtook the old man's body, and the group bore witness to the boy's grief as his older brother departed for war.

Patrick the child aged, becoming a dashing young man, a soldier in World War One, a participant in World War Two. Faster now, the many guises of Patrick Lovell flashed past: Patrick returning from war, beaming in civilian attire as he embarked on the next phase of his life. All too soon, his optimism had faded, and the group witnessed Patrick in army greens as he endured the Vietnam war. Home again, ageing, learning, passing on his wisdom to those around him, up to this moment when his human body called time.

A weary sigh escaped the old man's lips, and his head dropped to one side. The trees' song ended, and Nostradamus took the branches in his talons and flew out the window and into the night sky. The humans barely noticed his departure, their hands still clasped together, their eyes open but distant, witnessing the life of Patrick Lovell.

Andrew the cat climbed down from Mrs Bargwana's shoulders and crouched at the base of the bed. Everyone was waiting, but for what they were not sure, until a light began to build in a corner of the room. The light grew, taking the form of a beautiful, oversized hare. As the Seer materialised, the blinding light retreated into the star-shaped talisman at his neck. He removed the talisman, and standing at the head of the bed, the Seer rested the star on Mr Lovell's forehead.

Light burst from the star, illuminating the room, imprinting a flash of lightning on closed eyelids. The light penetrated all, electrifying skin and fur, crackling through paws and fingertips. The bond between the humans broke, and they stood apart, fingers tingling, mouths parted in wonder. The hare returned his talisman to his neck and lifted the body of Patrick Lovell into his arms. "Come, my friend," he whispered in the old man's ear. "It is time."

The hare raised his voice, addressing the gathering. "And so it is. Allow Patrick time to rest and to assimilate with his new body. Please assure him that his brother will be afforded full military honours in death."

The Seer was disappearing as he spoke, the body of Mr Lovell also fading in the hare's embrace as a fanfare of invisible trumpets marked the transition.

The music ended and everyone shook themselves, as if awakening from a dream. They all stared down at the bed. A black and white tuxedo cat lay sleeping, curled in the sheets that still bore the imprint of the man they knew as Patrick Lovell. Andrew tenderly touched the feline and drew his hand back in surprise.

The cat's face was damp with tears.

CHAPTER THIRTY-FIVE

"Morning, Dad."

Mr Adler was seated at the kitchen table with a coffee and the newspaper. He looked up as Andrew came in. "Hey, Andy! You missed some great Chinese food last night."

"Dad... there's something I need to tell you." Andrew sat down opposite his father. *Here goes,* he thought. He drew a deep breath. "Dad, Mr Lovell passed away last night."

Mr Adler put his coffee down and pinched the bridge of his nose with his thumb and forefinger. "I had an idea this was coming, especially after he didn't make it to the funeral." He glanced up, and Andrew saw tears in his eyes. "So soon after your mother. Was it old age, or something else?"

"Old age. His body just gave out on him." This was, at least, a true statement. "I'm sorry, Dad. I know how much he meant to you."

"Will there be a funeral?" Mr Adler's voice was hollow.

"Mrs Jordan mentioned a memorial service down at the park. Mr Lovell wanted to be reunited with his wife and child."

"Of course." Mr Adler swallowed. He closed the newspaper, folded it in half, and stood up. "You'll let me know when that is, Andrew." He hesitated, staring at his son. His mouth parted, as if he was about to say more, then he bit down on his lips with a slight shake of his head. He turned towards the back door. "I'm going out for a while. Call me if you need anything." He collected his keys and phone, and left.

"Great," Andrew slammed his hand down on the neatly-folded newspaper. "I've managed to upset my already upset father. Way to go, Adler."

Winston twirled around his legs beneath the kitchen table. "Andrew, there is no easy way to tell someone about a death. Perhaps one day you'll be able to tell him the truth of the matter."

"Without him saying I've completely lost my mind? I doubt it."

Winston clambered onto the table and sat down on the newspaper. "You haven't told me about—"

"Get off there!" Andrew interrupted him. "You know you're not supposed to sit on the table."

"Strictly, I'm not *on* the table," Winston said, washing a paw. "I'm on the newspaper. Now, where is Patrick, and how is he?"

Andrew rolled his eyes. "Okay, smarty pants. Just don't do it in front of Dad, he'll have a cow. As for Mr Lovell, Mrs Jordan said she'd take him and keep an eye on him. I'd better go and see how he is." He lifted Winston off the table and put him on the floor. "You might need to teach him a thing or two about being in a cat body. No bad habits, though, please!" He pointed his finger at the cat.

"How is he?" Andrew asked as Mrs Jordan ushered him inside. "Is he... is he really inside the cat?"

Mrs Jordan gave him a bleary-eyed look. "He is. It was a rough night, Andy. Patrick woke up, cried, muttered a few words, then went back to sleep. We repeated that for nearly five hours." They walked past the sunroom, and she pointed to the black and white cat curled up in a patch of sunlight on the floor. "He'll be okay. He was in his human body for a long time, now he has to get used to his new form."

The pair reached the kitchen, where they found Mrs Bargwana pulling cups from the cupboard and switching on the kettle. She offered Andrew a cheery hello. "Now, what happened with you?" she asked. "You went to 1947. Was that in search of Max?"

Andrew slumped into a chair, idly patting the three cats who had followed him into the kitchen. "Max was Winston Churchill's dog, would you believe. I went to 1947, but the Hag was already there, with some kind of protective bubble around that moment. I couldn't stop her! She took Max and disappeared." He gave the women an anguished look. "I've done all of this for nothing. Time stepping here, there, and everywhere to confirm that Max really is Max, and that he ended up with the Hag, but so what?" He shrugged. "They're still off-world, and the Hag is as strong as ever."

"There is a way," Mrs Jordan said, thinking out loud.

Andrew stared at her, his eyes narrowed. "How?"

"You've got the White Fire. You used it to get to Blair, who is 'off-world'. I suspect it will work for the Hag as well." She wrapped her hands around the cup of tea Mrs Bargwana handed to her.

Andrew shook his head. "I'm not so sure. Blair wasn't hiding. But the Hag... she doesn't want to be found. She feels safe taunting us from her lair. I bet she's got all kinds of protective spells cast around her hideout to prevent us from getting in."

Mrs Jordan took a sip of tea. "That's where Colleen and I come in. We're going to boost the White Fire's powers with other herbs."

Andrew was taking his own cup of tea from Mrs Bargwana, and his head snapped around in surprise. "Really?"

"Really," Mrs Jordan said firmly. "As you said, all that work for nothing? Not on my watch. And we'll ask Angus if he has any herbal tips too."

"Of course, Gus will save the day as usual," Andrew groaned. "What does he know about plants, anyway?"

"You'd be surprised," Mrs Jordan arched an eyebrow at him. "He knows more than me. We need all the help we can get, Andy. This will go far beyond your lucid dreaming experience. This will be a dream quest."

"And I'm coming too," Mrs Bargwana said as she sat down.

"What?" Andrew's eyes darted between the two women. "A dream quest? And no, Mrs Bargwana, I need to go alone. The Hag has been after me from the start, it's only right that I finish it."

"Perhaps so. But one of her dreaded dogs bit me, Andrew. I have her poison in my veins, a special connection, you could say." Mrs Bargwana's lips pressed into a thin line. "You may not be able to sense her, but I can."

"Lucy, no."

A voice in the hallway startled the group. Gus appeared, an apologetic smile on his face. "Sorry to make you jump, I let myself in and heard the tail-end of your conversation." He pulled out the remaining chair and sat down. "Firstly, Lucy: you can't come into the dream state, that will be Andrew's job."

"Thank you," Andrew said.

"But I'll go with him for backup," Gus added.

"Pardon?" Andrew burst out.

"Much better, Andrew," Deirdre spoke up from under the table. "Your manners are improving."

"Deirdre, be quiet!" Mrs Bargwana yelled in an uncharacteristic burst of anger. She turned to Gus. "Why can't I go?"

"There's no need to be indignant," Gus said. "It's for your own good. The Hag is an expert at zeroing in on our weaknesses, and you already have two strikes, don't you Lucy?"

Her face became guarded. "Two? The Hag's dog bit me. What's the other one?"

"There was an accident in Sydney, when you were a child. Your family was on holiday."

Mrs Bargwana froze, her face ashen. "How did you know about that?"

"I'm sorry to mention it." Gus bit his lip. "You haven't made the connection, have you? She was after *you* that day, but your father got in the way."

Mrs Bargwana stared at Gus, her mouth parted in shock. "I... I can't believe it." Tears appeared in the corners of her eyes. "I always believed Dad died in a random hit and run accident. No... it can't be true."

Gus leaned forward, his voice softening. "I'm sorry, Lucy. It's what she does. She steps out of the shadows, throws her daggers, and disappears. To beat her, we have to walk in the shadows too, and it's a dark and dangerous place."

"But I saw her house!" Mrs Jordan interrupted. "I stepped through the door in the Seer's Cavern and I saw a gorgeous little cottage in the forest, with an enchanting garden."

Gus smiled. "Funny you chose the word enchanting, Dorothy. You were enchanted by the Hag, and you saw what she wanted you to see. It was a glamour, just like her."

"I know I was lucky to get away," Mrs Jordan agreed. "My feet took me in the right direction, to Arleigh's Meadow. There's something about that place, it's like sacred ground. Her dog couldn't enter. Something to remember if you're in a bind."

"Okay, I think we all get it." Andrew held up his hand. "It's obvious that I need to go dancing in the shadows, but why do you need to come with me, Gus? You told me she can tap into you at any time. Won't you being there spoil the surprise?"

"Not this time," Gus's said. "We'll have a glamour of our own."

"To the pantry, Dorothy." Gus stood up. "I need to see what herbs you have."

"I have a reasonable collection." Mrs Jordan pushed the pantry door open, revealing shelf upon shelf stacked with little blue glass bottles, all neatly labelled and in alphabetical order.

Andrew's jaw dropped. "This is a reasonable collection? What does a great collection look like?"

Mrs Jordan ruffled his hair. "By reasonable, I mean I'm missing a few important herbs. I get most of these from your dad's work, Andrew. Healthy Herbs have a fantastic range!"

Colleen brushed past the humans and put her paws up on the lowest shelf. "You're right, there are a few gaps," she said, scanning the shelves. "We may need hyacinth, Angus. It cures fascination."

Gus said, "Any ideas for a replacement?"

"Pick me up. I can't read the labels of the higher bottles."

Gus lifted the tortoiseshell cat into his arms. Colleen's head craned backwards, taking in all the botanical names of the bottles on the upper shelves. "Alyssum," she raised a paw and pointed. "It protects from charms and fascination."

"Good. Now, thinking about a glamour, a disguise of our own..."

"Yes, yes. Give me a minute," the cat said. "Put me down." Back on the floor, Colleen scratched behind an ear. "I think a spell would be best for that, not herbs."

"I'm not sure I agree." Gus began to pull several bottles down from the shelf. "The Hag deals in spells and glamour. I think we need to counteract that with herbs." He placed the jars down on the kitchen table and turned to Andrew. "Would you mind ducking next door and grabbing the White Fire? I'll sort these herbs out while you're gone."

"Sure." Andrew shrugged. I'll be back in a minute."

Once Andrew was gone, Gus lifted Colleen onto the table. "What do you think of these? I've got mugwort and damiana to improve the dream state."

"Perfect," Colleen agreed. "And I can see you have the alyssum, good work."

"Plus I've added dragon's blood for energy, a touch of garlic—"

"She's not a vampire, Angus!" Deirdre interrupted.

"I know, I know, but it's good for protection too, as I'm sure you're aware, Deirdre." Gus replied. "My remaining herbs are mullein, yucca leaves, and comfrey."

"Yucca leaves?" Colleen said. "Are you sure about that one, Angus?" She glanced at her siblings for moral support.

"Don't look at me," Kevin said. "I didn't progress beyond a four-leaf clover."

"What's the issue with yucca, Colleen?" Mrs Bargwana asked.

"There's no issue with yucca!" Gus snapped. "Now, can we get on with this?" He turned towards the hallway, and his mouth parted in surprise. "Patrick! It's nice to see you up and about."

The black and white tuxedo cat padded into the kitchen. "Hello everyone. Thank you for looking after my brother last night. Did he get a good send off?"

"The best kind, Pat," Gus said. "The Seer escorted him on his final journey." He picked up his friend and placed him on the table. "How are you feeling?"

"It's a whole raft of emotions and physical sensations." The cat stared at Gus with Patrick's familiar blue eyes. "I'm an old bloke in a young body, and a young *cat* body, for that matter. My aches and pains are gone, but each time I go to get up, I still expect a struggle. Instead, my body launches forward as if my legs are spring-loaded! This is going to take some getting used to," he chuckled. "I'll be wanting some food in a moment, but first of all, bring me up to date on what's happening."

"We're preparing Angus and Andrew for a dream quest," Mrs Jordan spoke up. "We've got Angus using his old skills as an herbalist, and we're mixing up a special tea combined with White Fire. It's the final hurdle, Pat. We need to get Max and return him to his rightful owner."

"Is that right?" Patrick said. "And who is Max's rightful owner?"

"It's me, old boy." Winston trotted into the kitchen, Andrew a couple of paces behind. "Andrew figured it out, bright lad that he is." He leapt onto the table and nudged Patrick's head. "I must say, I'm pleased to see you adapting to your new body. Care to partake of a bowl of roo meat with me?"

"Winston!" Andrew thundered. "I've just fed you. What did I say about being a bad influence?"

Winston hung his head. "At least I thought to suggest you take a recording of my voice along."

"Yes, you did too," Andrew said as he threw the bag of White Fire down on the table. "Winston thinks it will help jog Max's memory."

Mrs Jordan clapped her hands. "Ooh, yes! Brilliant idea."

"I found his famous *We will fight them on the beaches* speech just now and recorded it onto my phone. Fingers crossed I can access it in my dream."

"Trust that it will work, Andrew," Mrs Jordan said, shooing the cats off the table. "We can only prepare so much, the rest we have to leave to trust." She pulled a mortar and pestle from the cupboard and starting adding ingredients to the bowl. "You and Angus get ready while the cats and I prepare the tea for you. It's going to be quite a powerful brew. If we look at how long you were asleep in the lucid dream, I'd expect the effects to last around nine hours. You *must* achieve your task in that time. After that, I'll waft a small vial of peppermint oil under your nose to bring you back from the dream."

It seemed preposterous to speak of a dream quest using rare and unique herbs, and then rely on something as common as peppermint to summon them back home. "Are you sure that will work?" Andrew raised his eyebrows.

Deirdre's tail lashed his leg. "Don't you doubt us, Andrew Adler, and don't doubt the power of herbs. Am I right, Angus?"

"She's right, Andy," Gus nodded. "It's a strong smell, and it will jolt us out of whatever situation we're in."

Andrew shrugged. "Whatever, you say, boss."

CHAPTER THIRTY-SIX

"Listen," Mrs Bargwana caught up to Gus as he left the kitchen, "I really think I can do this. I have a few tricks of my own up my sleeve. Surely three heads are better than two?"

Gus sighed and turned to face her. "Lucy, please. Let me and Andrew handle this. I wouldn't forgive myself if something happened to you." He neatly sidestepped her and proceeded to the toilet. "You'd better go too, Andy," he said over his shoulder. "Not unless you want to hold it in for nine hours."

Gus was waiting in the hallway when Andrew came out of the bathroom. He gripped Andrew's arm. "I'll take care of the Hag, is that clear? You focus on convincing Max to return to his previous life."

The boys locked eyes, a silent understanding passing between them. Andrew gave a short nod. "I'll do what I need to do, I promise you that."

"Boys, are you ready?" Mrs Jordan waved to them from the kitchen doorway. "Come in here and drink your tea."

The taste was quite awful, and both boys struggled to finish their cups. "Ugh," Andrew said. "Let's not make a habit of doing dream quests, okay? This stuff is evil."

"Agreed." Angus stuck out his tongue. "I've tasted some bad stuff in my time, but this takes the cake."

"Cake?" Winston's ears pricked up.

"Not now, Winston!" Andrew glared at him.

"Come into the sunroom, guys," Mrs Bargwana called. "We've prepared space in here."

There were two single mattresses laid out on the floor, each with a pillow and blankets.

"You may get cold during the journey," Mrs Jordan explained, her brow furrowed.

"We may also end up in the fires of hell, Dorothy," Gus said. Mrs Jordan uttered a horrified cry, and he held up his hands with a sheepish smile. "I was only joking! I'm sure we'll be fine."

The boys settled down on their individual beds, while Mrs Jordan and Mrs Bargwana brought chairs in from the kitchen. The cats streamed in, two tortoiseshells, a ginger, the large British shorthair, and last of all Patrick.

"Good heavens! Look at you all." Mrs Jordan placed her hands on her hips. "I suppose it was inevitable that I ended up being a crazy old cat lady."

Mrs Bargwana snorted. "Settle down, Dorothy, you've only got three! I've got a dozen waiting for me back home in Canberra."

"We're in esteemed company," Patrick said. "Can't you feel it? This group of people and creatures is quite the powerhouse, wouldn't you say?" He studied the faces of all present, his blue eyes gleaming. "Now let's pool together all our resources and good thoughts, and send these boys into battle. Any last words, fellas?"

"I think we're right to go," Gus said. "I can feel the herbs taking effect." He laid back on the mattress, his arms folded casually above his head. He showed no sign of nerves; he could have been stretched out on a picnic blanket, gazing at the clouds on a summer's afternoon.

Andrew took up position on his mattress, the boys laying head-to-head. He patted his pockets to confirm one last time that he had his phone. Winston was stomping on the blankets, claiming his spot before any of the other cats got ideas. All of a sudden, Andrew sat bolt upright on the mattress. "Wait. I need one more thing."

Mrs Jordan gave him a perplexed look. "What is it?"

"Strawberries."

The two boys groaned in their sleep. Their bodies shuddered as the herbs took hold, and Gus muttered something unintelligible. The cats glanced up at Mrs Jordan and Mrs Bargwana, their eyes wide.

"There's nothing we can do," Mrs Jordan answered their unspoken question. "We gave them nine hours to complete the task. We have to trust they will get all the way in, find the Hag and do what they need to do."

The comforting cloud that bore Andrew through his dream to Blair was sadly absent. Instead, he plunged through a dense cloud of smoke and into a blasted landscape below. He was awake almost immediately, his throat parched and his eyes smarting. Stretching below as far as the eye could see was a scene reminiscent of war. Through an eerie orange pall, Andrew saw trees reduced to matchsticks, derelict houses scattered across the burnt land, and a dry riverbed snaking across the countryside.

Despite his experience with Evelyn, Andrew had no fear of falling, only a grim anticipation of what was to come. Gus flew alongside him, awake and aware. In the distance they saw the dark outline of a stone cottage, the only intact building in the broken world. The pair shared a cautious smile as they descended towards the house.

They landed in the remains of a burnt-out building, a few steps away from the stone cottage. Crouching in the rubble, Andrew barked out a short laugh. "This is all your fault," he whispered. "You were the one who mentioned the fires of hell."

Gus rolled his eyes. "Trust me, I wasn't thinking of this when I said it."

Andrew patted the pocket of his jeans, reassured by the familiar shape of his phone. "Hey. Our clothes didn't change."

"No. We're dreaming, not time stepping. We're here, but we're not here."

"I don't understand." Andrew peered through the smoke. "Look at this place – it's destroyed. How could anyone live here?"

"The Hag doesn't live here," Gus answered. "She lives between worlds, and this world is paying the price for her duplicity." He spread his hands wide. "What you see here is a direct representation of her twisted reality. We need to finish this and get away from her madness."

"I get that, but I can't help wishing the Seer would turn up and help out."

"You know what he's like, Andy." Gus reminded him.

"I do, but why can't he give us some guidance?"

Gus shrugged. "It beats me. Anytime the Hag is involved, the Seer takes a back seat. Don't ask me why, I've never figured it out. For now, it's up to you and me. Let's get this done."

The boys crept through the orange half-light to the cottage. Keeping low they sidled up to the window and risked a glance inside. Andrew drew in a sharp breath. In a sight he blamed on the dream state, the woman's visage shifted before his eyes. At first, he saw a slim young woman with raven-black hair and the most stunning blue eyes he had ever seen. The next moment, she had changed into the stooped old woman he had seen at Chartwell. Rotting teeth protruded from her crooked mouth, and grey hair hung limp around her face. Her gnarled hands were propped on her knees as she spoke to the dog at her feet.

The midnight black dog and his master turned as one to stare at the boys outside, and a sudden realisation prickled Andrew's neck. This was not a time step where he was a harmless observer. He was stuck in a dream, and sometimes dreams turned into nightmares.

"I thought you said they wouldn't be able to see us," he whispered.

Gus kept his eyes on the Hag. "I guess I was wrong."

Chapter Thirty-Seven

"**M**ax, this is my lucky day."

Inside the cottage, the Hag spoke to her dog. "These two special boys have delivered themselves into my own hands. What a joy, what a delight!" She placed a hand on the dog's head. "It would be rude to keep them waiting. Go and open the door."

Outside, Gus grabbed Andrew by the shoulders. "RUN." His voice was hoarse. "Get out of here, now! Whatever you do, don't allow yourself to be caught by her. She'll kill you, do you understand?"

Andrew stared at him, uncertain. "She can't kill me in a dream!"

"We're in HER dream. And you're the grand prize. Move it! The dog will chase you. You know what to do."

"Okay, okay!" he said. "But don't go dying on me, Gus. I've lost too much this year already."

"I promise. One last thing: don't let anyone catch you wearing the necklaces. Put them in your pocket, out of plain sight. Now go!"

Andrew turned and ran. He risked a quick glance over his shoulder. The front door of the cottage opened, and the black labrador trotted outside. "Hello friends. Welcome to our world!" The dog smiled, baring a formidable set of teeth.

"We're not your friends!" Gus picked up a charred length of wood from the rubble and threw it in the dog's direction. "Get out of my way, Max. My beef is with the Hag, not you."

Gus's diversion gave Andrew enough time to put some distance between himself and the dog. He wanted Max to give chase, but he also wanted to be as far away from the Hag's cottage as he could before the dog caught him up.

He slipped the necklaces over his head and shoved them deep in his pocket. His mind worked furiously as he ran. Mrs Jordan was an unwitting visitor to the Hag's cottage in the past, escaping to Arleigh, the meadow of the Hares. She'd suggested the meadow was sacred ground, off-limits to the Hag and her dogs. *I need to find that meadow,* he thought.

But how?

He heard Max bounding along behind, with a steady rhythmic gallop that gobbled up the distance between them. "I'm coming for you, boy. The mistress wants you, and I'm not about to let her down."

Andrew didn't waste his breath on a reply. He focussed on thinking his way out of this increasingly dire situation. *Wait! What if I could get to the meadow through Blair's Heart of Hearts? What if all these places linked up?*

And pigs might fly, Andrew thought. He couldn't imagine two more different places than here and Blair's crystal home.

But as the thoughts took shape in his mind, he detected a change in the landscape ahead. Instead of the blasted orange land, there was a faint tinge of pink on the horizon. *Like a sunrise,* Andrew thought. The dawn of a new day. A new place. The meadow?

He put his head down and willed himself to run faster. His long legs were tiring over the rocky terrain, and a stitch was building under his ribs.

"You can't run forever, boy," Max panted behind him. "I won't hurt you, I promised her. Just stop running."

Not on your life, Andrew thought. *Or mine, for that matter.* The pink light brightened, and he saw the faint outline of a glowing tunnel hidden within the remains of a destroyed building. *I'll make it,* he thought. *You won't catch—*

"Got you!" The dog snatched at the legs of Andrew's jeans, and he stumbled forward onto his knees. "Don't struggle," Max growled. "I want you perfect for the mistress."

Andrew rolled over onto his back. The black labrador stood over him, his breath hot on Andrew's cheeks.

"Get up," Max growled.

"Give me a minute," Andrew panted. "Gotta catch my breath." An idea was forming in his mind, and as the pieces came together, he grew bold. "In actual fact, I've got a better idea," he said, grasping hold of the necklaces in his pocket. He grabbed the scruff of the dog's neck in his other hand. "Let's go visit someone else first, what do you say?"

The dog uttered a surprised yelp, and the pair disappeared.

"You could have left me the other one, Angus."

The Hag glided through the open door of her cottage, shiny dark hair cascading over her shoulders, her blue eyes gleaming. "He's so much younger than you. You're an old man and we both know it."

"Don't bother with the façade, Hag," Gus answered. "I know you, too."

The young woman shrugged. "So be it." Her youthful form melted away, leaving behind the stooped and scarred old woman. "Andrew would have appreciated my natural beauty," she sighed, flicking her lank grey locks over her shoulder.

"There's nothing natural about it." Gus's lip curled in distaste. "Besides, Andrew sees through most things. After all, you did kill his mother."

"She was in the way," the Hag sniffed. "Much as you are now. Let's be done with this idle chatter, Angus. Give me your talisman and you can go free." She was on him, her ragged nails raking across his arm. She lifted a hand to his neck and dragged him into the cottage.

"I don't have it," Gus croaked. The Hag dumped him on the floor, and he doubled over, wheezing.

"What do you mean, *you don't have it*?" Her eyes narrowed in anger. "You were destined to walk the earth for eternity with that stone. That's *why* you're called Angus Walker. Where is it, you vile excuse for a human?" She ripped his shirt open and scanned his body.

Gus flinched under the woman's touch. "You know you can't hurt me, so stop trying. I told you the truth. I don't have the talisman anymore."

"WHERE IS IT?" She slapped his face and he reeled backwards.

"Somewhere safe." Andrew rubbed his smarting cheek. "Somewhere unimaginable."

The Hag screeched in anger. "You've tricked me! You were here as a diversion and nothing more."

Gus grinned. "This is just like old times, you screaming, and me having a good old laugh about your crazy antics."

"I'm not that person anymore!" she shouted.

"Oh, but you are, in the same way I am an old man in a boy's body. Own up to who you are, and end this charade!"

The Hag touched the long scar on her cheek. "If you knew me, you'd know I will never give up, not until I get what is rightfully mine."

She waved her arm, blasting Gus backwards against the cottage door. His head whiplashed against the wood, and stars exploded before his eyes. Once his vision cleared, he saw he was alone. Oddly, he detected the smell of peppermint all around him, and the next minute, he was ripped away from the Hag's cottage.

Gus landed heavily on the mattress, the air pushed from his lungs. He jerked upright as Mrs Jordan's agitated face loomed above him.

"Angus, what the hell is going on?" she demanded. "Your body was attacked on the mattress. That shouldn't happen in a dream quest."

"It all went to plan, Dorothy." He dismissed her concerns. She thrust a glass of water into his hands and he took a long drink. "I had to fool Andrew into believing the Hag wouldn't see us."

"I knew it!" Colleen yowled. "The yucca leaves were a double-edged sword."

Gus rolled his eyes. "It was the only way to force him to run. And I knew Max would follow him. I fooled the Hag too, and she's livid. I'd better get back in there. My diversion only gave him a short amount of time, and she'll be after him now. Now, why did you summon me out of the dream?"

Mrs Jordan folded her arms across her chest, her head shaking in disapproval. "We needed you here. If you don't mind me saying, you took a massive risk by not being entirely honest."

"Why?" Gus frowned and turned his head towards the other mattress. Andrew was gone.

"What happened? Where did he go? Gus stared at Mrs Jordan.

"How on earth would I know?" The older lady's face flushed pink. "You were in there with him. He's gone, and so has Lucy. She was intent on stopping Max and she begged me to give her my Hag stone for protection."

"I told her not to go!" Gus clutched at his head. "Did they disappear at the same time?"

"More or less." She held her hands wide, pleading for understanding. "What was I to do? Lucy's been going on for years about her special connection with the Hag and her dogs."

"For crying out loud, Dorothy, they could be anywhere! How much time has passed?"

Mrs Jordan checked her phone. "Two hours."

Gus sighed. "Fingers crossed he had enough time to grab Max and do what he needed to do. And let's hope Lucy and Andrew are together. Lucy's skill with animals is indisputable, but if she ends up in the Hag's clutches..." He shuddered. "Andrew's herbs will wear off in roughly seven hours. To be honest, I'm not even sure they'll work now. He used his talisman in the dream, and it took him away." Gus paused, his mind working overtime. "Do you know what this means, Dorothy?"

She shrugged. "No, I don't."

"It means we can't get to them," Angus said. "There's no point me going back into the dream – the Hag won't be there. And I can't time step because I don't have my talisman. They're on their own."

CHAPTER THIRTY-EIGHT

Andrew's journey was short but turbulent, and when he opened his eyes, a thrill of elation rushed through him. He was back at Chartwell, exactly as he'd planned. Now to see if Max had come through the journey unscathed.

The big problem was that Max had disappeared in the transit.

Andrew's heart sank. *What happened to him? I was certain he came through with me!*

He scanned the area for the dog. He'd landed behind an ancient cypress tree, and no one had noticed his arrival. He could see Chartwell's grand front door from his position, and he felt a prickle of anticipation as the double doors were thrown open and maids hurried outside. They swept the entrance clean and dusted cobwebs from the eaves. The master of the house would soon be home, and everything had to be immaculate.

I'm early, Andrew thought. *They'll all be standing outside soon, waiting for Winston to arrive. The Hag will appear too, ready to steal Max away. How can I stop her?*

Someone tapped him on the shoulder, and he almost launched into the branches of the tree.

Mrs Bargwana appeared by his side, a black labrador in her grasp. "Hello, Andy. Fancy meeting you here."

"Mrs Bargwana!" he gasped. "You nearly gave me a heart attack. How did you get here? And is this..." He pointed to the dog.

"Yes, this is Max, or Rufus, as he is known in this time."

The dog's ears lifted at the sound of his names, and he growled. "You have unlawfully stolen me away from my mistress. Take me back, immediately!"

Mrs Bargwana gave him a stern look. "Your mistress stole *you* away, Max. We'll discuss that in just a minute." She looked at Andrew. "As to how I got here, I've no idea. I just took a punt. But there were a couple of things on my side." She pulled something from beneath her shirt, and Andrew saw a weathered old stone with a hole in its centre. A leather strap was looped through the hole, so the stone could be worn as a necklace. "One, I borrowed Dorothy's Hag stone," she said. "Incredibly protective, and given to her by the Seer. And two - and I've said it many times before - I have the Hag's creatures' blood in my veins, and that gives me an uncanny connection to them all. I grabbed hold of the stone and asked to be sent after Max. And hey presto, it worked. I arrived here, and Max was mooching around by my feet. I grabbed him before he could take off."

"So, what now?" Andrew said. "The last time I was here I couldn't do a thing, the Hag made sure of that."

"Oh, it will be different this time around." Mrs Bargwana crouched down beside the dog. "Give me those strawberries."

"Strawberries?" Max's ears pricked up. "You have strawberries?" He licked his lips and began to whimper.

Andrew handed them to Mrs Bargwana. "The final tell!"

"Indeed." Mrs Bargwana placed the squashed strawberries onto her open palm, and Max slurped them up. She allowed him a moment to savour the treat, then she asked, "Do you remember me? I knew you when you were a puppy."

Max cocked his head to one side in thought. "I see you, with my mother. You are younger. You are preparing food for my sisters and brothers."

"Do you remember how much we loved you, Max? You were precious!"

"It was short-lived. I remember the day *he* came and took Ralph. That was when it all went wrong," the dog sulked. "Why couldn't we have all stayed together? It was *his* fault."

"It was *not* his fault." Mrs Bargwana took the dog's muzzle and forced him to look her in the eye. "I *know* you, Max. I know you were decent."

"I wasn't that decent. My choice of master sent my sister to her death."

Mrs Bargwana paused, choosing her words carefully. "Be that as it may, you chose a master, and then you were stolen by the Hag."

"Don't call her that! She was the one who was wronged. You've seen the scar on her face."

"I have. But have you seen the scar on my arm?" Mrs Bargwana raised her shirt sleeve, revealing the hideous scar that ran the length of her left forearm. "Your predecessor did this to me. And your mistress, as you call her, has killed many times. She has cut short the lives of those we've loved the most: mothers, wives, husbands, fathers..." Her voice faltered.

"The day your mistress received that scar was the day she killed a defenceless little girl, Max," Andrew spoke up. "Her only crime was that she had blonde hair." He crouched down on the other side of the dog. "Please. Put things right. Go back to your real master. Don't you want to see him one more time?"

The dog was lost in thought. "I remember he was a kind man. He loved animals. But who was he?"

Andrew pulled out his phone, amazed it was still intact. "Listen, this is his voice."

The rich, rolling voice of Winston Churchill filled the air, and Max cocked his ears, a look of wonder on his face. "Rufus. That was my name! I used to ride in the car with my master. He was an important man, a busy man. I wanted to help him, ease his stress, but he was always surrounded by people. He left me at home one time and I missed him terribly. Each time he came home, I was so excited. I heard the car rolling up the driveway, and I couldn't wait to see him again..."

Andrew met Mrs Bargwana's eyes. By silent agreement, they linked hands and touched Max's glossy black fur. The shift was imperceptible, their only clue the dog's coat, which had reverted to the soft curls of a poodle.

The trio now stood amongst a crowd of people outside the entrance to Chartwell. Mrs Bargwana nudged Andrew's arm and pointed. A short distance away stood another poodle, in the grasp of a maid. Beside the maid, Clementine Churchill cut an elegant figure as she waited for her husband; her silver hair immaculate, signature pearls at her neck and ears. Andrew felt a longing to speak with her again, one last chance to reminisce about their unlikely friendship during World War Two. He shook his head. Now was not the time.

Keeping a tight grasp on Max's collar, Andrew ran with Mrs Bargwana to the side of the building where they took cover behind an old yew tree. A car was making its way up the long driveway. The window rolled down and the famous face of Winston Churchill appeared. "Hello, Cat!" he waved to his wife. "Hello, Rufus!"

Initially held in check by the maid, the small dog strained against his lead and broke free. Rufus dashed towards the car, and Mrs Churchill uttered a horrified cry of dismay.

All at once, the scene slowed, confirming beyond a doubt that someone was tampering with the timeline. Now, just as before, Rufus the poodle ran in slow motion towards his master's voice. Andrew closed his eyes at the point of impact, reopening them to see the Hag appear, a triumphant grin on her scarred face.

As the vehicle shuddered to a halt, the Hag scooped Rufus into her arms. Wrapping her cloak around herself and the injured dog, the Hag disappeared from sight.

"It's different!" Andrew cried. "It was different last time I was here."

"That's because we're here," Mrs Bargwana murmured beside him. "We're restoring the true course of history." She faced Andrew, her grey eyes melancholy. "And that means you have to let Max go."

They looked down at the brown poodle at their feet. The little dog was frozen in mid-leap, straining against Andrew's grasp as he yearned to reunite with his master.

Andrew's stomach twisted. Despite Max's misguided behaviour, the enormity of what was about to occur was too much to bear. How could he willingly allow Max to go to his death? *There has to be another way!* He closed his eyes, wishing time would correct itself.

"Andrew, look!" Mrs Bargwana shook his arm.

Andrew opened his eyes, and a spasm of fear shot through him. Max was no longer by his side.

The movie reel of time had rewound, and Churchill's car was once again purring along the driveway. In an eerie repeat of proceedings, Andrew saw that Rufus – their Rufus - had taken up position with the maid again. Churchill wound down his window and called to his wife and dog. Time ran at its normal speed, and in the blink of an eye, Rufus had broken free and was bounding towards the car.

"I'm so sorry, Max," Andrew whispered, a deep pain in his heart. He took his necklaces in one hand and Mrs Bargwana's hand in the other. As the pair tumbled back through time, Andrew felt Mrs Bargwana's fingers slipping from his grasp. He cried out to her, but she was gone.

He was alone, twisting through the darkness.

CHAPTER THIRTY-NINE

In Mrs Jordan's sunroom, the group waited. The male cats were restless, prowling in circles around the mattresses, while the two females hovered beside Mrs Jordan. The older lady glanced at the time on her phone for the hundredth time and sighed.

Gus gave her an irritated look. "Dorothy, stop it. Looking at the clock won't bring them back."

"It might!" she disagreed. "You don't know for sure."

They fell into an uneasy silence. Gus's eyes returned to the empty mattress on the floor. As he watched, he detected a faint sizzle of electricity in the air above the mattress. "Look, something's happening!"

Cats and humans alike gazed at the mattress. A rip opened up in the air beneath the light fixture, and Mrs Bargwana tumbled through it, her arms outstretched. Mrs Jordan leapt off the chair and swept her friend into a hug. "Thank goodness," she wept. "I thought you were gone! What happened?"

Mrs Bargwana sat up and gave them a blank look. "Max went back to Churchill. We fixed the timeline - we fixed it!" She looked around the room, her joy evaporating. "Where's Andrew? He was right with me."

"We meet at last, Andrew Adler."

The Hag hunched in a rickety chair beside the cold fireplace of her cottage. Andrew looked up from where he had landed on the floor. He was on his side, his hands and feet tied behind his back. A cold chill ran down his spine. There was no way he could reach the necklaces in his pocket. He was at the Hag's mercy.

"What do you want, Hag?" His voice sounded tired, even to his own ears.

"I want my dog back. What have you done with him?" She leaned forward in the chair.

"He wasn't your dog." Andrew said. "He's gone back to his rightful owner, so I'd say we're even. You'll never see Max again, and I... well, I'll never see my mother again, thanks to you."

Her laugh was a wheezing cackle. "I will find another dog. You, however..."

Andrew bit down on his lip. It took every ounce of his willpower to not respond to the Hag's cruel jibe.

"Ooh," she sneered. "The boy says nothing. How stoic." Her gnarled hands gripped the arms of the chair. "Your coming was foretold. I have tried in countless ways to alter your life path, but to no avail. I expected others' grief to impact you, but it appears you're immune to their suffering."

"Is that what you think?" Andrew's voice was choked with emotion. "You hurt all my friends and family just to get to me? That makes me all the more determined to finish you off."

"Fighting words, considering you're all tied up." The Hag's eyes glittered. "You're of no use to me anymore. I'm growing tired of throwing obstacles in your path. All I want is that black necklace Dorothy gave you. Say your final words and we'll be done."

Andrew was stunned. The Hag knew he had one special necklace, but was unaware of the silver necklace given to him by Mr Lovell! Why hadn't she found them when she tied him up? Was it possible they were invisible to her? If only he could reach them. He wriggled on the floor, and something touched the top of his hand. It was the chain from the silver necklace, dangling from his pocket. If he could just grab onto it...

"What do you want with my necklace?" he asked, stalling for time.

"It's not *your* necklace," the Hag snorted. "It's mine, and I want it back!"

"You must have searched me. You must know I don't have it."

Behind his back, Andrew twisted his long middle finger upwards to form a hook around the chain. Ever so slowly, he dragged his tied hands downwards, praying the necklace would follow. There was a moment of resistance where the sphere caught on the seam of his pocket, and then a bundle of cord and chain dropped into his upturned palm. His hand closed around the bundle, and he felt the sharp points of the black star on his flesh. Both necklaces were in the palm of his hand!

"And what are you going to do with it?" he asked, hiding his elation. He tested the give in his restraints. There was a tiny amount of slack in the rope, allowing him enough space to turn his palms to face each other. The necklaces were now cupped between his hands. A strange heat was emanating from the pair, as if they knew they were being spoken of.

"That's none of your business," the old woman snapped. "I have a score to settle, and with you gone, it will be smooth sailing."

Andrew passed the black star into his left hand, keeping the sphere in his right. It had opened when he pulled the necklaces from his pocket, and now it seemed the most natural thing in the world to slip the star inside the orb. "I wouldn't be so sure, Hag," he said. "You get rid of me, and someone

else will take my place. We've had enough of you interfering in our lives."
He snapped the orb shut, and a huge surge of energy rushed through
him. "Now leave us alone," he shouted, "and go back to where you came
from!"

The cottage exploded, and Andrew was flung into the smoky orange
sky. He had the odd sensation of a split, a ripping apart at the seams as
part of him hovered above the scene while his body appeared to vanish.
He was an observer, a witness to the Hag's demise, or so he thought until
he caught sight of the Hag cartwheeling through the tempest.

The old woman appeared lifeless, at the whim of the stormy sky. Andrew followed the Hag as her rag doll body drifted across the barren countryside, her dark robes flapping in the updraft. Little by little, the terrain
below showed signs of birth and regrowth. Andrew saw hills covered in
heather, dense, dark forests, and a river coursing across the land.

The old woman began an abrupt descent, plummeting through bruised
clouds, penetrating the roof of a stone cottage and crashing onto its dirt
floor.

Dust plumed upwards, and when it cleared, Andrew saw a large black
feather lying beside the motionless woman. Andrew raised his eyes to the
hole in the cottage roof. Had she collected a bird on the way down? His
eyes returned to the body on the floor. She wasn't dead, he saw, as he
detected a faint rise and fall in the woman's chest.

He had no idea how much time passed as he lingered above the scene,
but eventually the old woman rolled onto her side and got to her feet.
Clutching the feather in both hands, she staggered outside. She collapsed
into a chair on the porch, her hands in her lap, the feather standing
upright before the woman's chest.

The scene flickered, shifting into high-speed, and Andrew had the im-
pression of watching a time-lapse film. The woman remained motionless
in her chair as seasons changed and time marched past. The leaves on the
trees yellowed, dropped, and gathered around her feet. Frigid winds blew

past the cottage, but still the Hag did not stir. Spring came, with bright yellow daffodils bursting forth in the grass, and the woman did not move.

She's regenerating, Andrew thought, as the bright heat of summer baked the grass brown. One season overtook the other, and the Hag's hair grew down her back and her fingernails curled in corkscrews away from her hands. Soon the chair was covered by wiry white hair, while the yellowed nails continued their downwards growth towards the floor.

The galloping scene slowed, and the Hag shook herself, awakening from her hibernation. Groaning with pain, she stood and began to move towards the stream that ran past the cottage. Her hands were locked together by the snarl of fingernails, the upright feather a disturbing parody of a bridal bouquet. The Hag's white hair fell down her back to the ground, a tangled mass that pressed down on her shrivelled frame.

The old woman stumbled across the pebbles at the water's edge and waded into the stream. Without hesitation, she laid down in the stream, fully submerging her body. Her wilderness of hair softened around her, forming a white cocoon. The water frothed and fizzed as it washed over the still figure, as if cleansing the old woman in preparation for the afterlife.

Is that it? Andrew thought. *All that for her to end it here in the river?*

The Hag remained submerged longer than was humanly possible without drowning, and deep within, Andrew felt an odd pang of pity for the Hag. She had caused untold sadness and hurt over countless years, but at one point she had been a daughter, a sister, a spouse. It was a strange and lonely ending for the crippled old creature.

Or was it? There was a surge in the water and a bow wave spilled across the bank, stranding several small fish on the grass. Their flapping and floundering distracted Andrew until he noticed a movement out of the corner of his eye. In the middle of the stream, the Hag sat up. Water expelled from her nostrils, and she gasped for air. Her mane of white hair was gone, as were the hideous, curling fingernails. She raised her arms above her head in a stretch, and Andrew stifled a shout. The black feather had imprinted itself onto her left forearm, transforming into a large tattoo. *And the scar on her cheek has vanished*, he noticed as the beautiful, dark-haired woman waded through the water to the bank, her cornflower-blue eyes gleaming with purpose.

The young Hag strode into the cottage and lit a fire in the fireplace. Flames soon leapt up the chimney, and the young woman took up a large pot and went outside. A few minutes later she was back, the pot full of water. She suspended the pot over the fire, and it wasn't long before Andrew heard it bubbling.

Reaching into her dresses, the Hag retrieved a bundle of herbs and threw it into the roiling water. She raised her hands above her head and began to chant above the boiling pot. Steam rose, and Andrew smelled an unpleasant, grassy-green scent.

Still the Hag chanted, rocking on her heels, arms waving above her head. The water rose to the lip of the pot, and the young woman turned her attention to the feather tattoo on her forearm. The Hag began to pluck at the skin on her arm, as if scratching an annoying scab. She pinched something between two fingers, and bit down on her lip as she yanked a long black feather from the tattoo and threw it into the bubbling brew. With that, a dense smoke filled the room. Through the mist, Andrew caught sight of the Hag rising up through the roof of the cottage. Without thought, he followed. A pair of eyes penetrating the mist, a disembodied witness. The Hag rose into the sky, spiralling through time and dimension. Andrew sailed along behind her, unimpeded by a body, unaffected by the constraints of time stepping.

It wasn't long before the pair touched down in a place Andrew instantly recognised. Brown earthen walls, brown floors, and a brown ceiling, with ornate iron sconces on the wall. They were in Vellistrian, but for what reason? The next moment, Andrew understood. The Hag entered a lavishly-decorated bed chamber, surprising Jarl junior as he prepared for bed.

"Who are you?" The young Pisal backed away from the intruder.

"I'm your friend," the Hag said. "You're dissatisfied with the current arrangement in Vellistrian, aren't you? They don't respect you, do they? Well, allow me to fix that." She grabbed Jarl by the arm and thrust him beneath her cloak. The Pisal disappeared within the folds of material and was gone. With a cunning smile, the Hag lifted off the ground and rose up through the brown earth of Vellistrian.

Andrew willed himself to follow. He floated behind, silent and watchful. The Hag flew on, skirts and cloak fluttering as she twisted and contorted through time. There was no hesitation, she appeared to know exactly where she was going. Finally, the Hag lifted her arms and slowed. She descended through rock and stone, dropping into a sparsely-furnished cellar.

A Nazi German swastika was pinned to the wall, and a 1945 map of Europe stretched across a large wooden desk. A short man with dark hair and a peculiar flash of yellow in his eyes stood alone, a pistol raised to his head. "My name is Josef Goebbels, and I do this for Germany," he said.

"Now, don't be foolish." The Hag intervened, snatching the gun out of his hand. "You're coming with me." The pistol clattered to the floor. She grabbed the small man by the shoulders and stared deep into his eyes. "How delightful," she squealed. "It will be an absolute pleasure to work with you again." The raven-haired woman shoved the surprised Goebbels under her cloak, and he too disappeared beneath the heavy folds of material.

Oh, no, Andrew thought. *I know what she's doing - she's gathering a new group of henchmen.* The realisation gripped Andrew as the Hag disappeared from the cellar with her bounty. Their departure left a sudden void in the room, as if all the air had been removed. Time was hovering on the brink, waiting for Josef Goebbel's guards to discover that their leader had disappeared from the impenetrable Berlin bunker.

Andrew was in deep trouble. *I've got to wake up,* he thought. *She's changed history and now this particular moment is fragile.* Without a body, he could remain stuck in this timeline forever.

Can someone please open that bottle of peppermint oil and get me out of here? It was a silent, anguished plea and no one heard, no one answered. Andrew remained in the doomed cellar, thoughts going around and around in his head until one rose up: Leo's discussion of lucid dreams. *You realise it's a dream but you can control your actions.*

If I'm in a dream, he thought, *I can conjure what I need to get me out of it. What if I imagined the smell of peppermint?*

He remembered reading about an experiment where people were asked to imagine biting into a lemon. The mere thought of biting the sour fruit caused the participants to salivate. Could he replicate this experiment?

It's worth a shot. He pictured a Christmas candy cane in his head: the striped red and white cane and its fresh peppermint scent. He imagined the crunch as he bit off the hook, and the sweet and strong taste of peppermint in his mouth...

...And he was gone.

Andrew's eyes blinked. He felt a disconcerting shift, and then he had the strange sensation of arriving in his own body on the mattress in Mrs Jordan's sunroom, like a hand slipping into a glove. He sat up, his eyes squinting at the harsh overhead lights.

Three humans and five cats converged on him. "Oh, my goodness, you're awake! What happened? Did the Hag come after you? Where did you go? Seriously, are you okay?"

He flopped back on the mattress, passing a hand over his eyes. "I'm okay, stop fussing!"

"Here, drink this." Mrs Jordan held a glass of water in front of his face.

"Thank you." He rolled onto his side and drained the glass. "How long was I gone?"

"From when you disappeared, or from when you came back?" Mrs Jordan asked.

He frowned. "What do you mean?"

"You disappeared, and so did Lucy," Gus said. "I'm presuming this was when you were with Max. Lucy reappeared, and then an hour later, your body came back. We thought you were dead, Andy. It was like your body was here, but you weren't. We thought she'd won."

"Oh, I thought I was going mad!" Andrew felt a wave of relief wash through him. "On my side of things, I felt a separation. I seemed to be hovering above everything, watching it play out like a movie. It happened after my necklaces joined together, and I blasted the Hag."

Gus crouched down beside him. "You... *blasted* the Hag?"

"Not me. The necklace. Here, take a look."

Gus held the newly-formed necklace between his thumb and forefinger. "It's like they were meant to be together. Look at how the points of the star intersect with the filigree decoration. Brilliant craftsmanship."

"I knew I was meant to give you that necklace," Patrick pushed past the humans and sat beside Andrew on the mattress. "If only I'd thought of it sooner. Did this blast kill her?"

Andrew shook his head. "I wish. She took a big hit, and then I watched her regenerate. I don't really know what I saw, whether it was past, present, or future, but I know one thing for sure: the Hag is alive and gathering her troops. This isn't over yet."

CHAPTER FORTY

The group was interrupted by a flurry of knocks on the front door. Mrs Jordan excused herself, returning a moment later with an agitated Mr Adler. He rushed towards Andrew and swept him into a bear hug. "I was worried sick! You didn't answer my messages."

Andrew pulled his phone from his pocket. He'd missed five calls and half a dozen messages. "Dad, I'm really sorry, I had the phone on silent. We were having a get together to celebrate Mr Lovell's life."

"Peter, please don't blame Andrew," Mrs Jordan spoke up. "We should have invited you too, but we were worried about upsetting you..."

Mr Adler's smile was tight. "It's okay, Dorothy. I don't want you tiptoeing on eggshells around me. Helen's gone, and now Patrick's gone as well. I loved the old bloke. He could be a grumpy old so and so, but that was part of his charm, wasn't it? And he took care of me when I needed it the most. I'm going to miss him."

The black and white tuxedo cat let out a loud meow and trotted over to Mr Adler. The cat stretched his front paws up Mr Adler's legs, demanding to be picked up. "Oh, hello!" Mr Adler reached down and picked up the cat. "You're a friendly one. What's your name?"

A hush fell around the room as Dorothy said, "This is Patrick, Peter. I named him in honour of our dear friend."

The group waited as Mr Adler mulled the name over in his head. The cat rested in his arms, tucking his head beneath the man's neck and rubbing against his stubble.

"I like it." Mr Adler said, and everyone relaxed. "I like him too."

"I'm sure he'll come to visit, Peter," Dorothy beamed. "He seems to have taken a shine to you."

"I look forward to it." Mr Adler reluctantly placed the cat on the floor and scratched him behind the ears. Patrick purred loudly.

"Dad," Andrew yawned. "It's after midnight. Can we go home?"

"Of course." Mr Adler gave the cat one last pat before straightening up. "Goodnight, everyone."

On the way back to the house, Mr Adler said, "Has Dorothy gone a bit crazy with cats? I lost count of how many were in the room with us."

Andrew murmured through a yawn that a couple of them belonged to Mrs Bargwana.

Mr Adler nodded thoughtfully. "I liked that black and white cat, though. Patrick. He's a real character."

"He sure is, Dad. He's one of a kind."

Andrew awoke the following morning to a cat's paw in his face. "There's no food." Winston's whiskers tickled his cheeks. "I'm starving."

Andrew couldn't help but laugh. "You're fading away, aren't you, Winston?" He studied his cat's stubby form. "Didn't Dad feed you?"

"No, he left early. He was dressed for work."

Andrew swung his legs out of bed. "Work! That's good news. It'll be Dad's first day back since... since..."

"It's all right, Andy." Winston placed a paw on his arm. "I know what you mean. But seriously, I need food. Can't function without it. I was the same when I was in human form."

"Okay, okay!" Andrew padded down the hallway to the kitchen. He filled a bowl with cat food, then proceeded to the bathroom. In the shower, he realised he had none of the dizziness he'd experienced from previous time steps. "But this was a dream quest," he reminded himself as he sat down to eat breakfast. "Wasn't it?"

Like his father, Andrew planned on returning to school in a couple of days' time. Before then, he wanted to visit Ralph and bring him up to date with everything. He ducked next door to retrieve the bag of White Fire, and finding the front door unlocked, he let himself in. He heard gentle snores coming from Mrs Jordan's bedroom and the guest bedroom, so he tiptoed down the hallway to the kitchen. There he encountered four ravenous cats.

"Dorothy and Lucy are still sleeping," Kevin yowled. "With everything that happened yesterday, they forgot to feed us."

Andrew found the bag of roo meat in the fridge. "Apparently I'm on feeding duty today." He spooned meat into two bowls and left them to it. "I'll see you later. I'm off to visit Ralph."

Back at home, he tucked a few White Fire leaves into his pocket. He took hold of his necklace, enjoying the feel of it in his hand. "New and improved necklace, please take me to Vellistrian."

Once again, the shift was almost imperceptible. One minute he was in his bedroom, the next he slid into place beside Bodoron's desk in the head guard's office.

"Aargh!" Bodoron jumped, his chair clattering to the floor behind him. "Andrew, you have *got* to stop doing that!"

"I'm sorry, really, I am!" Andrew threw his hands up in apology. "My necklace's powers have changed, and I'm still getting used to it." He picked up the chair and motioned for Bodoron to sit back down. "I'm on my way to see Ralph, but there's something I need to tell you first." He explained his theory about a traitor at Nostalgia's hospital.

Bodoron scratched his jaw with a claw. "Someone leaked the details of the gifted hounds to the Hag? I'm disgusted!" He shook his head in disbelief. "I'll look into it, thanks, Andrew. I don't suppose you know any more about Jarl's disappearance?"

Andrew's heart sank. "He's still gone? I was hoping that what I saw was a dream." He shared his vision of the Hag stealing the young prince away.

The head guard's orange eyes flared with anger. "Now she's made it personal," he said. "Do you have any idea how she achieved this kidnapping?"

Andrew shrugged. "Magic. I know it's not the answer you want to hear, but it's what I saw. As to when she took him, I don't know. But we're going to need your help to get him back, Bodoron."

"You can count on it," he nodded. "I'll get the Miniature Pisal to look into it immediately. Let's hope science can beat magic."

Later on, Andrew broke the news of Max's death to Ralph. The dog's initial shock turned to acceptance. "I'm sorry he's gone. He was a clever one. I guess that's what made him attractive to the Hag. But you fixed it, Andy. You repaired the timeline and returned Max to Churchill. Not a happy ending but the best we could hope for."

The old friends strolled away from Nostalgia, enjoying each other's company without the need for words. As the pair approached Reminiscent Town, their thoughts turned to happier times.

Snow had introduced the unique town to them three years ago. Through a trick of sight, it afforded visions of times past for any who approached. For Andrew, it had been a memory of playing with Ralph beneath the peppercorn tree in their backyard. For Ralph, it had been a romp on the grass with his mother and siblings at Mrs Bargwana's house in Canberra.

As the memories flickered at the edge of his vision, Andrew paused and turned to Ralph. "Let's focus on the day we met." They sat together on the side of the cobbled road and waited. Soon enough, the memories consumed them: five beautiful labrador puppies frolicking with their mother, a shy, long-haired blond boy claiming Ralph as his own, and Mrs Bargwana waving the happy family goodbye. The pair continued to watch the passing of time at Mrs Bargwana's house. The Seer materialised and shortly after, he whisked the remaining puppies away. The scene then took on a rosy hue as a tall, long-limbed man appeared and claimed Abi, the mother dog. The man was tanned, with long hair and a beard, and he was dressed in a t-shirt and jeans. His eyes were compelling; an amber orange that was at odds with his human form, and Andrew smiled with fondness at the man he knew as Blair. He took the White Fire leaves from his pocket and placed a couple in Ralph's mouth. "It's time."

The pair chewed on the leaves. They laid down beside the cobble-stoned road, and within minutes they were asleep.

Andrew awakens. He is elated to see they are in Blair's Heart of Hearts. From across the rosy cavern, Blair raises an arm and waves. "Greetings, friends." Andrew hears the words in his head. "Welcome."

Andrew smiles and waves back. The stress of his dream quest slips away, and he basks in the warm glow of Blair's home. He beams at the sight of mother labrador Abi reuniting with her only living child. Ralph has reverted to his golden colour, Andrew notes with surprise, as his old friend nestles against the face of his mother.

Andrew listens as Ralph speaks with Abi. "I am thrilled to know you are alive, and to find you again. I'm so happy we've made it through to the other side."

Abi gives him a puzzled look. "My child, we are not on the other side. If truth be told, we may only be approaching the middle of this ordeal. My master watches, as does the Seer. We will see our way through, but not without some heartache. My only hope is to see you again one day."

"That is my hope also."

The two dogs sit with each other, enjoying a relationship believed lost in the portals of time. Time slows, but the inevitable moment arrives when both dogs stand and nuzzle each other in farewell.

Andrew rises from his crystal lounge. He offers Blair his thanks, and takes one last look at the Heart of Hearts before leaving. There, down one of the arteries, Andrew catches sight of his mother. She puts a hand to her heart and blows him a kiss. Through his tears, Andrew sees an object coming towards him. A bright orange leaf twirls along the artery and into his hands.

Late afternoon sunshine slanted across the backyard. After his visit to Ralph, Andrew had returned home, eaten lunch and he was now outside under the peppercorn tree. It was a gorgeous spring day, and the bulbs his mother planted last year were in bloom. Beautiful blue irises, bright yellow and orange daffodils, and the scent of freesias floated on the breeze towards him. *I wish she was here to see them,* he thought.

There were five cats in the yard with Andrew. The two female tortoise-shells lay side by side on the grass near the flowers, basking in the gentle sunlight. The other three cats, a ginger, a large grey, and a black and white tuxedo cat frolicked nearby. It had all the makings of a brilliant Instagram photo opportunity, but Andrew knew better. Kevin, Winston, and Patrick were fiercely debating a hot topic from World War One. He caught a few of their words, *bully beef... tinned jam... beer,* and he smiled. The topic inevitably turned to food and drink whenever Winston was involved.

Andrew rested his head against the tree and closed his eyes, thinking back over his trip to the Heart of Hearts. After some deliberation, he had folded the orange leaf from his mother over and over, until it was a small, lopsided square. He placed the leaf inside his talisman, and now the black star rested inside Cecil's silver necklace, a warm glow on his chest. The warmth radiated through his body, and he felt his head nodding...

"Wake up, lazy. We need to talk!"

A shadow fell across Andrew and he opened his eyes. Leo stood over him, a cheeky grin on his face. "Hello, Lambie," he said. "Who are you calling lazy?"

Leo set his bike down and leaned against it. "Don't call me Lambie. A little tired, are we? Is that because you did it again?"

"Did what?"

"Don't act innocent. You used the White Fire again, didn't you?" Leo tapped the skin beneath his glasses. "Your eyes have that weird light in them, like they did after the experiment. Where did you go this time?"

"I don't know where I went," Andrew answered. "And my eyes did most of the travelling, so it's not surprising they look weird. But I do know I was lucky to see what I saw. Problem is, I don't know *when* it all happened. I have a feeling I glimpsed into the future, but how far into the future, I couldn't say."

His friend was quiet, mulling over his words. "Was it bad?" He stared at Andrew. "Were you successful?"

"Yes, on both counts. We returned Max to his correct time, where he met with his intended fate. But the other bit..." Andrew paused, a muscle flickering in his jaw. "It was ugly. The Hag went into the past and stole your old nemesis, Owen trapped inside Josef Goebbels."

"What?" Leo's face paled. "I thought he died of self-inflicted wounds."

"She got to him before that happened."

Leo swore under his breath. "What else? There's more, isn't there?"

"She wasn't content with one, or two, if you count Owen. She went to Vellistrian and stole Snow's first-born, the heir to the throne." Andrew scratched the back of his head. "I think that one happened in real time, because Jarl is missing."

Leo gave him a confused look. "I don't understand."

"I'm not sure I do, either. But here's my theory: The Hag is preparing for a showdown, and she's mustering her forces." He ripped at the tendrils of grass beside him. "I watched this creature regenerate, Leo. How long did that take? I watched the seasons go by, her hair grew down her back and her fingernails were long and curling - just disgusting!"

"I get it, I get it," Leo said. "This could be going on right now, or ten years down the track." He paused as a gust of wind lifted the feathery tendrils of the tree above them. "Listen, can I drag you back to the present for a moment?"

"Sure. What's going on?"

"I had a chat with Teresa yesterday."

Andrew rolled his eyes. "Oh yeah? What did she have to say for herself?"

"She wasn't making much sense," Leo answered. "I said all three of us should catch up, you know, for old times' sake, but she wasn't into it. She said she needed time alone, and she was going into the city by herself."

"Hmph. Whatever."

Leo grimaced. "Look, there's no easy way to say this to you, but she was rambling on about Gus. From what you said, she doesn't stand a chance with him - she's only going to get hurt." He took a deep breath. "I thought we should step in and do something."

Andrew's heart thudded dully in his chest. There would be no coming back if he chased after Teresa and attempted to fix things. In fact, he could make things worse, and risk looking like the biggest green-eyed monster on the planet.

His mother had raised him to be respectful of all women. But respect had to be mutual, and Andrew knew that while Teresa obsessed over Gus, his actions would go unnoticed, much less respected. That meant it was time to withdraw. He looked up at Leo and shrugged his shoulders. "You know what, I can't worry about this anymore. She doesn't care about me, that's obvious. Why should I care?"

Leo's mouth fell open. "But... Andy, this is Teresa!"

"I know. Look, you know how I feel about her," he said, dropping his eyes. "Nothing's changed. But Dad said something to me while I was driving the other week. He said I have to keep my eye on what's happening down the road, not just what's in front of me. Here in the now, Teresa has her eye on Gus, not me. I have to accept that. So that means I have to concentrate on me and my future."

Leo laughed awkwardly. "Okay, sure. Just don't forget about me, Andy-Pandy."

Andrew punched his friend's arm. "I could never forget my Lambie. But I'm having an idea about something else." He tilted his head to one side, deep in thought. "Why not," he said, almost to himself. "Gotta go, Leo.

I'll catch up with you." He shot to his feet, waved goodbye, and jogged to the shops on Lincoln Street.

Some of the shops were closing for the day, but the newsagent remained open. Inside, Andrew spotted Rachel, her dark head bent over the till as she counted the day's takings. He wasn't sure if his heart was pounding from the run or from what he was about to do. He went up to her and smiled. "Hi, Rachel. I'm Andrew Adler."

The girl finished counting and shut the register. She met his gaze. "I know who you are."

"Good. That saves me a heap of time. Do you want to go out and see a movie together?" Rachel's eyes flew open, and Andrew noticed flecks of hazel in her brown eyes.

"Wow. You don't mess around, do you?" she said. "Sure, I'd like to see a movie with you, Andrew Adler." Her mouth tipped upwards in a mysterious smile.

Across town, Teresa was riding a bus home from the city. She'd imagined shopping would cheer her up, but it had only made things worse. She'd visited Myer and David Jones, and the large Dymocks book store on George Street. Everywhere she looked, there were young couples arm-in-arm. Couples sharing a kiss, sharing a laugh, blissfully unaware of the world around them.

Why couldn't she have that? She wanted more with Andrew, but her father had swiftly put an end to that relationship. Now she felt there was something between her and Gus, but he only wanted to be friends. It was so unfair! Her shoulders shook, and she wiped at the tears on her cheeks.

There was another girl sitting beside her on the bus, and she turned to Teresa, a concerned look on her face. "Are you okay?"

Teresa studied the girl's face. She was a similar age, with long black hair and vivid blue eyes. She had a caring look on her face, and that persuaded Teresa to open up. "It's just a boy. I like him - even my father likes him, which is a rarity. But he doesn't seem interested."

"I've had that same problem myself," the other girl said. "What's his name?"

Teresa sighed. "It's Gus. Well, actually, it's Angus, but everyone calls him Gus."

"Do they?" the girl said, a look of keen interest on her face. "That's an uncommon name."

"He's an uncommon guy. He's such a mystery to me!" Teresa blushed, pushing a stray curl of hair off her face. "I want to know everything about him."

"I'm sure that will happen." The girl placed a hand on Teresa's arm, revealing an intricate tattoo of a feather that ran the length of her forearm. "All in time."

Afterword

Previous readers of my stories will know how much I love history, but any good story needs fiction interwoven with the truth. Here is the history behind a couple of the scenes in *The Hag:*

Winston Churchill was a great animal lover, and it is true that he owned two poodles called Rufus. Churchill and Rufus I were inseparable, and Rufus interrupted important war meetings from time to time, as described in *Time Stepping*. Unfortunately, Rufus was hit by a car in 1947 and died. Churchill was away at a political conference, and was inconsolable at the news. Another poodle was presented to Churchill, who he named Rufus II. He was unconvinced that Rufus II could fill the hole that Rufus I left behind, but in the end, Churchill warmed to his new friend. Rufus II lived a long, pampered life, and when he died in 1962, he was buried at Chartwell beside his beloved namesake.

In the Great Scottish Witch Hunt of 1597, over 400 people were charged with witchcraft, leading to the execution of approximately 200 people. A large trial in Aberdeen charged Janet Wishart and accomplices with using spells to bewitch others, resulting in sickness and death. She was further charged with using a 'nightmare cat', apparently leading to diabolical dreams and sleep paralysis. Janet Wishart and one other witch were sentenced to death by burning.

Finding 'tells' for the gifted hounds was fun. My own cat Max is a great fan of a robust pat on the rump, and he loves his fur being stroked the wrong way. He also loves food, and I have often wondered if he is a labrador in disguise! Villain Max's love of strawberries came from my lovely friend Jodie and her dog Molly, a cavalier King Charles spaniel. Molly used to creep into the vegetable patch and eat the strawberries straight off the plant!

About the author

Kim Rigby was born in the island state of Tasmania, Australia, where she was encouraged to write by her school teachers. She grew up (a little!) joined the Royal Australian Navy, and returned to writing in 2015. *The Hag* is book six in the Black Fire Chronicles series.

Connect with Kim:

Web: http://kimrigby.com

Facebook: https://www.facebook.com/kimrigbywriter

Instagram: https://instagram.com/kimrigby27

A personal message from Kim...

If you enjoyed this book, please leave a review on Amazon, Goodreads, or social media. Your comments and encouragement inspire this author to keep writing!

Also by

The Black Fire Chronicles – *One Magical Day* – *Andrew and Ralph Meet* – Prologue

The Black Fire Chronicles – *Origins* – Book One in the series

The Black Fire Chronicles – *Revenge* – Book Two

The Black Fire Chronicles – *Time Stepping* – Book Three

The Black Fire Chronicles – The Guardians – *Dorothy the Dreamer* – Book Four

The Black Fire Chronicles – *The Hag* – Book Six

The Black Fire Chronicles – The Guardians – *Angus the Ageless* – Book Seven

The Girl from Berchtesgaden – a World War Two historical thriller co-written with Alistair Birch

www.ingramcontent.com/pod-product-compliance
Lightning Source LLC
Chambersburg PA
CBHW020350120726
47904CB00002B/530